Agony & Hope

L.L. Diamond

Agony and Hope
By L.L. Diamond
Published by L.L. Diamond

Cover and internal design © 2021 L.L. Diamond
Cover design by L.L. Diamond/Diamondback Covers
Cover photos: Winter Sunset in Snow Covered Park by Phant via Shutterstock, Regency Man by Period Images, Window picture by L.L. Diamond, Two Brandy Glasses by Studiovin via Shutterstock

ISBN-13: 978-1-7373356-2-7

Facebook: https://www.facebook.com/LLDiamond
Instagram: @l.l.diamond
Twitter: @LLDiamond2
Blog: http://lldiamondwrites.com/
Austen Variations: http://austenvariations.com/

Other works by L.L. Diamond include:
Rain and Retribution
A Matter of Chance

For my family and my friends,
who have supported me more than I ever could've
imagined.
Love to all of you!

L.L. Diamond

Chapter 1

February 10th 1813

The earl's eye twitched as he prodded the desk with a pointed finger. The mannerism was one that never failed to occur when his uncle struggled or someone tested his ire. The habit did nothing to help his uncle's ill-favoured appearance, and at this moment, his irritation drew out the worst in his countenance. "I will brook no opposition to my scheme, Darcy. You require a wife, and you shall find no better candidate than Lady Prudence."

Darcy pulled in a deep breath while his uncle spoke, measuring the draw of air into his lungs to maintain an illusion of calm. He was by no means ill-at-ease, yet his uncle's demands had grown wearying. How many times had the man sat in that very chair and made the self-same demand? He was in no mood to entertain his uncle's selfish dictates tonight. If only he would leave so Darcy could spend the remainder of his evening in peace.

"Uncle—"

The earl wagged his finger at Darcy's chest. "No, I will accept no excuses. Georgiana requires a sister, a lady to teach her and guide her and to prepare her for marriage. Your sister, with her thirty-thousand pounds as well as her status as the granddaughter and niece of an earl, should expect a splendid match—one worthy of the first circles. She must be prepared for the future. Lord Denbigh has expressed an interest, though he understands, of course, that he must wait until she is out."

Darcy fisted his hands, digging his fingernails into his palms, while he struggled to prevent his eyes from rolling towards the heavens. Why his uncle assumed Darcy would accept his advice for Georgiana when he refused under any and all circumstances to consider it for himself was a mystery. "Lord Denbigh is thirty years her senior and an unrepentant rake. Georgiana would be with child and diseased within a year. I would prefer her to make a love match, which in my opinion, is of greater importance than the gentleman's standing within the *ton*."

"Enough of this." His uncle's voice emerged at a low growl. "You will wed Lady Prudence at the end of the Season."

"No, my lord. I shall not." Darcy endeavoured to keep his breathing even. He would not lose his composure. "The lady I court will be of my choosing and no one else's." Darcy had been fending off his uncle's matchmaking schemes since he left Cambridge, though the earl's determination proved more tenacious as of late. His excuse that Georgiana had need of a sister had been employed before; however, the lecture on how the simpering, fawning daughter of another earl would make an exemplary model for his sister was new, but made no difference to Darcy. He would never marry, though he had no intention of revealing that resolution. His uncle would never understand because the man lacked the depth of feeling required to experience any empathy and kindness—even love.

The earl rose and proceeded to pour himself a generous glass of Darcy's best brandy. Lord Fitzwilliam's manner had always been officious. Darcy's decision not to offer refreshments was to ensure the visit remained brief, yet his uncle appeared prepared to visit until Michaelmas if afforded the opportunity. How the man tested his resolve! Darcy still prayed his uncle could be persuaded to depart before too long.

Otherwise, the patience he strove to maintain would be drawn so thin the fragile cord might snap.

"I care not for your preposterous notions," said the earl. "This family has always married for money and connections, and you will be no different. I shall inform Lord Seldridge in the morning of your grateful acceptance."

Darcy shook his head, his fingernails burrowing further into the tender flesh of his palm. Did his uncle not find these futile arguments as tiring as he did? "Uncle, I shall never capitulate to your wishes. For years, you have proposed dismal candidate after dismal candidate—"

The earl's shoulders stiffened and his chin hitched back. "I have never proposed a 'dismal candidate' as you suggest." His voice drawled in a manner not heard thus far during this evening's call.

"If you remember, Lady Cecilia wed a mere fortnight after you forwarded her as a potential match," said Darcy. "The lady then entered her confinement no more than six months after she wed. Bingley's older sister could not cease gossiping of how rosy and robust the child was for one born so early. Lady Cecilia was fortunate her husband's age and desperation for an heir allowed her to raise the child. Another man would not have accepted a cuckold with such grace. He would have found a suitable home rather than allow the child to inherit his title and his estate."

His uncle gave a flippant shrug. "I admit to being misled by Lady Cecilia's father, but the inconvenience of the child would have been but a small price to pay for her fifty thousand pounds."

Darcy pressed his hands atop the dark, polished oak of his desk. The piece had belonged to his father as well as his grandfather before him and was as much of a Darcy tradition as the inheritance of Pemberley. "No amount of money could persuade me to accept a lady of your choosing. I refuse to sully the Darcy name and reputation by accepting one of the insipid daughters of your political allies.

"And since disease has been mentioned, I would be remiss if I did not ask of Carlisle? Does the mercury seem to have cured the pox?"

Lord Fitzwilliam sucked in as much air as his chest would accommodate, holding the breath until he changed an interesting shade of puce. He then released it all at once. "You dare use my son's condition against me? I could not have known his wife—"

"No, you could not have, could you?" Darcy kept his tone light as if discussing a trivial matter and not a topic his uncle took great pains to conceal. "Particularly since you made no effort to discover why her father was so determined to be rid of her. I have not forgotten Carlisle's blind acceptance of his bride."

"You dare—"

"Have you visited Carlisle of late or have you neglected to inconvenience yourself?" Yes, his manner was harsh, but the truth of the matter was the earl's lack of attendance at the sickbed of his eldest son and heir was due to appearances. He would not want to be seen entering or exiting the hospital. God forbid someone recognized him!

Spittle flew from his uncle's lips. "I am the head of this family and a peer! You will afford me some respect! Your mother would be appalled at such horrid treatment of your nearest relation!"

"She would be appalled at your attempts to elevate your own importance at the expense of her children. You arranged Carlisle's union to that woman with nary a question of her father. The mercury failed her too, did it not? Rumour has it she has been ill after the loss of a child, but I imagine when she still showed signs of disease, you hid her away in the country." Darcy's voice stayed flat and calm while he delivered the accusation.

His uncle sniffed and brushed non-existent dust from the leg of his breeches. "If you will not have Lady Prudence, she will do for Richard."

A bitter laugh burst from Darcy's chest. "I would not count on Richard's agreement."

"I can and will disown him," said his uncle, his hand shaking while he stared into his glass.

"After Carlisle's illness, he will never provide an heir, and that is even should the mercury be successful and he live to be an old man." How many times had Darcy relaxed in this very chair while he and Richard shared conversation over Port or brandy? They had spoken of the earl's selfish and conniving nature on many occasions. Instead of the earl, Richard had long thought of Darcy's father as his own, regardless of how the sentiment angered Lord Fitzwilliam. "You cannot disown Richard since you have no one after Carlisle to inherit not only the title but also your estate. Protecting your younger son's life should be your objective over all else."

Darcy rose and rang the bell. "I beg you not to importune me further on this matter as I shall never be amenable to any suggestion of a wife from you. I shall further warn you not to so much as mention Georgiana as a possibility to your allies. My father knew better than to entrust you with her future, which is why Richard and I share her guardianship. She *will* have a choice in the man she weds, and *we* shall ensure her choices are suitable."

His uncle slammed the brandy on the desk, the liquid splashing. Thank goodness it did not spill onto Darcy's nearby ledger. "You dare treat me with so little respect! I can ensure you marry a lady of my choosing. A well-timed letter to the papers—"

"And the condition of Carlisle's wife, as well as Carlisle, become fodder for society."

After a gasp, his uncle stood, brandishing a quivering finger in Darcy's direction. "You would humiliate your cousin?"

"You forget that under your lifelong tutelage, Carlisle has been abominable. He is cruel and has been since he was a child. I care little for preserving his reputation when he has never afforded me one ounce of respect, and since I have no interest in maintaining any appearance of ease between us, I have no reason to give consideration to you or your eldest son." He had not told a falsehood. Carlisle had always been horrid, yet Darcy would never reveal the nature of Carlisle or his wife's maladies, but would his uncle apprehend that he was prevaricating?

The door opened and Watson stepped inside. "Yes, sir?"

Darcy glared at his uncle. He could not waver or allow any hint of weakness to be evident in his manner. "Pray, escort Lord Fitzwilliam to his carriage. He will be leaving."

His uncle's chest puffed and his cheeks reddened. "This conversation is not over."

"In that, sir, you are mistaken. Good evening, Lord Fitzwilliam." Darcy stepped around his desk to stare out the window, turning his back on his uncle.

"My Lord," said Watson, pressing his back to the door so the earl could depart.

Heavy footfalls stomped from the room. They paused for but a moment before the front door slammed. Darcy did not sit but waited until Watson entered. "Did he not put on his coat?"

"No, sir, Lord Fitzwilliam ripped it from my hands before rushing through the door. The weather is frigid. I wager he will stop to don it soon. Otherwise, he will catch his death."

Darcy rolled his shoulders to relieve a certain amount of the tension from his uncle's call. "In the future, I am not home to Lord Fitzwilliam."

"Yes, sir."

After Watson departed to see to his duties, the overwhelming silence of the empty room swallowed Darcy whole. The heavy and suffocating silence squeezed with a painful pressure upon his chest and prompted him to rub the oppressive ache.

At one time, he had not minded his own company, yet he had changed. He was not the same man he was a year ago. Blast! He was not the same man he had been a mere month ago. How often could one find themselves altered yet still recognise themselves? It was as if one day he would stand before the mirror and not know the man reflected back to him.

He downed the remnants of the brandy he had poured before the earl's unwelcome call and rose to pour another generous glass. Perhaps two or three more glasses full would be enough to fall into a dreamless abyss where he could no longer hear the bubbling laughter that haunted him, that brought to mind a pair of fine eyes that still captured him with their intelligence and sparkle.

The owner of those fine eyes had ruined him with her challenging repartee and intelligent opinions. Her teasing smile and humour had pleased him in a way no other woman could hope to duplicate. She freed him from those expectations that had been heaped upon him since his parents' deaths, representing a future he had never before considered possible. He could never love any but her, thus he could never marry. His heart was no longer his to give. She possessed that fragile organ that still beat so faithfully in his chest and she always would. His eyes burned, and his throat itched as though it might squeeze closed. No other lady was her equal. He had ruined his one chance at happiness, his one chance to have her as his bride.

No other woman could be Elizabeth Bennet, but he could not have Elizabeth Bennet. Elizabeth Bennet was dead.

Chapter 2

February 10th 1815

"Brother?"

At his sister's voice, Darcy abandoned his all too familiar occupation of watching the flames flicker in the grate and waved her inside. "Are you well?"

"Yes," she said, sitting on the sofa beside him. She was attired in a modest dressing gown and her hair was in a simple plait that hung over her shoulder. "I am finding it difficult to sleep even though I am assured Lady Catherine is settled for the evening."

The glow of the fire on her ginger-blonde fringe transported him to when he was a boy. How many times had he sat in his mother's lap while she sang to him, the fire rendering a similar effect upon her hair? These past few years, Georgiana had grown so. She had become a true lady and so much like his mother. His parents would be immensely proud of her. Would that they could have lived to see her grown and married! He took her hand and squeezed. "You should at least try. You do not want to appear fatigued on your wedding day. What if Witney takes one look at the dark circles under your eyes and cries off?"

Georgiana nudged his shoulder with hers. "Stop." The slight lift of her lips belied the serious tone of her voice.

"You could fall asleep in the midst of your vows, or you could faint as the vicar pronounces you man and wife."

Her voice broke with her laughter. "Then James would prevent me from falling."

The lightness of her reply brought a smile to his countenance. James Ivey, Viscount Witney, was not only a good man, but also the perfect match for his sister. "I believe he would. He would likely sweep you up into his arms, much to the shock of all the guests. You would be the talk of London for the Season."

His sister rolled her eyes. "He would know what to say to put a halt to the gossips' tongues. He is much better with those of a slight acquaintance than I." The couple shared many of the same interests, including horseback riding and music, as well as long conversations about the most trivial matters with nary a pause between them. Darcy could not have wished for a better husband for his sister. "I am certain he would."

"You *will* visit us at Loughton Hall for the summer, will you not?"

His gaze returned to the fire. "I have not yet any fixed plans, but I am certain I shall be required at Pemberley before long. You know how much business awaits me there after the Season."

"Pray, say you will come," she said. "I do not like to think of you all alone." Her concern for him was obvious. She had made no secret since her betrothal of how she despised leaving him without a "companion." He swallowed back his distaste at the word. She made him sound as if he were a young lady of a particular standing, not a bachelor who lived in his own home.

"You know Richard shall force me to visit our club while we remain in London. I shall not suffer for company." If only she would abandon her attempts to have him stay with them. She would not desire his mournful presence dampening the happiness of her first months of marriage. He would need to visit her in the future, but when the last of his business in town was finished, he yearned for the peace of Pemberley. He longed for home—not to be a guest of his newly married sister.

Georgiana placed a palm to his cheek and turned his head until they faced each other. "Do you promise not to hide from our cousin? Do you promise to speak to someone besides the servants from time to time?"

Her eyes searched his, seeking nothing more than the absolute truth. The expression she wore was identical to his mother, so much so that he had to blink and look once more to be certain he was not gazing upon a ghost. "I promise, but while we are speaking of the future, I require a vow from you as well."

With a start, her eyebrows lifted. "What is it?"

"I want you to promise you will not fret over me."

She sighed and relaxed into the cushions. "You need someone to be troubled for you. If I do not, I fear..."

"I am certain Mrs. Northcott will perform the task admirably. In fact, I have reason to believe you charged her with the duty a week ago."

Georgiana rested her elbow on the back of the sofa. "I understand what happened two years ago hurt you greatly, but the idea of you hiding yourself away in this room pains me."

"Georgiana," he said with a low drawl.

"No, you will listen—even though I know you have no wish for the conversation." She leaned forward and put her hands atop his shoulders. "Would it make Miss Elizabeth happy to know how you have closed yourself off from life?"

When had that boulder appeared in his throat? Even as he squeezed his eyes shut and swallowed hard, the obstruction would not give way. "I have not shut myself away."

"Fitzwilliam." She shifted and cradled his cheeks in her hands, making it impossible to avoid her steady gaze. Why could she not leave this be? "You only returned to society when I decided to come out, and I know you have despised every single moment. I do not want to think of you sitting in this room, night after night, in the same attitude while you drown yourself in brandy."

He pulled his face free and shrugged. "I do not drink brandy all of the time." He rubbed his thighs. No doubt, his sister's eyebrows drew together in that expression she wore when she was confused. "Sometimes I drink Port."

"Oh, you are so infuriating." Her weight fell against the sofa cushions. "Pray do not become cross, but Miss Elizabeth would hate how much time you spend alone. I know we did not know each other a long—"

"You spent a mere few days with her at Pemberley." Georgiana had been with him that dreadful January day when he had happened upon Mr. Gardiner at Hatchard's. He had been ecstatic when Elizabeth's uncle had invited them to dinner at his home in Cheapside. Thus, his sister knew all. She also knew his heart was not his own.

Georgiana rested her head upon his shoulder. "Yes, but I could tell how much Miss Elizabeth adored laughing as well as the simplest of pleasures. She would not wish you to spend the entirety of your days mourning her."

"I beg you, do not pretend I can go on as if I never loved her." Blast! He hated when his voice became hoarse. Why could he not speak of Elizabeth without his voice cracking or becoming rough? In the past two years, her steadfast grip upon his heart had not relaxed in the slightest. His heart would always belong to her, and truth be told, he had no desire for her to so much as loosen a finger. He never wanted to forget her, and if that meant he was never whole, then so be it.

His sister looked at him and frowned. "Do you think me so unfeeling?"

He groaned and shook his head. "No, forgive me."

"I shall never forget that evening—how the blood drained from the Gardiners' complexions at your enquiry after the Bennets. Poor Mary," she said in a soft tone. "The manner in which she collapsed into the chair and began to sob. To lose two sisters in such a way..." She shook her head. "My heart broke for her."

Georgiana and Miss Mary Bennet, now Miss Bennet, had first been introduced at that particular dinner. The two had since become the best of friends, with Miss Bennet standing as Georgiana's bridesmaid on the morrow.

"As dreadful as their reactions were, I never dreamt I would see you so devastated," she said.

His eyes burned and flooded with tears while he swallowed over and over again. "I have no wish to speak of it."

"But you are not to blame." Georgiana rose and poured herself a small measure of brandy. He should never have introduced her to spirits and should have insisted she drink sherry, an indulgence more appropriate for refined ladies. "You are no fortune-teller and could not have known what would happen."

"Georgiana—"

"And you have no proof that miscreant knew of your attachment to Miss Elizabeth." She set down her glass and held out her hands. When he took them, she pulled until he stood. "No more. Over the past few years, we have exhausted this discussion more times than I can count. You cannot continue to wallow in this misery and recrimination."

"Very well," he said, in his usual timbre. He had not the slightest intention of forcing a cheer he did not feel.

Georgiana narrowed her eyes and crossed her arms over her chest. She did not believe him, but would she wish to argue? "I believe we should retire. Tomorrow will be a long day."

He stepped over to the brandy to pour another glass. "I would prefer to remain a while longer."

His sister's eyebrows rose. "Pray, do retire. I do not want you sick from overindulgence when you give me away."

"You know I would not!" Heat flooded his face, and he snapped his mouth shut. It would not do to make an intemperate comment.

"I know you would not do so intentionally, but I marry James tomorrow. I wish for nothing more than the perfect day."

One side of his lips quirked up. "Nothing more than the perfect day? You do not hold high expectations, do you?"

"I do not believe them to be too high. I love my betrothed, so I am already much closer to perfection than most ladies can claim." She grasped his hands. "If you had not allowed me to decide when I would come out and insisted I do so at seventeen, I would not have James."

"You may not have married your first Season. After all, you did not care for the callers you received at the beginning of last Season. If Witney had not returned from Ireland before those last few balls, I believe you would have met him this year, and your life would have taken much the same turn."

After bestowing a quick peck to her forehead, he coughed and stepped back. "I could never have forced you into society when I detest it so. Besides, you are tolerable company. Why would I part with you sooner than I must?" He may have been teasing, but what had he said that was not true?

She rolled her eyes and smiled. "You are the best of men, Fitzwilliam. I am proud to call you my brother."

For the second time that evening, his eyes burned and he blinked rapidly. Life would be quite dull with Georgiana gone. Whatever was he to do?

———————◆———————

The day had dawned bright and clear. The sky boasted of a brilliant sun in a clear blue sky that, along with candles, had illuminated the drawing room well. The crystal sparkled, the silver shone, and the house had been in perfect order. Yes, his servants had outdone themselves giving Georgiana a day she would never forget. Her wedding feast had been lovely.

"Have you seen my mother?"

Darcy glanced over his shoulder where Richard peeked from behind the heavy draperies. A fair number of guests had departed, but family and a few close friends remained. "She is speaking to Lady Chester by the fire. What are you about?" Lady Chester was a great friend and confidante of Lady Fitzwilliam.

"She mentioned introducing me to Lady Chester's daughter." His cousin rose onto his toes and peered around the room.

"Lady Helena?"

Richard lowered and shrugged. "I believe that was the name. Do you know which one she is?" He leaned closer. "Would she be the one who bears a passing resemblance to my father's horse?"

"I have heard of her, but know no more" said Darcy, "though I doubt the poor lady deserves such a comparison." His cousin no longer wore the uniform of the Regulars, but at times, he still sounded as though he spoke to his men. At least he lowered his volume, which lessened the possibility of offending a passing relation.

"Forgive me." Richard removed a flask from inside his topcoat and took a generous gulp. "Father summoned me to Belgravia yesterday. I fear I have been rather intemperate since."

"I cannot credit that you attended him."

"I cannot credit it either." He replaced the cap and tucked the silver piece back into its hiding place. Georgiana would never forgive him if she caught him drinking anything other than wine today. "I should have known he wanted nothing more than to tell me what a miserable failure I am and how superior my elder brother was."

"How is your brother?" Darcy spoke low. As far as the *ton* was concerned, the former Viscount Carlisle, Ambrose Fitzwilliam, had returned to the country after a trifling cold went to his chest. Last autumn, he was said to have succumbed, yet Darcy and his cousin were not fooled by the earl's ruse. At his father's behest, Richard had sold his commission. He now held his brother's title and lived in his brother's former homes. His father even begrudgingly allowed Richard to keep the profits from the Carlisle estate, even if Richard had been entitled to them when he assumed his brother's title and place as heir.

"Mother saw him a month ago. She travelled to Yorkshire after father departed for town. She claims Ambrose is becoming more and more insensible, though she is not certain if it is from the disease or a result of the mercury." Richard stopped speaking until a servant passed. "If you remember, he was terribly weak after the treatments and did not remember Mother or me. The servants have said he does not always remember my father, which is why he has remained hidden away. Father hoped he would rally, but Mother says that has yet to occur. At times, he blusters and is full of bravado but can also become angry or despondent in a matter of moments. Oh, and he drools."

Darcy winced and shifted on his feet. With Richard's description, he could not be surprised at his uncle claiming his eldest son had died. He was surprised his uncle kept him in a cottage on the estate and had not had him locked away in Bedlam. "How is your mother?" His aunt, Lady Evelyn Fitzwilliam, appeared a formidable lady in company, yet after thirty years of marriage to the earl, she was quite adept at disguising her true feelings.

"Ambrose treated my mother as dreadfully as father always has. She is saddened as any mother would be at the illness of her child, but you know they ceased to have a familial relationship years ago." That much was true. Ambrose was his father's son through and through, and his aunt's marriage had for all intents and purposes ended thirteen years ago. Neither he nor Richard knew what the earl had done, but his aunt had insisted his uncle move his belongings to his mistress's house and leave her in peace. In fact, the marriage had been so poor, his uncle had not argued. An anomaly, to be sure.

Richard lifted his chin towards a group in the corner, the less than dulcet tones of Lady Catherine's conversation carrying over the murmur of the remaining guests. "Our aunt is much the same as she has always been. I understand she did not open her own house but is staying here." Richard's attention shifted as Georgiana wrapped her hand around Witney's arm and leaned a hairsbreadth closer to whisper in his ear. "Did you ever believe this day would come? All I can remember is the little head of ginger-blonde curls that would follow me around Pemberley and beg to ride my horse."

"I often feel as though I see my mother before me. Georgiana favours her and has her natural grace."

"She does, though as much as I love the little imp, I am exceedingly relieved her care now falls to Witney. Some days, I felt as though we navigated a battlefield rather than raised a girl. Have you ever wondered if marriage is not so dissimilar? The thought is terrifying, is it not?"

Darcy frowned and scratched his cheek. "I do not know." He could not imagine Elizabeth's emotions turning in the same rapid fashion as Georgiana's had for the past eight years, though Georgiana's temperament had become more even in the past year. Had Elizabeth's been just as volatile in her youth?

Richard kicked Darcy's shoe. "So, why has Georgiana charged me with dragging you kicking and screaming from this house whenever I can? She also told me you have a secret—a sorrowful one—and I am to persuade you to share the tale."

Darcy groaned and shook his head. "Georgiana is telling a falsehood."

Richard's lips curved to one side. "You are the one who is lying. Once the last of the guests depart, you will tell me over brandy in that study of yours. If Georgiana believes what you have concealed is important, then I shall drag it out of you one way or another. You keep too much bottled inside."

"This is not necessary, Richard. I am quite capable of managing—"

"Damn! I have been spotted."

When Darcy faced the room, Lady Fitzwilliam crossed with purpose as Richard shrank back behind the drapery.

"You know how my sister frets," said Darcy over his shoulder. "I am certain that is all it is."

Richard's gaze once again darted across every feature of Darcy's face. His cousin had an unnatural ability to know when someone lied. Darcy could sometimes fool him, but more often with subjects not so close to his heart.

"You are usually more adept at hiding your falsehoods, which means Georgiana is correct to insist you tell me. You will need a willing ear when hers is not available. Since I shall be no more than a quick walk away in Berkley Square until the end of the Season, I am your best option."

"Richard James Albert Fitzwilliam." Lady Fitzwilliam took the last few steps and whipped the drapery aside. "You are being ridiculous."

"I am capable of finding my own wife, Mother."

"Are you?" She glanced back and forth between them. "Is that why you are hiding like a small child?"

Darcy stared at the carpet while he tried to keep his shoulders from shaking with his laughter. "Perhaps if he could first see Lady Helena without the introduction? When he approached, he made mention of a horse."

His aunt drew back and gasped. "If you made that unflattering comparison, I am certain you have never set eyes upon Lady Helena, who is one of the loveliest and most accomplished young ladies of my acquaintance. Your insinuation makes me seem no better than your father, who would auction you off to whoever offered him the most political leverage. I would wager *he* would marry you to a horse if it benefited him."

"Forgive me," said Richard. He narrowed his eyes at Darcy while his aunt peered behind her.

"Enough of that." She grasped her son's ear and tugged him towards the opposite side of the room. "You will meet her now, and I warn you, I will not tolerate a refusal."

Richard dragged his feet as he followed—not that he had any choice in the matter. He took two steps, turned, and mouthed, "You will tell me."

"Darcy!"

He turned in time to shake Mr. Gardiner's outstretched hand. "Mary and my wife are wishing Miss Darcy well before we depart. Our youngest complained of a belly ache this morning, so my wife is eager to return home. I hope you understand."

"Of course. I would be concerned in your place. I hope he is well."

"Thank you," said Mr. Gardiner as he released Darcy's hand.

"We are pleased you came. Georgiana was quite adamant to have Miss Bennet stand up with her. Thank you." His arm relaxed at his side. Had he finally managed to find some semblance of calm? His shoulders were now sore from being so tightly wound for such a long time.

Mr. Gardiner grinned and glanced about the room. "Mary was honoured to be asked, I assure you. Miss Darcy's friendship means a great deal to her."

"My sister treasures Miss Bennet's friendship as well."

The man glanced across the room and startled. "Ah, forgive me, my wife is sending me a look." He bowed. "I do hope you will come for dinner soon. You are always welcome."

"Thank you," said Darcy, returning the bow. "I shall send a note."

"Excellent." After one more swift handshake, Mr. Gardiner hurried across the room.

Darcy's gaze happened upon Richard and his back stiffened. Under most circumstances, he could confide in his cousin without reservation, but why would he want to speak of what happened with Elizabeth to another person? Speaking of her to Georgiana was painful enough. The last thing he wanted was another well-meaning relation poking about in his personal affairs. But, what to do?

Watson could escort his cousin from the house when breakfast ended, but Richard knew how to navigate the servants' passages and would find a way to sneak back inside.

Georgiana had known the exact foil to use to trap him into a corner, and she had wielded it with flawless precision. Fending off Richard possessed about as much appeal as a ball or dinner the *ton* called "the event of the Season."

He clasped his hands behind his back and rocked on his feet. How could he sneak out of the house before Richard sharpened his foil and used it to ferret out the truth?

Chapter 3

After the last of the guests departed, Richard motioned in the direction of the study. "I believe we were to have a glass of brandy."

"This truly is not necessary." How could he muster the fortitude, not to mention the equanimity, to confide in Richard? Georgiana had set her trap, and he could not very well chew off an arm or a leg to free himself. "I am not Georgiana, who needs to speak of every happening and every emotion she possesses."

"Richard!" His cousin winced, and Darcy pressed his lips together to keep from laughing. The reaction to Aunt Catherine's tone was the same now as it was when Richard was a boy. "Do you not have your own home? I am sure Darcy wishes to retire after such a long and trying day."

"We were to have a brandy, Aunt." Richard's shoulders were rigid. He had always required at least a half-hour complete to relax in their aunt's presence. "I am certain my cousin does not object to a bit of gentlemanly conversation before he retires."

His aunt jabbed at Richard with her walking stick. "If the conversation is with you, I am certain it is far from 'gentlemanly.'" Darcy coughed in a failed attempt to restrain his mirth. "Besides, I have estate matters to discuss with Darcy that cannot be delayed. I depart at first light, and I have no intention of rising at some ungodly hour so you can conduct your 'gentlemanly conversation' tonight. You live close enough to come again on the morrow if Fitzwilliam desires your company."

Richard stepped beside Darcy, leaning close to his shoulder. "I shall not forget Georgiana's concern. You *will* tell me."

Darcy stared straight ahead and said nothing. His aunt had granted him a much-needed reprieve, and he would make the most of the opportunity she was affording him. The moment the door closed, his aunt drew herself up and resituated her walking stick. "I overheard his conversation with Georgiana. If in your place, I would not be pleased with her interference into my affairs. As far as I am concerned, you are entitled to keep your own counsel. She had no right, regardless of her good intentions."

"I appreciate your aid, Aunt."

"Yes, well, I recognise grief when I see it." She held up a hand and shook her head. "I do not require an explanation unless you wish to tell me. After Anne's death, Lady Fitzwilliam tried to force me to speak of my feelings when what I desired most was solitude. You have helped with Rosings and brought Georgiana to visit while allowing me to grieve as I needed. I wished to afford you the same opportunity." She walked towards his study. "Now pour me a glass of sherry."

He offered his aunt his arm and helped her to the sofa. When he handed her the glass of wine, she huffed. "With Georgiana gone and you not entertaining, no one else will be drinking the sherry. Do not be stingy."

He bit his lip and topped off the glass before pouring himself a sizeable brandy. A fire had already been lit and the room was warm in preparation for the remainder of his day. His servants knew his current habits well. They had also lit the two candles near his desk, which he would extinguish once his aunt retired.

"Your sister made an excellent match. You should be proud."

He sat in one of the chairs near the fire and nodded. "I am. She has become a poised and intelligent young lady. I cannot be anything but proud."

"She seems blissful, and he is obviously taken with her. I believe they shall do well together." His aunt held the delicate crystal glass just below her chin while she stared into the fire. "I once hoped for a match such as that your sister has made. I was never so fortunate." She had never before spoken of her marriage. Georgiana's wedding must have brought those memories to the fore.

"Were you dissatisfied with Sir Lewis?"

After a laborious inhale, she sighed. "Your mother never told you of my marriage." It was more a statement than a question.

"How do you mean?"

Her hand holding the sherry lowered to rest on her leg. "As much as I had hoped for a successful first Season, I was greatly disappointed. I could blame it on the quality of the ladies who debuted that Season, but I am certain the same could be said of every Season. I smiled and attempted to impress the gentlemen, but the few who called were more interested in my fortune than me."

He rested his elbow on the arm of the chair. "How did you come to wed de Bourgh?"

"After my fourth Season, my father died. My brother had been a spoiled, selfish prig for as long as I could remember, and

I was unwilling to entrust my future to him. I had met Sir Lewis during my first Season. He was just returning to society after losing his wife, who had died during childbirth. We developed a friendship over the years. After my father passed, he called upon me and offered his hand. He was ill. He knew he did not have a great deal of time remaining and had not found a lady he desired to marry. He said he preferred our conversations on politics and literature to the remarks of other ladies on the weather and the latest fashions." She took a sip of her sherry. "He hoped for an heir, and I needed to escape. He did not love me any more than I loved him, but we were dear friends. In the end, we both benefited. Unlike his previous children, Anne survived her first year, and I cared for him until he succumbed."

He furrowed his brow and let the crackling of the fire in the grate soothe him. "I do not remember much of him, but I do remember he was quite fond of Anne."

A slight smile graced her face. "Rosings was not entailed, so he was well-pleased with a girl. She was, as the bard would say, the 'apple of his eye.'"

"Have you ever thought of marrying again?"

She straightened with a jerk. "Why should I do that?"

"For love," he said in a soft voice.

"Nephew, Anne inherited Rosings when she came of age, and you inherited it with her death. I am indebted to you for allowing me to remain in my home."

"I have no need to force you to the Dower house—"

She shook her head. "I enjoy not being under the rule of a man. I have no desire to humble myself when I take great pleasure in presiding over my home."

He could not help but smile. "Is that why you choose parsons who bow and scrape—"

His aunt scoffed and pointed a bony, knotted finger in his direction. "Impertinent boy. Never forget that I know of your exploits, young man."

"I have never had exploits." He relaxed back into his chair and crossed his ankle over his knee. Who could have known his aunt would be so altered after Anne's death? She had become rather likeable as opposed to the domineering woman who had once insisted he wed her daughter. "You are confusing me with Richard." His humour faltered, and he trained his eyes on the flickering shadow of the flame on the carpet. "How is your new companion?"

"Frightened of her own shadow, not that I blame her." His aunt sighed and shrugged. "She is tolerable company and has become accustomed to the household servants. They are considerate of her, even though they do not understand why she is so timid."

"Does she still have nightmares?" His eyes met his aunt's. "You made mention of them some time ago."

"They are not as frequent." She stood and filled her glass. "Truly, she is much improved. She takes walks in the gardens near the house, accompanied by a maid and a footman when I do not wish for exercise. The pianoforte lessons you provided were appreciated—she often shuts herself away in the music room to play while I have callers. Since my eyesight has begun to decline, she reads to me. I purchased the latest Radcliffe from Hatchard's yesterday as a gift for when I return. I also purchased some fabric for new gowns. The bonnets and trimmings you sent for Christmastide were well-received. She passed a great deal of time decorating her new hats. She even smiled."

"Then I am pleased." He watched the fire until his aunt sat in her chair once more.

"Did you ever find the blackguard who did this to her?"

He nodded, still staring into the fire. "I did."

She lifted her generous eyebrows. "Well? Tell me he cannot harm another young lady, and I shall be satisfied."

He stood and propped his arm on the mantel while he poked the fire. "He is gone. He cannot harm another young lady."

"Are you certain he cannot return?"

"He is working as a labourer at a port in the East Indies. The company is aware of his past and has told the captains he is not to be given passage to any destination to prevent him from making a circuitous route back to England. Even should he somehow acquire the funds, he cannot return."

His aunt took a long draw from her sherry and gave a low laugh that sent a chill up his spine. "I am not sorry. He deserves every bit of unhappiness, for it will never equal her suffering. Your father spoilt that young good-for-nothing. I am proud of you for correcting his mistake."

"He never appreciated what he had. He always wanted more." His voice was soft, but his aunt's shake of her head demonstrated that she had heard him.

"No, and I daresay Richard would heartily approve if he knew. Do not dare feel guilt for his fate, Fitzwilliam," she said in a firm tone. "He coveted your position and wealth and was willing to hurt others for a piece of it. Harming servants and those he could not use for profit was for nothing more than entertainment, and when he ceased to find sport in it, he abandoned them. In the case of that poor girl, she would have rotted in the back alleys of Saffron Hill if not for you. No, he deserved far worse, but I would not have you responsible for his death. This is a much better solution."

He indulged in a sizeable sip of his brandy and closed his eyes as he swallowed. His aunt's company was in no way objectionable, but how he longed for solitude. The house had been a hive of activity since breakfast. He needed quiet.

"You appear tired, Nephew," said Aunt Catherine.

"I am weary. I am thankful I was spared speaking to Richard this evening, but behaving as though I am a social creature to those at the wedding and breakfast was a chore."

She set her glass on the side table. "You did well. You are a good brother."

He blinked a few times and smiled. "Georgiana has said as much. I am glad she is contented, but I am going to miss her."

"It would be strange if you did not." When she began to stand, Darcy made to rise with her, but she stayed him. "No, I require no fuss. I shall see myself to my chambers." She patted his shoulder, situated her walking stick, and took a step. "Do not hide yourself away. I expect you at Rosings before too long." She opened the door, peering back once more before leaving. "Good night, Fitzwilliam."

He tipped his glass in her direction. "Good night." As soon as he was alone, he swallowed the last of his brandy and poured himself a second helping. Once he had the full glass in hand, he stepped before the window and stared without seeing across Park Lane and into the dark shadows of Hyde Park.

Tomorrow, the knocker would be removed from the door. Now that Georgiana was wed, he had no reason to accept callers. When he met with Mrs. Northcott and Watson in the morning, he would also ensure Richard was kept at bay for the time being. They could post footmen at the entrances to the servants' passages. Richard had hoped to journey with Darcy to Pemberley in a month or so, but perhaps he could conclude his business and away to Pemberley before Richard was ready to depart. In the perfect plan, Georgiana's request would be long forgotten by the time they were in company once again.

He sighed and rested his head against the cool glass. He should retire. The sitting room attached to his bedchamber boasted of a supply of brandy. He took a sip, relishing the bite, and made his way to the stairs. The sooner he found sleep, the sooner he could dream of a happier life—a life with Elizabeth by his side.

Chapter 4

The frigid February air stung Darcy's nose and cheeks as he walked along Piccadilly. With the cold weather, few milled about the street, but the lack of people stopping him to speak or to bring their daughter to his attention was not a disappointment. On the contrary, the scarcity of his acquaintances was a blessing.

A man tipped his hat as they approached, and Darcy reciprocated the gesture before they passed. He could not say the fellow was an acquaintance, yet his face was familiar. Perhaps they had acquaintances in common? He had attended many events over the course of the last Season, so the man could have been invited to any number of balls or dinners. Thankfully, he did not seem inclined to keep him and continued on.

When he reached Hatchard's, Darcy ducked inside the popular bookseller's and began to search the shelves. He could not say what he sought, yet he had the urge to find something—anything to appease his housekeeper in some regard. Lady Catherine had journeyed back to Rosings, as planned, the day after Georgiana's wedding. Since her departure, he had been content to remain in his study from the moment he rose until he retired, but after three days, Mrs. Northcott began to regard him with a gimlet eye and her lips pursed. To prevent her further study, this afternoon, he made a swift escape from the confines of Darcy House, though not without an odd look from Watson when he refused a carriage and insisted upon venturing out on foot.

"Sir, may I help you find a particular book?" He straightened to tower over an elderly man whose sparse hair stuck out in white tufts around his ears.

Darcy glanced around. He knew the shop well enough. If he made an excuse to continue his search on his own, he could pass a vast amount of time doing no more than staring at the titles. "What of poetry? Is there something new?"

The old man wagged a finger at him. "I remember you, sir. You have not come in for some time, but if I recall correctly, you have purchased Lord Byron and Wordsworth in the past. The latest from Lord Byron is 'The Corsair' and the latest from Wordsworth is 'The Excursion,' but both volumes are from last year."

"I do not have either." He followed as the little man trotted towards a shelf along the opposite wall. "Would you have two copies of each?" He always purchased one for Darcy House and another for Pemberley. On occasion, he travelled with a book to pass the time, but he did not like to carry too many. This prevented the necessity.

The little old man bounced on his toes while he collected the volumes and hurried with them to the front of the store. Once they were bought and wrapped, Darcy stepped into the icy wind and continued along Piccadilly until he reached Bond Street where he turned, roaming along the pavement. For some reason, a shop ahead arrested his attention, so he paused and stared at the sign for what could have been a full minute. The owner had been his mother's favoured jeweller. Without considering why, he pushed open the door, the bell ringing merrily with the movement.

"Mr. Darcy!" The man behind the counter straightened and grinned. "How are you, sir?"

"I am well, thank you." He approached and tried to force a smile. "I hope you and your family are well?"

"Yes, sir, thank you." The man pressed his palms together. "Searching for a gift for Miss Darcy?"

He glanced up. "Perhaps, but my sister has lately become Lady Witney."

The owner gasped, and if possible, his grin grew larger. "Congratulations, sir. I wish her joy."

After a nod, he returned to the shop owner's wares. "Thank you, she is overjoyed. I shall pass along your good wishes." His gaze flitted from a pearl comb to a sapphire necklace then to countless other pieces. Why was he searching for jewellery? Georgiana had no need of jewels. With her marriage, she gained those from the Witney estate. One day, she would inherit those of the earldom. Just as he was about to wish the proprietor a good day, a glimmer of green drew his notice, and he pointed into the case. "May I take a closer look?"

The man hurried towards him and set the piece upon the counter. "You have a superior eye, sir. Nine emeralds of excellent quality between two gold chains with a teardrop-shaped emerald at the base. I also have ear drops that would match well."

Darcy ran his fingers along the gold, the image of it resting against a pale neck invading his mind. "I shall take it."

"Would you like the ear drops as well?"

"Yes, I would."

The man took a box from a cupboard behind him and began to wrap the pieces. "This is a beautiful set, sir. The lady who receives it will be thrilled."

He nodded and sighed. The likelihood the emeralds would ever grace flesh and bone was non-existent. What was he doing? The man would think him addled if he changed his mind now, so he forced a smile and slipped the wrapped package into his great coat pocket. "Thank you."

When he stepped back outside, a light snow had begun to fall, and he remained frozen in place while each delicate snowflake drifted on the cold breeze until it landed gracefully on the street. In his imagination, Elizabeth lifted her face into the falling snow and let it caress her cheeks, pink from the chill of the day.

After a shuddering breath, he turned and continued, his hand cradling the jewels. Would they do nothing more than sit in his safe until he gave them to his sister or he died? He could afford the purchase, but it was such a waste. The emeralds would never grace the neck of a living soul. They would sit in a box until the end of time.

He came to an abrupt halt and blinked at the sign over the shop on the corner. How had he reached Brook Street so quickly? Darcy glanced about, but few horses and carriages occupied the roads today so his legs carried him with swift steps across Bond. He walked along Brook Street towards Hyde Park, quickening his pace at Berkley Square, else Richard see him and chase him down. When he reached Park Lane, he climbed the steps of Darcy House where Watson admitted him without delay, but before the butler could remove his coat, he stayed him. "Pray, put the books on my desk, and the other parcel in my rooms."

Before Watson could enquire of his plans, Darcy departed once more. This time, he crossed Park Lane to enter the Grosvenor gate of Hyde Park. Mrs. Northcott would be beside herself at his continued exposure to the weather, but he craved a quiet he would not find inside the house. For some odd reason, Hyde Park seemed the ideal place to find solace. Few would consider a walk in the park during the snow a pleasant idea.

The park was not its usual verdant green, but instead, boasted of barren trees and grass that appeared a little darker than straw due to its dormant state. His feet followed the paths until he reached the Serpentine where a bench beckoned him to sit. He brushed off a place for himself and relaxed while the flakes fell around him like a dream world. He tipped his chin towards the heavens, welcoming the damp sting of the icy crystals on his face. For one brief second, the numbness he endured disappeared despite the aching hole that remained. The hole had been part of his everyday life since he learnt of Elizabeth's death—a not-so-subtle reminder of her importance as well as of her absence. He felt for the Gardiners. After all, they did not just lose Elizabeth; they had also lost Miss Bennet. The Bennets had faced so much tragedy since their youngest sister's folly. The family would never recover—they could never be as they once were.

He shivered but did not take it as a hint that he needed to return home. He had been correct about the quiet of the park. Other than an occasional person who appeared to be rushing through the paths in the hopes of finding refuge from the weather, people did not promenade or mill about. The beautiful stillness brought a peace he sought, not a feeling borne of happiness or contentment but of something else he did not recognise. While he remained, the flakes became fatter and the snowfall became heavier. The snow began to collect on the grass, and the blackness of the Serpentine stood out in stark contrast to the white as it covered the ground.

With no one to please or to importune him, he sat and stared until he started at the growing darkness engulfing him into its fold. A mist hung over the water, and he blinked. How long had he remained upon that bench?

His pocket watch read half five. He had not glanced at his watch when he entered the park, so he could not say how many hours he spent gazing at the prospect. With a heavy exhale, he stood and took one last look at the Serpentine before walking in the direction of the Grosvenor gate.

In the time he had been in the park, the few people on the pathways had vanished and left the space deserted. He did not happen upon a soul as he exited the park and crossed the street, which suited him well. When he reached Darcy House, no sooner had he placed a foot on the step than the door whipped open and Watson ushered him inside. After helping him remove his great coat, the staid butler regarded the damp garment with a slight flare of the nose as he handed it to a footman. When Darcy was free, he strode into the library and removed the crystal stopper from the brandy.

"Mr. Darcy! Thank goodness you have returned!" Mrs. Northcott's hand was splayed across her chest as she bustled into the room. "Water is heated for a bath, and I shall have coffee brought to your chambers to help put you to rights."

"Thank you, but the coffee is not necessary."

"Tea then," she said in a higher tone.

"No, the brandy will warm me." He poured a full glass and cradled it in his hand. "I shall have Morton attend me. Thank you for heating the water so it would be ready upon my arrival."

"Of course, sir."

Mrs. Northcott stood stock-still near the door, watching him as he exited. In all likelihood, she thought him in his cups—not that he was concerned if she did. He would indeed have his fill of brandy before he retired.

"Mr. Darcy," said Morton when he entered his rooms. "Your bath is prepared. Would you prefer comfortable clothes for the rest of the evening or your nightclothes?"

Darcy set down his glass and closed his eyes while the valet fussed over him and tugged his topcoat down his arms. "Comfortable will do."

"You must have spent some time in the weather, sir, but we shall soon see you warm and fed for the evening. I am certain Mrs. Northcott—"

"Pray, no food."

"Sir?"

He shook his head. "I have no wish for coffee or tea, and I am not hungry. The bath and the brandy will do admirably."

"Of course, sir." Morton followed him into his dressing room and collected the rest of his clothes. When Darcy sank into the steaming water, the heat seeped through to his bones, and he melted into the liquid warmth with a sigh.

"Morton, I seem to have left my brandy in the bedchamber."

Within moments, his valet held his glass before him. "Sir," he said with a slight bow.

Darcy took a generous drink of the liquor and savoured the burn as the spirits swirled in his mouth. After swallowing, he slid down a bit further so he could rest his head against the back of the copper tub. "If you lay out my clothes, I can manage for the rest of the evening."

"Yes, sir."

After a few minutes, the room was silent with the exception of the water lapping against the side of the tub. He lifted his head long enough to take a sizeable sip of the brandy before setting his head once again upon the edge and closing his eyes. What he would not give to ready himself for bed without such a fuss. He had no desire to trouble himself over what he would wear or whether he would eat.

When the bath cooled, he towelled himself and donned the clothing Morton had left for him. Brandy—he needed brandy! He poured another glass from the decanter in his sitting room and paced around his rooms. His feet led him into his bedchamber where he paused inside the door, staring at the package upon the bed. Had his father felt this same emptiness after the death of his mother? How had his father survived for so many years in such a state? He rubbed the ache in his chest. His father had been much older. His nightmare had been of shorter duration. For Darcy, the future stretched out before him, day after tedious day to pass before he could welcome the night with open arms. How many years would he have to live in such misery?

Darcy picked up the parcel. What had possessed him to purchase it? He unwrapped the paper, opened the box, and ran his fingers along the vivid green stones. The emeralds would be striking against her pale skin and would complement the flecks of green in her fine hazel eyes. He could imagine them around her neck, glimmering in the candlelight.

He set the package on the bedside table before moving to the window. Big, white snowflakes still fell from a pitch-black sky as he stared into the darkness of the park below. He turned his back on the window and scanned the empty bedchamber. He gulped the last of his brandy and coughed at the burn. His legs dragged some as he stepped to the bed. He climbed atop, propped himself against the pillows, and sighed. The sooner he found sleep, the sooner he could find the sole happiness available to him, his dreams. Outside the window, one fat snowflake drifted in a dream-like fashion down, down until the darkness enveloped it and him into its warm embrace.

Chapter 5

Darcy stood before the windows of his study as the sun set over the treetops of Hyde Park in a brilliant wash of vibrant reds and oranges then lingered as the moon began its ascent into the night sky. This day had resembled the others that had passed since Georgiana's wedding, tedious task after tedious task while he anticipated the evening to come. How he welcomed this time of day—welcomed the hour when he could pour his first sizeable glass of brandy and work towards the dream world he sought without one ounce of reserve.

A fire burned in the grate, providing a modicum of light to the one room he regularly inhabited other than his bedchamber, lest his servants believe him in need of a physician to balance his humours. After all, what servant worth their salt would not act if their master remained in his cups and abed for days at a time?

The paltry light of two candles illuminated the untouched tray of food upon his desk. Mrs. Northcott would "tsk" and shake her head at another meal ignored in favour of spirits, yet he would find sleep sooner without the food in his belly.

He stared into the dark window, but the reflection of the room caught his attention. Elizabeth reclined against the far end of the sofa, her one eyebrow arched, and her lips curved into a tempting smile. Her expression beckoned him to abandon his place and love her. Oh! How he wished he could!

His eyes itched, and he fought the urge to blink, a trivial physical requirement that never failed to disappoint him in these situations. Finally giving in, he allowed his eyelids to close for a fraction of a second. When he reopened them,

Elizabeth had vanished. His heart cracked and bled with every sighting his conscious mind allowed then stole away with a cruelty that pained him. At least in sleep, her departure was rare before the bitter glare of dawn.

The amber liquor slid down his throat with ease as he finished the first glass. He poured another and focussed on the darkened street. Park Lane, while not a busy thoroughfare, had an occasional carriage that passed, heading to one ball or another. Darcy no longer read the invitations. Why would he do so when he could task his secretary with sending his regrets? With Georgiana's marriage, he no longer had reason to don an air of civility and bear those insufferable matchmaking mothers and their tedious, cloying daughters.

At the creaking of the door, the glass reflected Mrs. Northcott as she entered. True to character, she took a long look at the laden tray before her eyes met his in the window. "Sir, Cook would be pleased to prepare a meal more to your liking. If—"

"Pray, do not put her to the trouble. I am not hungry." The housekeeper opened her mouth to speak. "Beg her forgiveness. I know she has put a great deal of effort into the food tonight. I am appreciative of her dedication."

Mrs. Northcott's lips pressed into a thin line before she gave a curt nod. "Yes, sir."

At a knock on the front door, the housekeeper uttered what resembled a growl. "Who calls at this time of day?"

Darcy twisted and placed a hand to the back of his chair. "If it is Lord Carlisle, I am from home."

"Yes, sir," said Mrs. Northcott. He was thankful she had not mentioned Richard's near daily attempts to call. Since

Georgiana's wedding a week ago, Watson had thus far managed to keep Richard from accessing the servants' passages. Darcy had been blessedly left to his own company.

When his eyes returned to the park, a hackney stood before the house. He frowned. Who had come? Richard lived on Berkley Square and would never hire a hackney to carry him, for all intents and purposes, around the corner. His eyes lit on the silhouette of the horse harnessed to the carriage, a nag too thin to haul anything of considerable weight. How had the poor beast even managed with the vehicle it pulled? The individual at the door could not be Richard. For that matter, none of his acquaintance would require a hackney. "Mrs. Northcott?"

As she paused in the doorway, an unintelligible voice carried into the study with Watson's loud reprimand following, prompting him to set down his drink and follow the voices towards the hall. "Miss, if you have business with this house, I am certain it should be conducted at the servants' entrance. If you make your way to the mews, you can enter near the stables and apply to the housekeeper, a Mrs. Northcott."

"Thank you, but I am not here to see the housekeeper. I am acquainted with Mr. Darcy and must speak with him on an urgent matter that cannot be delayed." He frowned. He knew that voice. The frantic and insistent tone caused him to increase his pace. He followed close behind Mrs. Northcott, almost pushing her into the hall, then leaned forward in an attempt to see around Watson's broad back. Whose voice was that? He had heard it before, yet could not place to whom it belonged. He needed to see her face.

"Miss, I sincerely doubt you are acquainted with the Master. As it is, he is not at home to callers."

With five large steps, a small portion of the caller's left side became visible. Golden blonde hair peeked from a worn straw bonnet followed by a face that nearly brought him to his knees. How was this possible? He shook his head and looked again, standing dumb just behind Watson's left shoulder. Had he lost consciousness at his desk? Could he already be asleep and dreaming? If so, where was—

"Sir!" Darcy, who had been swaying in his spot, startled at Watson's cry. "I am terribly sorry! I told the woman you would not see her, but she insisted. I was about to demand she depart—"

"No!" Darcy lunged forward and grabbed the edge of the door as Watson dodged his movement. Darcy blinked and stared, disbelieving his own eyes. Dark circles marred the undersides of her eyes, her buff-coloured pelisse was worn and threadbare, and her figure thin, but...but... "Miss Bennet?" This was impossible. She was dead, was she not?

She curtseyed, her expression tight. "Good evening, Mr. Darcy."

"Forgive me." He shifted aside and held out an arm, gesturing her into the hall. His entire body shook in a manner he had never experienced. If Miss Bennet lived, dare he ask what had become of Elizabeth? They were together when they disappeared, were they not?

With all he had, he fought against the urge to grab Miss Bennet by the arms, shake her, and demand her sister's whereabouts. He gulped down the trembling in his chest and endeavoured to breathe in an even manner. "I fear you have given me quite a shock. Your aunt and uncle will be overjoyed. They were told you and your sister are dead."

Her eyes widened. "You must not tell them." She spoke forcefully, far different from the gentle manner he had witnessed so often in Hertfordshire. "I shall explain," she said in a calmer tone, "but they cannot know." When she stepped inside, the shabby condition of her bonnet as well as the appalling frayed and stained hem of her gown became more apparent. Bingley's sisters would be merciless if they were to see her in such a state. "Forgive me for the intrusion, but I am in desperate need of aid and knew not who to ask. When you came to mind, I hoped you would be amenable. Lizzy—"

"Lizzy?" He became lightheaded and staggered back into the wall. He had hoped— "I..." His heart pounded against his ribs. "Do you mean Elizabeth is alive?" He propelled himself from the wall and bolted towards the door. "Where is she? Is she in the hackney?"

"Mr. Darcy, she did not accompany me." He made an abrupt stop, his stomach dropping like a weight to his feet. Miss Bennet gasped and reached for him as he stumbled into a chair Watson kept nearby. "Sir, she is alive!" He covered his face and struggled to contain the torrent of emotions that threatened to burst from his skin.

"Sir?" When he removed his hands, Mrs. Northcott knelt at his side. "Are you well?"

"Yes," he said. "I..."

"I fear I have caused him a shock." Miss Bennet clasped her hands in front of her. "Forgive me, Mr. Darcy. My sister is alive, but quite ill. She is why I have come." She took a small step forward but then seemed to think better of it and retreated back. "Sir, I am afraid for her and did not know where to turn. She confided in me long ago what occurred at Rosings as well as your time together at Pemberley. What she divulged gave me reason to hope you would help. She is very poorly." Her shiny eyes had a well of tears resting on her lower eyelids and her lip quivered. "We have managed the best we can, but we cannot afford the apothecary. I do not know what to do. She is all I have. I cannot lose her."

He drew himself up and nodded. His beloved needed him. He had failed her when he did not follow the Gardiners to London, but he refused to fail her again. "Watson, have the stables prepare the carriage. Mrs. Northcott, we shall require rugs to bring Miss Elizabeth here, and send one of the men for Mr. Acker."

"A friend hired the hackney that brought us here," said Miss Bennet. Her eyes shifted to the door and back. "I cannot leave without word—"

He looked to Watson. "Pay the hackney driver and bring the gentleman inside. We shall journey to..."

Miss Bennet glanced from Mrs. Northcott to Watson and took a breath. "We are on the corner of Mercer and Castle Streets in St. Giles, a short distance from Seven Dials." Her voice was weak when she gave the direction, and her eyes still darted from person to person as if she braced for a reaction. At the mention of Seven Dials, his housekeeper's nostrils flared for but a moment. Watson said nothing, but hurried outside while Mrs. Northcott bustled off, no doubt to gather supplies.

As soon as they were alone, he clasped his hands behind his back. "Miss Elizabeth told you I proposed?"

Miss Bennet's lips curved ever so slightly. "She did."

Before he could ask another question, Watson stepped back inside, his expression odd. Darcy opened his mouth to ask what was amiss when a man taller than his own six feet followed his servant inside. He turned to Miss Bennet. "Would you do me the honour of an introduction?"

"Mr. Darcy, may I present Mr. Erasmus Cooke," said Miss Bennet, holding out a hand in the man's direction. "He and his wife live in the home next to ours."

A comment made by Mr. Gardiner shifted to the forefront of Darcy's mind. During his search for his nieces, he had spoken of a Black man of substantial height who worked in the stable of a coaching inn. "You spoke to Mr. Gardiner when he was searching for the Miss Bennets."

The man nodded while his hands clenched and released at his sides. "Yes, sir. My wife and I knew Miss Bennet and Miss Elizabeth did not want to be found, so when he knocked at our door and asked if we knew the ladies, I told him the story my wife and I discussed with the Miss Bennets."

Miss Bennet smiled and gave a dip of her chin. "He is an excellent neighbour."

"We have loaded some rugs into the carriage, sir," said Mrs. Northcott as she entered from the servants' entrance. "The driver will bring it around in but a moment." Her head shifted back and forth between the men and Miss Bennet. "Do you wish me to accompany you?"

He had not considered the necessity of her presence until now. Depending upon Elizabeth's condition, his housekeeper's knowledge could be beneficial. "Yes, I would appreciate your experience. Thank you."

"I have placed Elsie in charge of preparing rooms for the Miss Bennets. Will the gentleman require a bedchamber as well?"

Mr. Cooke's eyebrows lifted high on his forehead. "I accompanied Miss Bennet out of concern for her safety, but upon our return, I am needed at home by my wife. Thank you."

A footman handed Mrs. Northcott her spencer, bonnet, and gloves, which the woman began to don. "The carriage is being brought around," said the girl, who curtseyed and hurried back into the servants' passage.

The four of them met the equipage when it came to a halt at the kerb. They settled themselves inside, Mr. Cooke riding atop to direct the driver to the correct location. Darcy had a thousand questions spinning and churning in his brain, but he kept them to himself for the almost half-hour trip.

Truth be told, he stared without pause at the dim figure of Miss Bennet across from him. A part of him still could not credit she was alive, and he would soon see Elizabeth. His body trembled, and his knee bounced in a constant motion. Would Elizabeth be much different from the lady he had known a few short years before? Living in St. Giles could have caused a drastic change in her personality, could it not? And what of her health? Miss Bennet said she was ill, but would she be as thin as Miss Bennet? If Cook had laid eyes upon Miss Bennet, she would have vowed, in the next breath, to fatten her up. She had said those same words often enough about him in these past two years.

When the carriage slowed to a stop, the footman placed the step and opened the door. Miss Bennet was swift to alight and move towards a basement dwelling. He followed behind, struggling not to recoil at the filth that covered the windows and seemed to permeate the neighbourhood.

Mr. Cooke climbed down and bowed. "I fear I shall be in your way, so I shall take my leave. Good evening, Mr. Darcy, Miss Bennet."

Once Darcy bowed to Mr. Cooke and thanked him, he followed Miss Bennet, his body somehow taut despite his incessant quaking. He clenched his hands at his sides while he ducked his head to enter. When he straightened, a single room lay before him. A smoking tallow candle lit the space, set in the middle of a table that leaned as though it might fall into pieces at any moment. Two wooden chairs were at the table and two worn chairs, marred by the stuffing peeking from the fabric, stood before a large fireplace where a fire crackled in the grate.

"Thank goodness you have returned." The owner of the voice strode around the screen and into the firelight as she spoke. The lady, who he assumed was Mrs. Cooke, was also Black with wide brown eyes and her hair in tight curls framing her face below her cap. "Her fever has risen since you left and her breathing has worsened. I have been bathing her with cool water for some time." Miss Bennet removed her bonnet and placed it on the table while the lady stepped outside of the door. The sound of pouring water could be heard before she stepped back inside, a sizeable bowl in her hands. "I am glad Erasmus replenished the bucket before you departed." She looked at Darcy and paused. "Forgive me. I fear I have been rude."

He dipped his chin at Miss Bennet's glance. "Mr. Darcy, this lady is Mrs. Gemma Cooke. Gemma, Mr. Darcy also brought his housekeeper, Mrs. Northcott."

He had not introduced his housekeeper but was not surprised Miss Bennet paid close enough attention to know her name. He nodded and cleared his throat. "I must thank you and your husband for your excellent care of the Miss Bennets."

Mrs. Cooke smiled though her eyes never left him, seeming to study every detail. "They are good neighbours. We have enjoyed their society these past two years, and we have done well to find work together. Three ladies can sew much more than one alone and are more attractive when the dressmakers have a large order to fulfil and require extra hands. They are also of great help with my son. He adores them both."

"One of us watches young Michael while the other accompanies Gemma to the dressmakers and tailors," said Miss Bennet. "We take in sewing for them and sometimes the homes of the *ton* to support ourselves."

With a small jump, Mrs. Cooke made her way around the screen. "I should put a cold cloth on Lizzy's head instead of chatting away as I am." Miss Bennet joined her, their voices lowering to hushed murmurings that could not be understood.

"Mr. Darcy, if you intend for these ladies to come to Darcy house," said Mrs. Northcott, distracting him from the happenings behind the barrier. "May I suggest we remove their hair and burn their clothing to minimise the vermin that may accompany them." Before he could respond, she continued, "I know lice are quite common. From what I have read in the former housekeeper's journals, your grandmother struggled with them for most of her life. They burned the bedding as well as her clothing and wigs upon her death. After, your mother was meticulous about her hairpieces to keep them at bay. She boiled them and replaced them often since she had no wish to remove all her hair."

Darcy glanced around the room and revolted. How could he insist that Elizabeth's beautiful auburn curls be cut? "I cannot ask that of them."

"I do not mind." His head whipped around to Miss Bennet, who had somehow crept around the screen without capturing their attention. "Since living here, Lizzy and I have tried to do what we can. We have rubbed castor oil into our hair and our scalps as well as other remedies, but to no avail. I believe they are in our mattresses, but we cannot afford to replace them. I would hate to bring this into your household, particularly when you are being so kind."

"The best remedy would be to remove your hair." Mrs. Northcott gave him a quick glance. "I took the liberty of bringing a blade in the event you were amenable."

"Miss Bennet," he said, "I do not expect this of either of you. We can consult with the physician."

Miss Bennet shook her head. "No, I would prefer to bow to your housekeeper's wishes and greater expertise in the matter. After all, she is the one who must deal with the problem once we are gone. If she would remove our hair before we depart, I would be grateful." She brushed her hands as though they were covered in dust. "In fact, if Mrs. Northcott wishes, she may start with me."

His housekeeper hurried to the carriage and Miss Bennet placed a hand to his sleeve. "I know it is not proper, but

Gemma's son needs to be taken home and put to bed. Would you mind sitting with Lizzy? I do not want her to be alone."

He took a deep breath and stretched his fingers in an attempt to calm himself. "Of course." His hands continued their futile motions as his feet crept closer and closer to the edge of the screen. His lungs fought to draw in the air that had somehow become thicker as though he were trying to breathe treacle. When he walked around the partition, Mrs. Cooke stood against the wall to allow him to pass. In her arms, a small boy, who bore more than a passing resemblance to his father, rested his head on her shoulder.

Darcy moved in the direction of the bed. How many times had he prayed for one last glimpse of Elizabeth—for one more chance to correct his mistakes? His heart picked up its pace, and he closed his eyes. Even though he had intended for them to be closed for but a moment in order to bring himself under better regulation, they struggled to open. How many times had he blinked only to have her apparition disappear? He held his breath and began to draw open his eyelids. Whatever would he do if he suddenly woke to find this a dream? How would he survive?

Chapter 6

As the room flickered into view, a tallow candle next to the bed provided enough light to discern a lone figure lying among the bedcoverings. Her head rested upon a pillow with a folded, damp cloth across her forehead. He took two steps closer, and when Elizabeth came into clearer view, his greedy eyes roamed over her while his heart hammered against his sternum. The dim light prevented him from examining her in great detail, but she was thinner and her beautiful curls lay lifeless, several damp and plastered to her flushed cheeks.

Miss Bennet squeezed by and removed the cloth, dipping it into the bowl Mrs. Cooke had just replenished. As it was placed back on Elizabeth's head, she gave a high-pitched inhale and began to squirm. "I know it must feel like ice, dearest, "said Miss Bennet, "but we must leave it if we are to lower your fever." She walked over to him. "If you would rinse and replace the cloth so it does not warm, I would be most grateful."

He nodded and turned sideways to allow them to pass in the confined space. "Of course, Miss Bennet. I shall do whatever task you require of me."

"I promise not to take advantage then."

With a glance over his shoulder, he noted that she was no longer on this side of the screen. Mrs. Northcott's lower tones created a hum in the room, but he could not make out what the two ladies said.

He flipped the cloth over on Elizabeth's forehead so the cooler side was now in contact with her skin. Unable to resist, his fingers traced down her cheek, which burned with the fever, until he reached her chin then pulled away. As much as he wished he had the right to touch her, he could claim no such privilege. Instead, he took her hand in both of his. "You cannot know how relieved I am you are alive," he said in a soft voice. "Once Mrs. Northcott and your sister have everything prepared, we shall take you to Darcy House for your recovery. Whether you choose to marry me or not, I shall ensure you never need live like this again, my love."

Her eyes squeezed tighter, and she whimpered.

"Elizabeth?" Her head began to thrash back and forth while she made unintelligible noises—almost as if she were talking in her sleep but could not speak. "Shh, all will be well. I promise."

He spent the next ten minutes rinsing the cloth and reapplying it until Miss Bennet returned, rendering him speechless. Mrs. Northcott had shaved Miss Bennet down to her bare scalp.

"Miss Bennet?"

She ran her hand along the smooth skin and blinked rapidly. "Do not distress yourself. I instructed Mrs. Northcott to do so, and she did as I asked. I shall be pleased to be free of the itching, I assure you." She brushed the back of her hand against her sister's face. "Mr. Darcy, would you be willing to help Mrs. Northcott while she tends to Lizzy? She requested I sort our belongings so we can bring our items of value, even if they are of nothing more than personal value. I assure you we do not have much, mostly a few books Lizzy managed to bring from Longbourn."

"I would never have you abandon your belongings. When you have prepared a trunk, the grooms can load it onto the carriage. I am fine to assist Mrs. Northcott."

A moment later, his housekeeper entered with the candlestick from the other side of the screen and set her supplies on the small table beside the bed. "Perhaps we could move her so I am not hampered by the wall? Rotating the sheet would help us with our task without disturbing the poor dear too much."

Mrs. Northcott set to work as soon as Elizabeth was moved. He watched as his housekeeper placed a towel on the floor under Elizabeth's head and cut as much as she could with a pair of shears, removing the cut tresses as soon as they were free from her scalp. By the acrid smell that had overtaken the room, Elizabeth's hair joined her sister's in being tossed into the fire.

Before he was prepared for the sight, Elizabeth's head was wiped clean to resemble her sister's; however, despite the absence of her lush curls, she remained the most handsome lady of his acquaintance. The loss of her lovely hair did naught to dampen her beauty.

His housekeeper replaced the bowl of cool water, and instead of placing the cloth on Elizabeth's forehead, she draped it over her scalp as well. "The lack of hair may benefit us in keeping her fever at bay."

When Miss Bennet returned, she glanced about the room. "The grooms have loaded the valise under the seat of the carriage. I also took our clothing to a fire down the street and tossed it all inside, lest the room reek of burnt fabric as well as hair. At least those who have no shelter may gain some warmth in this frigid weather."

"I hope nothing of value was discarded," he said.

"I fear our gowns were in poor condition. Lizzy and I have delayed their relegation to the rag pile by waiting until our gowns were too worn to be serviceable. We had just saved enough for the fabric to replace one gown each when Lizzy fell ill."

"Miss Darcy left some gowns and undergarments for me to distribute to the maids and to give to the ragman," said Mrs. Northcott. "I am certain we shall have enough until a dressmaker can come to the house to measure you for new gowns."

"Oh, no!" Miss Bennet shook her head. "Not a dressmaker. We do not want to be any more of a burden than necessary."

Darcy steepled his hands. "I would never consider either of you a burden, regardless of how much you spend at the dressmaker. You came to me for assistance. Pray, allow me to provide it." In the dim light, he could not be sure, but Miss Bennet seemed to turn a bit pink.

"Thank you, Mr. Darcy."

"Now," said Mrs. Northcott, who dipped her chin and gave him a stern but motherly expression. "If you will leave us, Mr. Darcy, Miss Bennet and I shall remove Miss Elizabeth's clothing and wrap her in rugs so she can be carried to the carriage."

"Mrs. Northcott," he said with an authoritative voice. "I understand what propriety demands, but no footman or groom will carry Miss Elizabeth. If she needs to be lifted for any reason, I am the only man you are to call." If he had his way, Elizabeth would be his wife. No man would hold her in such an intimate embrace but him.

His face burned as he strode around the screen. He needed to divert his attention to the small details of the room to distract himself from what was occurring behind him. He stared at the dirt that obscured the view of the street from the window, the stained cloth of the chairs by the fire, and the worn, splintered tabletop where Elizabeth had dined every day. He gritted his teeth and moved to the fire, staring into the dark recesses of the grate.

After almost five minutes, he was summoned, but stopped by Elizabeth laid out on a rug upon the floor. Another rug covered her to preserve her modesty. Miss Bennet then proceeded to wrap Elizabeth until her face was the sole bit that peeked from the coverlets. "If you will pick her up, we can put another rug over her head and tuck it to keep her warm. I do not want her catching a chill when you take her outside."

When Elizabeth was in his arms and covered from head to toe, he carried her to the carriage, as instructed, and settled inside with her cradled in his lap. The position was far from proper yet necessary. She could not very well support herself for the journey to Darcy House, and in her current condition, the blankets would fall if he did not ensure she remained covered.

Miss Bennet and Mrs. Northcott joined them a moment later, and he knocked the wall behind him to signal the driver. While they travelled back to Mayfair, Darcy held Elizabeth as close as possible. Who knew when he would once again have the opportunity, so he would make the most of every second of having Elizabeth in his arms. She whimpered each time the equipage struck a hole in the road, and his heart found a small sliver of peace at ensuring she remained steady and murmuring words of reassurance to soothe her distress.

Upon their arrival at Darcy House, he alighted to find they were at the back of the house near the stables, which was odd. He had not given the order and assumed Mrs. Northcott instructed the driver to do so. The plan had been quite prudent with the current state of Elizabeth and Miss Bennet as neither would desire to be seen in their current state by anyone walking down Park Lane.

Mrs. Northcott led him up the servants' passageways to Georgiana's former bedchamber where a fire burned merrily in the grate, heating the room in preparation of Elizabeth's arrival. "Place her on the chaise. Once Elsie and I have her bathed and dressed, we shall have a footman place her in the bed." He glanced around since Elsie had not followed them upstairs, but the young maid entered a second later with a bucket of water in one hand and a stack of towelling under the opposite arm. "I have placed Miss Bennet in the next bedchamber down. Clare is showing her to her rooms and seeing to her bath."

He cleared his throat and nodded. "Very good. And Mrs Northcott?" When the housekeeper looked up, he dipped his chin a small fraction, mirroring her posture at the Bennets' small hovel. "I was in earnest in St. Giles. If Miss Elizabeth should require moving, you will notify me, and I shall perform the task myself." At the housekeeper's agreement, he breathed somewhat easier. He may have no rights to Elizabeth as things stood, but he would be the one to care for her if a man's aid was required. "I shall refresh myself and await your summons."

All of four steps carried him down the corridor to his rooms where he rang for his valet. When Morton entered, he executed a quick bow. "Sir, I took the liberty of preparing a bath."

"Excellent," said Darcy. "I shall require clean clothing. I do not yet wish to retire."

"Of course, sir." Morton poured one last steaming bucket into the large copper tub. "You may want to know that Lord Carlisle did indeed call after you departed. Watson informed him you were away from home but did indicate that Lord Carlisle did not appear to believe him."

"I am not surprised. I have been unavailable to him for the past week. I am certain he will try again. I shall speak to Watson about my cousin in the morning."

"Yes, sir."

Once Darcy lowered himself into the water, he scrubbed away the dust as well as the stench of the acrid smoke from the Bennet ladies' small home. The combination of burnt towelling and hair had left a foul odour, though not as putrid as that of the Thames in certain weather. Darcy did not take his time and linger in the hot water, but washed with haste. He wished to be dressed when Mrs. Northcott sent for him.

Morton had his clothing prepared, so in no time, Darcy sat in a chair a footman had placed outside of Elizabeth's bedchamber. He hopped up when the door finally opened and his housekeeper peeked outside. "I did not expect you to have returned as yet." She opened the door further to allow him to pass.

When he entered, Elizabeth lay on the chaise atop a pristine white sheet with a coverlet to prevent a chill. The rugs from their trip to Darcy House were gone. Given Mrs. Northcott's thoroughness when it came to the ladies' removal from St. Giles, she was certain to perform a detailed cleaning of anything brought from that neighbourhood.

Darcy slipped his arms under Elizabeth, and with great care, lifted her slight frame, placing her into the turned down bed. He then looked away so his housekeeper could remove the blanket and tuck Elizabeth into the fresh bedding.

"Cool water and clean towelling are on the table, Mr. Darcy. If you would like to sit with Miss Elizabeth, Elsie will remain for propriety's sake. If you would prefer to retire, Elsie will care for her."

He placed the back of his hand against his beloved's forehead. She was not as warm, likely due to the invalid's bath Mrs. Northcott and the maid provided. "Thank you," he said in a hoarse voice, not lifting his eyes to those of the housekeeper. He swallowed down the lump in his throat and moved a chair to the side of the bed.

"The word from below stairs is that Matthew has returned and Mr. Acker should not be long behind him."

"Very good. Pray, bring him here directly."

Once Mrs. Northcott departed, he glanced at Elsie, who took up a piece of fabric she set to work sewing. He slipped his hand around Elizabeth's with care and stroked her fingers with a delicate touch. She appeared to sleep more peacefully than before, though her calm could be a result of the reduced state of her temperature rather than any comfort derived from being within his home. He could, however, wish it were the latter.

The bare flesh of her scalp was covered with a fine sprigged muslin cap he recognised. Georgiana had preferred them to bonnets when she was younger. He was thankful they could be put to use rather than wasting away in a trunk in the attics.

Elizabeth's eyes fluttered open, and he froze, his fingers stilling near her wrist. Would she be angry with him for taking the liberty of holding her hand? Her opinion towards him had been different at Pemberley, yet even then, they were not on such familiar terms.

She blinked several times, her forehead creased, and she gave a rattling gasp. "Fitzwilliam." Her voice held a hoarse quality it did not usually possess. "You are here."

The glassy appearance of her eyes made him once again press the backs of his fingers to her forehead. He winced. The fever was no longer being held at bay by the bath. "I am, my love," he said, taking the opportunity since she had addressed him in such an informal manner.

Before he could say more, her eyes drifted closed. He exchanged the cloth from her forehead for one from the cool water while her rasping breaths filled the room. The congestion in her lungs that had barely been noticeable a few hours prior was worsening.

He closed his eyes and rested his forehead on top of their joined hands. What would he do if she succumbed? After all, people died of trifling colds, so a tragic outcome for whatever ailed her was not beyond the realm of possibility, but how would he bear it? Despite her illness, hope had bloomed in his chest when he had learnt she was alive, filling that hole that had for so long ached to be filled. He said a prayer, then again swapped the cloth. She had to be well. She had to be.

"How is she, Mr. Darcy?"

His attention jumped to Miss Bennet, who entered from the family corridor. "The bath cooled her some, but the fever is returning. She opened her eyes for a moment and said my name."

"If she was not angry, I would guess she thought you a dream," said Miss Bennet with a smile.

His heart split in two. "Would she not want to see me?"

Miss Bennet sat upon the bed on her sister's other side. "You ask a complicated question." She brushed her fingers along Elizabeth's temple. "If the dreadful situation of our family could somehow be remedied, then I am certain she would welcome you and your suit."

"I am aware of your youngest sister's elopement with Wickham and the death of your father." Miss Bennet gasped. "You forget I have spoken to the Gardiners." Why had they left Gracechurch Street and the safety of their uncle's protection and how? He opened his mouth to ask but was prevented by the entrance of Mrs. Northcott and Acker.

"Darcy," said the physician with a warm smile. "I am relieved to see you looking so well."

Darcy stood and shook Acker's hand. "I am quite well. I requested you here for Miss Elizabeth Bennet." He shifted towards Miss Bennet. "Miss Jane Bennet, may I present my physician and good friend, Mr. Mathias Acker. Acker, Miss Bennet enlisted my aid when her younger sister's condition worsened."

Mr. Acker, said Miss Bennet with a curtsey. "Any assistance you can provide will be greatly appreciated."

The physician nodded. "I am pleased to make your acquaintance, Miss Bennet. Darcy, you should leave us so I can examine Miss Elizabeth." Elizabeth's body convulsed as she let out a horrific cough. Acker shook his head and set down his case. "I have a tincture I shall leave you for that rattle. We do not want that to settle into her chest any more than it already has."

After one last long look at Elizabeth, Darcy cleared his throat. "If you would come to my study when you have completed your examination."

The physician took a quick glance over his shoulder. "Yes, of course."

Upon his departure from the bedchamber, the empty sensation surged to the fore with a vengeance, increasing with every footstep away from Elizabeth. That all too familiar pit had been a part of his everyday life for so long, and he had only just noticed its absence before it settled back into the place it had once occupied. Elizabeth had been back in his life for no more than a few hours, but her mere presence had lit a flame in his chest, thawing the ice that had consumed him when he had believed her dead.

As soon as he entered his study, he strode to the brandy but paused before removing the crystal stopper. He had spent years drowning himself in spirits in order to seek Elizabeth in the sole form he could possess. Tonight, she lay in Georgiana's old bedchamber ill, yet very much alive. He had no need to smother his misery as long as Elizabeth breathed and he still had some chance of making her his wife.

Darcy took his usual place before the windows, staring into the darkness. The moonlight glimmered off the leaves of the trees. For the past two years, a nightly habit of standing at that window, staring into the darkness, had been his wont. Yet, during that time, he had not seen the brilliance of the scene, only the blackness consuming what had been light a mere few hours before.

His mind shifted to Elizabeth as he dreamt of a future he once thought impossible—marriage, children, a lifetime—until a knock at the door jolted him from his reverie. "Come!"

"Sir, you wanted to speak to Mr. Acker?"

Darcy blinked and shook himself to pull his mind from the last vestiges of the fantasy. "Yes, thank you. Show him in."

"Would you care to sit?" asked Darcy as soon as they had privacy.

Acker sat in the chair opposite him and set down his case with a smile. "May I be so bold as to assume this young lady is the reason you have been a perpetual disappointment to the mamas of the *ton*?"

Darcy groaned and sat in his own chair. "I know we have been friends since Eton, but must you be as insufferable as Richard?"

Acker laughed and lifted his eyebrows. "Well, if I merely suspected when I found you holding her hand, my confirmation would be your current churlish disposition."

"I am not churlish."

"I beg to differ." He pointed to the spirits. "Why do you not pour me a glass of Port?"

"Then will you tell me of Elizabeth?"

"Oh, so it is Elizabeth?" At Darcy's sudden halt and turn, Acker put up his hands. "Yes, we shall discuss Miss Elizabeth's condition. Now, pour me that glass. 'Tis been a long day, and I am in dire need of fortification."

Chapter 7

Darcy crossed his arms over his chest while Acker sipped his Port and savoured the fruity vintage before swallowing. "So, what of Elizabeth? Will she live?"

"Quite an informal mode of address." Acker snickered, resting his glass on the arm of the chair.

Darcy thrust out a finger to point at Acker and opened his mouth—

"I believe she has Grippe," said Acker before Darcy could speak. "After examining her and listening to her breathing and cough, I do not think the malady has settled deep into her lungs as of yet, which is good." He took another draw from his glass and tilted his head as he swallowed. "Your housekeeper already had willow bark tea prepared and cooled. Miss Elizabeth will need to regain some consciousness to administer it using the invalid's feeding cup, but Miss Bennet and Mrs. Northcott are prepared. I left Miss Bennet a small bottle of the tincture I mentioned. I shall bring more on the morrow. I also gave your housekeeper a recipe for a poultice of sorts: a mixture of syrup of violets and sweet almond oil covered with a plaster of candle wax, nutmeg, and saffron. In the meantime, I showed the sister, your housekeeper, and the maid a method of pounding the back to attempt to expel some of the congestion and prevent this from worsening. I warn you the process appears rough, but I have found it to be effective in my patients and preferable to bleeding."

Darcy swallowed hard and grimaced. His remedies sometimes seemed odd, but Acker was a good man and an excellent physician. Darcy trusted him. The main reason

Darcy had come to prefer Acker over other physicians was not only their long-standing friendship, but also Acker's lack of faith in bloodletting. He tended to employ those more traditional methods as a last resort, even experimenting before cutting a patient. Darcy admired his friend for his ingenuity. "Whatever she requires will be done. Do you understand? Treat her as you would your own wife and children."

"I treat all my patients as I would my family," said Acker, his voice hard.

"Forgive me." Darcy covered his face with his hands before dragging them back through his hair. Why could he not better regulate himself when it came to Elizabeth? "I am tired and intemperate."

"I would say lovesick." One side of his lips curved. "I was beginning to think I would never see you so afflicted. I am glad to know you will not live as a monk for the rest of your days. People have stopped wagering at White's on your wedding, did you know?"

"I have not visited White's in some time. I knew they placed wagers on me, but I cared not. You should know that." At times, he despised his club.

Acker finished his port and set his glass on Darcy's desk. "I should be going, but do send a servant if Miss Elizabeth worsens or has need of me."

Before his friend reached the door, Darcy took a step forward. "Acker, thank you."

"Do not thank me yet." His friend laughed softly. "If you recall, the last time I treated Miss Darcy, I told you the fees for treating you and your family had increased due to your horrible impatience."

"I am not impatient."

Acker rolled his eyes and smiled wider. "You insisted I come out at dawn to treat your sister's cold, do you remember?" His friend proffered a finger, pointing at Darcy's chest. "Do not say you are no physician. She had a slightly runny nose and was sneezing. She never even had a fever, and you insisted on my daily examinations." Acker started towards the door but doubled back. "I shall, however, return on the morrow to check Miss Elizabeth." He put on his hat and tipped it. "Good evening, Darcy."

He was wild to see Elizabeth. As soon as Watson escorted Acker out, Darcy hastened up the stairs to her bedchamber and rapped upon the door. Miss Bennet answered swiftly and moved aside for him to enter.

"Your doctor is quite a gentleman. I know Lizzy is ill indeed, but he had some suggestions I have never seen before. I am very appreciative, sir."

"Pray, do not thank me for a service I am happy to provide." One glance at Elizabeth, and he balked. "She is so red and damp. Let me send a servant after Acker. He could not have seen her this way."

Miss Bennet grabbed his arm before he could depart. "Her appearance is the result of one of his treatments."

Darcy stepped around Miss Bennet in order to gain a better view of Elizabeth. "But she appears worse than before."

"He assures me she is well." She glanced back to a small table set by the fire. "Mrs. Northcott had a tray sent up. She has been exceedingly kind. She found us clothing and slippers as well as caps. Lizzy roused enough for us to administer a little of the willow bark tea. I am hoping her fever will abate enough for her to wake for longer. She needs to take the tincture Mr. Acker left."

The backs of his fingers brushed Elizabeth's forehead. Her fever had not broken. "I do not wish to disturb your meal," he said. "I can return." How he wished he could stay! But he would not impose himself upon Miss Bennet; He would not make her uncomfortable with his unwanted presence.

"If you would prefer to sit with Lizzy, I do not mind." Miss Bennet again peered over her shoulder at the table. "I hope I am not too forward, but if you have not eaten, you could join me. Then, you could tell me of my aunt and uncle as well as remain near my sister for a while longer."

The suggestion had merit. He had not eaten, and taking a meal with her would allow him to linger in Elizabeth's room. He would also be more aware of her condition and nearby in the event she had need of him. "Elsie," he said to the maid still seated in the chair. "Would you request a tray from Mrs. Northcott? I believe I shall join Miss Bennet for supper." Elsie curtseyed and hurried through the door. "Do not feel you must wait on me. I shall sit with Miss Elizabeth until the food arrives."

"Have you word of my mother, Mr. Darcy?"

Once he was seated in the chair beside the bed, he propped his elbows on his knees, his fingers laced in front of him. "The Gardiners have indicated she is well as are Miss Kitty and Miss Mary. Miss Mary lives with your aunt and uncle and helps with the children."

"I am glad to hear it. My mother has always been hard on Mary. I am certain Mary is much improved by my aunt's influence and company."

"She has become quite accomplished. They hired a piano master and ensured she was educated. She is betrothed to a Mr. Goodwin, a gentleman with a modest estate in Norfolk."

Miss Bennet paused and stared. "You mean Lydia's folly did not damage her prospects?"

"Miss Mary became very good friends with my sister, Georgiana. Mr. Goodwin is a cousin of Georgiana's husband, Viscount Witney. Witney first introduced them at the end of last Season at his mother's ball. The couple became engaged a month ago. Mr. Goodwin appears to be a man of sense and respectability. Miss Mary seems pleased with the arrangement."

Miss Bennet pushed her food with her fork while she listened. "I am happy for her. It was very good of your sister to befriend her. No doubt, my sister's eligibility was elevated by the association."

He frowned and shook his head. Credit for the match could not be attributed to him or Georgiana, particularly considering that Mr. Goodwin requested the introduction. "My sister and I are not so dissimilar, though Georgiana is more circumspect in her words than I once was. She has always been uneasy amongst the *ton*, yet never found herself ill-at-ease with your sister. I have been grateful these past two years for Miss Mary's honest friendship. My sister blossomed with the companionship of someone she could trust."

After swallowing, Miss Bennet smiled. "What of Kitty? Do you know of her?"

"Your uncle has indicated she is much the same. He means to have her live with them once Miss Mary is wed." By Mr. Gardiner's description, Miss Kitty had lost a little of her impetuousness but had become more indulged since Miss Lydia's absence. The Gardiners hoped to temper her behaviour and see her married as well.

The housekeeper bustled in and set a tray across from Miss Bennet. "Here you are, sir. If you want anything else—anything at all—"

"I shall ring," he said stifling a laugh. His plate was piled so high it was no wonder the food was not spilling over the sides. She departed and Elsie assumed her previous place in the chair along the wall. He released the laugh when he sat down. "I have not had much of an appetite for some time."

"Your housekeeper seems to have taken your request as an opportunity to fatten you up." Miss Bennet grinned.

"I suppose so." Their laughter gradually faded, and he furrowed his brow. "Earlier you said Miss Elizabeth told you of Rosings?"

Miss Bennet glanced at her sister. "Yes, she told me of your proposal. Later, when she returned from Derbyshire, she spoke of your kindness at Pemberley. She felt terrible leaving without speaking to you herself."

He blinked to stop his eyes from stinging. "I have wished many times since discovering the truth of the situation, that I had followed them to town. I could have located Wickham. If anything, he is a creature of habit and predictable. All of us could have been saved a great deal of heartbreak."

She took a sip of her wine. "Are you still friends with Mr. Bingley?"

Her eyes dropped to her plate, and she fidgeted with her utensils. Could she still have feelings for Bingley after all this time? "Last I heard from him, he was well. He wed a lady last year, and they live at a small estate he purchased in Bedfordshire. They will not travel to town this Season as they expect their first child next month."

The corners of her lips lifted a little as she met his eye. Her smile, albeit weak, was genuine. "I am pleased for him. I wish him happy."

"I believe he is content. His sister was displeased by his choice of bride." He laughed and relaxed back into his chair. "Mrs. Bingley's father is a tradesman. He lives three doors down from Mr. Gardiner."

"Oh," said Miss Bennet. "You must mean Mr. Evans's daughter. If my memory serves me, her name is Ophelia."

Her response disconcerted him. He should have known they would be, at the very least, acquainted. "You know her."

"I do, though we are far from intimate friends. Her mother kept her much occupied with masters. I rarely spoke to her unless Uncle and I happened upon her walking with her father. She seemed agreeable." Miss Bennet surely once thought Miss Bingley agreeable as well. Despite Miss Bingley's vehement dislike of the new Mrs. Bingley's origins, Mrs. Bingley bore more than a passing resemblance in disposition to Bingley's affected sister. Miss Bennet's countenance had paled since she enquired of Mr. Bingley. He needed to change the subject.

"May I ask if Miss Elizabeth ever spoke of more than what you mentioned earlier? Had her opinion of me changed?"

Miss Bennet's smile grew. "After Derbyshire, Lizzy's opinion had changed. I shall not tell you more since I feel I would be betraying a confidence by revealing what is in her heart." She set down her knife and fork and placed her hands in her lap. "I must warn you that when Lizzy awakens—really awakens—and realises we are in your home, she will be furious with me."

His heart cracked, causing a ripping sensation to tear down his chest. "I thought her opinion of me had improved?"

"I should have phrased that differently," said Miss Bennet. "I should say that I suggested requesting your aid when Lizzy first required a physician. Her fever was not as high, and she still had her wits about her. She refused." He blinked and stared at his plate. "You must understand she had concerns about your sister's reputation as well as yours. She also did not want you to see us in such a state. We may have chosen our poverty—we left our uncle's home of our own accord—but our former acquaintances seeing us in such meagre circumstances was—is mortifying."

"I would hope you are not embarrassed, Miss Bennet. I have always imagined you and Miss Elizabeth had your reasons for leaving your uncle's protection. I would never think to look upon you with disdain due to where you and your sister have found yourselves."

Miss Bennet fidgeted and grabbed her utensils, putting all of her concentration into cutting her beef. "At the time, we felt ourselves a burden to our uncle."

Darcy furrowed his brow. "I can assure you he did not think of you in those terms."

"He said as much to us, but Lizzy overheard him speak to our aunt of the problems he was having at the warehouse. He was concerned how long he could afford to maintain us as well as pay for some of Mama's more frivolous expenses since she refused to economise. Lizzy and I knew Uncle would never allow us to help him at the warehouse. We tried becoming companions. We hoped an old widow would not care of Lydia's scandal, yet we were unable to find positions. We sacrificed some comforts by living in St. Giles, but we found solace in that our uncle could better provide for our mother and sisters as well as his own family."

He turned his glass of ale while Miss Bennet spoke. Regardless of the reduced circumstances she had inhabited, she did not appear sad or regretful of her actions. "Tomorrow, I shall send a note to Madame Villers, so new gowns can be made for you and Miss Elizabeth."

"Mr. Darcy," said Miss Bennet. "While I appreciate your offer, we cannot afford Madame's creations, and we would never expect you to purchase such expensive finery for us. If you could send a servant to a warehouse for the materials, I can sew myself a new gown. Your housekeeper was good enough to find us suitable items to wear for the time being as well as give me the older gowns your sister left behind. Those are still serviceable and better quality than we need or can afford. I can adjust or rework most of them for Lizzy and me without much expense."

He set his napkin beside his plate and shook his head. "I do not expect you to sew your own clothing while under my roof or make adjustments to what Georgiana left for the servants or for the ragman—particularly when you are caring for your ill sister. Pray, allow me to treat you and Miss Elizabeth as I would any guest who stays in my home. I am certain you will appreciate having the freedom to tend to her."

Miss Bennet exhaled and crossed her arms over her chest as she dropped back into the seat. "Very well, but not Madame

Villers. I am certain your housekeeper knows of another dressmaker who would suit."

He nodded and held out his hand as though he was shaking a man's hand. "Very well. As long as you are not toiling away when I am more than capable of providing for the both of you."

She grinned as she took his hand and allowed him to give it a brief up and down movement. "You have done more than I could have dreamt by simply caring for Lizzy, sir. I refuse to take advantage."

"You cannot know how relieved I was to discover the two of you are alive."

As she withdrew her hand, she lifted a shoulder. "I believe I have some idea of your relief. Your informal address of Lizzy spoke of how shocked you were at my appearance as well as the possibility of Lizzy being alive."

He winced. "Forgive me. I meant no disrespect."

"I know," she said with a tilt of her head. "At that moment, I understood how strong your feelings for her must still be—how faithful you must be."

Darcy cleared his throat. "I do not mean to sound as though I am bragging, but I shall never spend all of my income on my own. I would never resent any money spent to provide you and Miss Elizabeth some relief."

An incoherent mumble came from the bed, and Darcy jumped up and rushed over to Elizabeth's bedside. "Miss Elizabeth?"

Elizabeth's eyes opened slowly, as if it took all of her energy to accomplish, and blinked several times. "Fitzwilliam," she said in a breathy manner. Her hand lifted to cradle his cheek. "You are here."

He covered her hand with his, his heart beating with so much force it could have burst from his chest. "Where else would I be?" Her eyelids fluttered as she smiled. "Elizabeth?" With her use of Fitzwilliam, would she object to him addressing her in a similar manner?

"Hmm?"

Miss Bennet pressed her hand to her sister's forehead. "Her fever has risen." Her voice was soft while she pointed to the invalid's cup on the table beside him. "See if she will take some."

"Elizabeth." He spoke louder than was his wont to prevent her from slipping back to sleep. "Let me help you sit up and drink this tea." He slid an arm under her shoulders while Miss Bennet assisted. Together, they raised her from the stack of pillows behind her. Thankfully, she accepted the invalid's cup he brought to her lips, so he tipped it back and let the willow bark tea trickle into her mouth.

After several swallows, she pulled away. "'Tis bitter."

"I know, but it would be best if you could drink it all." She opened her eyes just enough to see what would usually be their vivid hazel colour, though tonight, they were dulled by the illness. He touched the cup to the tip to her lip, and she took it until the last was gone, and she pulled back with a grimace.

"No more, I beg you," she said hoarsely before breaking into heavy coughs, wracking her small frame. When she sagged against him, he allowed her to recline back into the pillows, and Miss Bennet adjusted the cap so it remained on Elizabeth's head. Lines marred her forehead in a frown before she fell back to sleep. Had she truly been awake or had it been a hallucination that would prevent her from remembering what had occurred once her fever broke?

Miss Bennet placed another cool cloth on her sister's forehead. "Her cough is worsening."

"I agree. Should I send for Acker?"

"No, he said this may happen. He will return in the morning." Miss Bennet wrung the spare cloth and swapped it with the one on Elizabeth's forehead. "I believe we can wait until then."

His hand curled around Elizabeth's, holding it tight. She would be well. She had to be.

Chapter 8

Darcy shot up and took stock of the darkened room while he shook off the last vestiges of sleep. Had that sound been a wail or had that been part of his dream? He threw his legs over the side of the bed and sat for a moment, his heart racing and the hair on his arms standing on end. Dreams often times diminished in clarity as time passed, and some more quickly than others. He could not remember dreaming, but perhaps the memory faded upon waking?

While he scrubbed his face with his hands, he slid from the mattress, his bare feet sinking into the soft carpet. He stretched his arms over his head and relished the satisfying clicking of his joints.

With a bit of a tremor still in his hands, he lit the candle at his bedside and carried it to the clock. How had three in the morning come so quickly?

A noise came from somewhere inside the house and he frowned. Since he had slept in his breeches and a shirt, he considered himself more or less dressed, so he padded to the door and opened it, leaning out and peering in both directions. A sudden cry tore through the silence, and without thought, he rushed into Elizabeth's bedchamber, finding Mrs. Northcott kneeling over Elizabeth and holding her arms at her sides. "Mr. Darcy! Thank goodness you have come."

He set down the candle and approached. As soon as he placed a hand upon Elizabeth's arm, he recoiled at the heat radiating from her skin. She was burning up!

"No," Elizabeth in a weak voice before dissolving into a spasm of coughing. Every two or three coughs, she would heave in a great inhale and manage another "no" before succumbing once more.

"What upset her so?" He took her arms from Mrs. Northcott and held them with a gentle pressure.

His housekeeper retreated to the chair at the bedside. "She is frightened because she does not know me, sir. Before she opened her eyes, she called for her father, but when she saw me, she began to struggle."

"Elizabeth!" He spoke loudly so she would hear him over the wretched coughs wracking her petite frame.

Her eyes opened, she gasped and turned her hand to grab his. "Mr. Darcy!" She attempted to hold in the next cough, though she remained silent until she managed to catch her breath. "Thank God! Mr. Darcy, you must help him!" Two more coughs ripped through her before she groaned and dropped back into the pillows, closing her eyes again. "You must help my uncle." During her plea, her voice rasped and a tear escaped one eye to track down her temple.

Mrs. Northcott handed him a fresh cloth, which he pressed with his free hand to Elizabeth's forehead. "Shh," he said in soft tones near her ear. "Why does your uncle require my aid?" He was certain how she would respond, but he asked in the event he was mistaken.

"'Tis Lydia. She has run away...with Wickham." She sucked in a tremendous breath of air, coughed three more times, then swallowed hard, wincing before her eyes reopened. "You know too much of his character to doubt his intentions." He glanced at his housekeeper, but Elizabeth gave a strong pull at his arm for someone so ill, drawing his attention back to her. "You must promise me!"

"Yes, of course." He took her cup from Mrs. Northcott and raised her from the pillows. "But first, you must drink this tea. As soon as you finish, I shall find your uncle and search with him. Do not fret. We shall force Wickham to marry your sister."

He put the cup to her lips, and this time, she took the entirety without complaint. Once he settled her back into the bed and her eyes drifted closed, Mrs. Northcott blew out a noisy exhale. "Elsie was exhausted, so I allowed her to retire. Miss Elizabeth had been so quiet. I thought I could manage on my own. When she panicked, I had no one to call for aid, and I did not know how to calm her."

"Do not fret." His eyes traced Elizabeth's beloved face while he cooled the rag to place back upon her head. The cloths would need to be replaced often if he was to have any success in controlling her fever.

"She was remembering a horrible time for her family. She may have been upset with anyone who tended to her."

"Mr. Wickham is known to the Miss Bennets then?"

He took a spare cloth and placed it into the water. He sat back onto the mattress and dropped his head into his hands. "Yes, the autumn, when I resided with Mr. Bingley at Netherfield, Wickham was encamped with the militia in the local village. As was his wont, Wickham charmed the ladies and the men alike until he departed with his regiment to Brighton. Miss Elizabeth's youngest sister was invited to be the companion of the colonel of the regiment's silly, young wife. Wickham persuaded Miss Lydia to elope. The blackguard never intended to marry her. When word reached her father, he died of an apoplectic fit."

Mrs. Northcott squeezed her eyes closed and shook her head. "He was a scoundrel, that one. I am relieved he has not visited this house in some time. Good riddance I say."

"I am surprised Miss Bennet has not come with Miss Elizabeth's wailing," he said while he glanced at the door.

"The poor dear looked exhausted, so I persuaded her to drink a draught. With both of them sleeping in that one bed and Miss Elizabeth being so ill, I doubt Miss Bennet has had an entire night's rest for the past se'nnight. I cannot fathom how she still managed to stand and smile so sweetly."

"She has always been very pleasant." He wrung the excess water from the spare towel and placed it over Elizabeth's arm, which rested on top of the coverlet. "Miss Bennet, Miss Elizabeth, and Miss Mary are all amiable ladies. I know Miss Elizabeth often felt protective of her elder sister. Miss Bennet was once reserved, though I believe their circumstances may have forced her to be more forthright than in the past."

Mrs. Northcott took a cloth he had dampened and repeated the action on the opposite side. "It speaks well of the sisters that they care for each other as they do."

"Yes, it does." He frowned as Elizabeth shivered, her teeth chattering lightly. "Is she worsening?"

His housekeeper touched Miss Elizabeth's forehead. "I believe she is much the same. You must be prepared; her illness could linger for some time. Even once the fever breaks, the cough and fatigue will take time to remedy themselves."

"Then she will have the care she requires." He combed his fingers through his hair. "If she will have me, she will never have to return to that wretched neighbourhood."

"But what if she refuses?" His head shot up. Whether Elizabeth would accept him or not was certainly in question, but what did his housekeeper know that he did not? "I ask because the Miss Bennets seem proud—in the very best sense of the word, of course. Miss Bennet has said naught of her sister's feelings to me."

"I shall make arrangements for them regardless of whether Miss Elizabeth accepts me or not. I appreciate that Mr. Cooke and his wife sought to be of aid and to protect two ladies so wholly unprotected. Lord only knows what could have happened if they had been without anyone at all, but they do not belong in that squalor, and I will do all I can to prevent their return."

Mrs. Northcott lifted her eyebrows and gave a slight laugh. "Be warned, sir. I do believe these two ladies are capable of telling you 'no.'"

He was unable to stop one side of his mouth from curving upwards. "If you only knew how capable this Miss Bennet is." He tipped his head towards Elizabeth while he spoke. "Why do you not try to sleep? I can manage until Miss Bennet wakes. 'Tis late and no one will be the wiser."

"Are you certain?" She bent forward about to stand, but waited before she actually rose to her feet.

"Yes, Miss Elizabeth has yet to be agitated with me, and morning is but a few hours away. If you could prepare another cup of willow bark tea in the event she awakens, I believe I shall manage."

He concentrated on Elizabeth while Mrs. Northcott moved about the room. He exchanged the cool cloths and watched, waiting for some change or sign of improvement, despite that logical part of him that knew time was required for any alteration to occur.

"I added to the fire," said Mrs. Northcott. "One of the footmen brought two pails of water should you need to replenish the bowl. They remain in the dressing room. With no fire in there, they should remain cool." She pointed to the tea service. "The invalid's cup has a fresh batch of tea set to cool for the young miss when she awakens." She bobbed a curtsey. "Good night, sir."

"Good night."

The door to the servants' corridor closed, and he sighed, using a feather-light touch to shift the soft cap back from her forehead. "My love, you must be well. You must."

Darcy sat up with a start and perused the room, blinking madly. When his eyes set upon Elizabeth, he jumped forward and pulled the damp cloths, now warm, from her forehead and arms and dropped them into the cool water. Damn! How could he have fallen asleep!

Before replacing the compresses, he pressed his palm to her forehead. How warm her skin was against his fingers. If he had not fallen asleep, her fever would be more controlled. How could he be so careless? As much as he wished for a visible improvement, none was to be had. Her fever still raged and her breathing remained laboured.

"Jane," she whispered. Her tongue peeked out, moistening her lips, and her eyelids fluttered before their hazel irises appeared. Her forehead crinkled as she took in the room. "Jane?" Her voice was still hoarse, but a bit louder.

"My housekeeper gave her a sleeping draught last night. I do not know if she has awakened yet."

Elizabeth stared at him. "Mr. Darcy, why are you in my bedchamber?"

"You have been ill. Your sister is asleep so my housekeeper and I passed the night sitting with you." He removed the towelling on her arms, careful not to touch her skin.

She coughed from deep in her chest while she pulled the cloth from her head. "No, this makes no sense. I came to Netherfield to care for Jane. I must go to her." Elizabeth threw the coverlet from her legs, pressed her palms to the mattress, and attempted to shift her legs to the edge. Darcy jumped forward to stop her from standing, but she dissolved into another fit of coughing.

"Elizabeth, you have been very ill. If you will but remain in bed, I shall call for a servant to fetch your sister so she can verify I speak the truth." He grabbed the bedclothes to cover her and placed a hand to her shoulder.

"No! I need to dress and go to Jane!" With a surprising amount of strength, she batted his arm away from her. "You should not be in my room or address me so informally," she said forcefully. She doubled over while she suffered a deluge of coughs, heaving in breaths when she could manage to speak. "I have no wish to be forced to marry you, and you surely do not want to wed someone you find merely tolerable."

"Lizzy!" At Miss Bennet's sudden appearance at the bedside, Darcy stepped aside to make way. Miss Bennet, with careful hands, pushed Elizabeth into the bed by the shoulders. "You are burning up."

"No, I came to Netherfield for you. I am here to nurse you!" Her voice held a gravelly tone that her swallow did not remedy.

"Dearest," said Miss Bennet, with a wide-eyed glance at him. "You did care for me, but you became ill, and Mama insisted I remain with you."

Elizabeth hacked out a laugh. "She hopes Mr. Bingley will propose."

He received a glance and an ever-so-slight smile from Miss Bennet. "She does indeed. But you must be well, or I cannot leave you to spend time with him." As much as he despised the deception, if it calmed Elizabeth, then Jane's illusion was necessary.

"Oh, Mama will blame me if he does not propose."

"Do not fret over Mama. All will be well." Miss Bennet tucked the coverlet around her sister. He winced as she dropped her head back into the pillows.

"Why am I so tired all of a sudden?"

He offered Miss Bennet the invalid's cup. She nodded and sat beside her sister. "This will help you feel better." When she passed him the empty cup, he handed her the tincture and spoon.

"Jane?" asked Elizabeth weakly. "Where are Mama and Papa? Why am I not at Longbourn?" He stiffened. Could Elizabeth see his face? He could not guarantee his ability to maintain his equanimity.

"We are at Netherfield because you cared for me until your fever started." She wrung out a cloth and laid it upon her sister's forehead. "Mama was here a few days ago—just before you fell ill." Elizabeth's eyes gradually closed as she shook her head. Her breathing evened and her eyelids fluttered as if she was dreaming.

Miss Bennet's shoulders slumped, and she shook her head. "I should not have let your housekeeper give me that draught. I should have slept in here with Lizzy."

"No, you required the rest, and until this morning, she has not been uneasy in my presence. She woke several hours ago and became upset at Mrs. Northcott's tending to her, but I was able to settle her. Since she seems to be having waking dreams, she could become disquieted by any of us—especially if her dreams cease to be rooted in reality. At the moment, she appears to be re-visiting the past."

"The previous time, did she believe herself at Netherfield?"

"No, she begged my help to find Miss Lydia and Wickham." He scratched the back of his neck. "I coaxed her to take more willow bark tea, and she settled swiftly." With a step to the side, he placed himself so he had a better view of Elizabeth. "How long has she been insensible?"

"Since the day I begged your aid. When I awoke that morning, her fever had become more severe, and she called for different members of our family while she tossed and turned. She also called for you." His head jerked from Elizabeth to Miss Bennet, though she continued to watch her sister. "Gemma and I took turns nursing her, but she had need of a physician, regardless of the expense. The Cookes offered to help, but they have a young son, and I refused to allow such a sacrifice. They are saving in the hopes of leaving the city. They want to raise their son in the country. 'Tis why they live in St. Giles over a more costly neighbourhood." She faced him and rested her hand upon his forearm. "I must thank you for everything you have done. I am certain Lizzy would be lost to me without..."

"I am pleased you felt safe coming to me," he said, meeting her eye. "You must have faith in your sister's determination, Miss Bennet. She will be well."

Miss Bennet's eyelashes fluttered and a tear dropped to her cheek. "I am trying, sir, but I have never seen her so poorly."

He covered her hand with his. "Let me ring the bell. A tray can be brought up since you will not wish to leave your sister. Mr. Acker should be here soon as well."

"Thank you, Mr. Darcy."

"I do not mean to diminish your gratitude, but do not thank me for something I am happy to do." He swallowed back the emotion that rose into his throat. "You have done me an immeasurable service by requesting my aid. Because of you, I now know your sister is alive. That knowledge is more valuable to me than all I possess."

Chapter 9

Darcy scrubbed his face with his hands before setting his attention back to the ledgers before him. The problem was no matter how diligently he tried to concentrate, his thoughts never failed to return upstairs to the room where Elizabeth rested. She was still insensible, at times crying out in her sleep, or as she had with him, reliving their heart-breaking past. He lived for those brief moments when she turned to him with love in her eyes and called him by name.

Acker had checked on Elizabeth the past three days as well as come this morning, as he had promised, but as of the last Darcy had seen her, she had not improved. More than once, she had awakened as one would from a night terror, crying out and thrashing. Two at a time had been required to attend her since they restrained her lest she do herself harm.

He dropped his head against the back of the chair and stared at the ceiling. Would Acker find her worse than yesterday? Her cough pained him to hear, and her fever was so high. Darcy could not imagine how she could become worse without—No, he could not think of it.

A knock on the door made him lift his head. "Come!"

Watson entered but never ventured past the doorway. "I beg your pardon, sir, but a Mrs. Cooke is requesting to call upon the Miss Bennets. I was unsure—"

Darcy stood and stepped around his desk. "Mrs. Cooke is welcome to visit her friends as often as she wishes." When he reached the hall, he stopped and frowned. She was not in the entrance hall. Where was she? "Watson, did you leave her outside in the cold?" Snow had fallen again during the night, leaving a delicate white blanket upon the ground that would soon be churned up into sludge by the carriages and horses braving the weather.

"No, sir. She came to the servants' entrance."

Without a pause, Darcy strode in the direction of the servants' passageways, making his way to the kitchen. When he entered, Mrs. Cooke waited near the fire. She stood straight as an arrow while she clutched her reticule as if someone might snatch it from her hands at any moment. "Mr. Darcy, forgive me for disturbing you. I have been distressed for Miss Elizabeth and hoped to visit her and Miss Bennet, if you do not mind."

He bowed at her curtsey and held his hands up with his palms facing her. "Pray, Mrs. Cooke, you have no need to apologise. I am certain Miss Bennet would be pleased to see you and tell you of Miss Elizabeth's condition." He held out an arm towards the stairs. "Let me show you to her rooms."

When they emerged into the hall, her eyes widened, and she pivoted in a circle. "Mr. Darcy—"

"I know you would use the servants' entrance when searching for work, but when you call upon a guest in my home, I hope you will knock at the front door. You are welcome to visit the Miss Bennets anytime—even when the knocker is down."

"Thank you," she said as her entire body released some of its tension.

He started up the next flight of stairs. "If you will follow me."

When they reached the bedchamber, he knocked with care not to be too loud. Elizabeth seemed to be sensitive to loud noises and bright light. He refused to disturb her any more than was necessary.

Miss Bennet opened the door, her face lighting up at the sight of her friend. "Gemma," she said. "I am so pleased you are here." The ladies hugged and Darcy stepped back to provide them some room.

"I say! Darcy, who is that?"

Mrs. Cooke and Miss Bennet both drew back to look in the direction of the voice while Darcy practically growled as he set off towards Richard, who walked with a determined stride in their direction.

"Keep your voice down," said Darcy in an emphatic hiss.

"I have been trying to call since the wedding, but today was the first time I managed to make it into the passageways. Watson has had someone guarding the entrances day and night. If I chose, I could be quite offended at your unwillingness to accept my call." Richard side-stepped Darcy and proceeded to approach Miss Bennet and Mrs. Cooke. "Are these ladies why you have been avoiding me?"

Darcy hurried after his cousin and reached twice for his arm before catching the sleeve of his topcoat. Richard never faltered and tore his arm from Darcy's grasp, continuing towards Elizabeth's bedchamber.

"Fitzwilliam, I have not spoken to you in an age," said Acker, who emerged from the room. He held his hand out to Richard.

Richard peeked back over his shoulder at Darcy. "Acker? What brings you here?"

Darcy lunged forward to grab his cousin and haul him away from the door, but Richard tilted his head and slipped into the bedchamber. "I say! I know her." Poor Miss Bennet hurried after him, taking a protective stance near the bed.

"Richard," said Darcy, waving his cousin out of the room. "Come to my study and we can talk."

"Is that not Miss Elizabeth..." Richard's eyes narrowed and his forehead creased while he stared at Elizabeth, who as luck would have it, remained oblivious to the intrusion. "What was her surname? I remember she visited the wife of Lady Catherine's vicar at Hunsford several years ago. During Easter, was it not?"

Darcy sighed and pressed his fingers against his eyes. "Bennet. The name is Bennet." Had Elizabeth not been in such a delicate state, he would have hauled Richard from the room as one would a bag of refuse, but he did not want the commotion that would ensue. This was bad enough.

"Yes, that is it. I remember quite enjoying how she set down our aunt without rudeness." He looked from person to person. "Will you not introduce me?"

Darcy dropped his arm to his side. He would never remove the blunderbuss without revealing a certain amount of information first. "Richard Fitzwilliam, The Viscount Carlisle, may I present Miss Jane Bennet, Miss Elizabeth's elder sister, and Mrs. Gemma Cooke, their good friend."

With a bow, Richard allowed a grin to spread across his face. "A pleasure, ladies. I hope my dour cousin is treating you well." He swallowed back a groan at Richard's ridiculousness. In these past weeks, Richard had claimed a talent for charming the ladies. His cousin was more than likely deluded since the ladies laughed at his banter and had not taken the time to enlighten his cousin to the absurdity of his behaviour.

Hopefully, a lady would set his cousin down and remedy the situation without his interference.

Darcy clenched his hands to keep from covering his face and shaking his head. Meanwhile, Miss Bennet fidgeted with her cap, curtseyed along with Mrs. Cooke, then continued to tug at the fabric near her ear. "Mr. Darcy has been very kind," she said, her eyes darting between them.

"Richard, we should leave them—"

"No!" They all rounded to Elizabeth, who thrashed and gasped. "No!" She fell into a paroxysm of coughing.

"Lizzy!" Miss Bennet rushed to her sister's side, wrung out a fresh cloth, and pressed it to her sister's cheek. "You are well, dearest. Can you not wake? Gemma has called."

"No!" Elizabeth's head lifted and her eyes opened, but when she saw Acker and Richard, she flinched and recoiled back into the pillows. When her eyes set upon Darcy, she reached for him with both arms. "Mr. Darcy! Pray, you must help us!"

He took her hands and sat upon the edge of the mattress. His cousin would be shocked, but at that moment, he could care less if he offended his cousin's sensibilities. He would comfort Elizabeth if she required it. "Of course, Miss Elizabeth." He took the invalid's cup Miss Bennet offered him. "But you must first drink this." He wrapped an arm around her shoulders and propped her a bit straighter, ensuring every drop made it into her mouth between her hacking coughs. Once the cup was empty, they allowed her to relax.

"All is well," he said, in a low, soft tone. "I shall take care of everything."

Her eyes fluttered. "Lydia... Wickham..." She tossed her head from side to side. "Papa," she whispered before quieting once more.

"Excellent, Darcy," said Acker in a soft voice.

"She is so flushed. I do not even need to touch her to know she is burning up," said Richard as he looked between them. "Whatever you are giving her is not enough. Put her in a cold bath. Surely you have a barrel of icy rainwater in the mews."

Acker winced. "The shock could kill her."

"And the fever will not?" Richard lifted his eyebrows, daring Acker to argue. "I saw my fair share of fevers on the continent. Those where the fever was this high and allowed to rage rarely survived."

"Many of those men were wounded, were they not?" asked Darcy. His cousin was going to upset Miss Bennet if he did not cease his infernal interference.

Richard gave a one-shouldered shrug. "Some, but not all."

At a sniff from his side, Miss Bennet's tear-filled eyes were enough for Darcy to rise to grab his cousin in a firm grip. "I believe you have said enough." He pushed Richard through the door and closed it behind him. "My study, now."

"What is the matter with you?" His cousin wrenched free and straightened his topcoat. "I mean well."

When they reached the bottom of the stairs, Watson stood in the hall, his jaw dropping like a rock upon setting eyes on Richard. "Sir, I am sorry. I do not know who abandoned their post, but I assure you, I *will* ensure they are reprimanded."

Darcy acknowledged Watson while he gave Richard another shove towards his study. As soon as they were inside, Darcy slammed the door and fisted his hands at his sides. "You are the closest thing to a brother I possess, thus I have always given you free reign of my homes. You have been welcome, even when I was not in a mood for company. I told you at Georgiana's wedding , I did not wish to speak of personal matters. You insisted—"

"Because you *are* my brother," said Richard, leaning somewhat forward. "With Georgiana married, you cannot remain so alone—so isolated in this house. Do you think I have not seen your suffering? I knew you were plagued by some memory or happening, but I left you to your own counsel until Georgiana insisted you had need of me. I do not want your sister to fret for you when she is newly married. This should be one of the happiest times of her life." He straightened with a deep inhale. "Have you kept me away to avoid a painful conversation or because you have brought these ladies into your home? And what has Wickham to do with Miss Elizabeth?"

Darcy pinched the bridge of his nose and squeezed his eyes shut in a futile attempt to ward off the slight throbbing near his temples. "The story is indeed a long and painful one, and I had no wish to share with anyone before Miss Bennet came to me for help. So much has changed in these past few days, yet in some ways nothing is different. I still do not want to speak of it, but perhaps if I do, I can gain some much-needed clarity."

"I do not understand what you mean, but I have nowhere to be. Do you?" Richard sat in a chair by the fire and crossed his arms over his chest. Richard could be as stubborn as an ox, and his stance was a familiar one. He would not leave without an explanation.

Darcy poked his head through the door. As he had suspected, Watson had posted a footman across the hall. "Pray have a tray of tea and refreshments sent to the Miss Bennets and their guest in Miss Elizabeth's room, and my cousin and I shall have coffee."

"Yes, sir," he said with a swift bow. Darcy closed the door, sat upon the sofa, and straightened his topcoat, steeling himself for the arduous task of telling such a personal history.

"Does Georgiana know of Miss Elizabeth and her sister? Does she know they are staying under your roof?"

"Georgiana once met Miss Elizabeth at Pemberley, but no, she does not know they are here," he said, shaking his head. They both stopped speaking at a knock, and a maid entered with a tray. Once the service was settled on a table, she poured coffee for Darcy and his cousin before she hastened back to the kitchen. Richard lifted his eyebrows. "So, we are alone. What is this secret I have been waiting to hear?"

"'Tis not a secret. I have simply never felt the need to speak of it."

His cousin crossed his ankle over his knee and relaxed into his seat. "You told Georgiana."

"Georgiana happened to be with me when I discovered some tragic and distressing news, and was confused by my reaction. The day she insisted I tell her, she hid my Port and brandy and threatened to send for you if I did not confess what had upset me."

"And you indulged her?" He laughed low as he lifted his cup to his lips, pausing before taking a sip. "I have done her a disservice. I had not expected her to possess the fortitude to prise information you did not desire to share. I am impressed."

Richard's insufferable crooked grin disappeared as he sipped his coffee.

Darcy sighed while he rested his cup on his leg. "I refuse to tolerate your jests. I would have had no patience with them at that time, and I confess I lack the patience for them today."

His cousin's smile vanished when he set his cup back upon the saucer. "Forgive me. I am glad to know you could confide in Georgiana. You have a habit of keeping more inside than you should." He turned the cup on the saucer. "I know we have a great deal to speak of, but what I must ask before we continue is: How do the Bennets know Wickham, and what does Wickham have to do with Miss Elizabeth?"

Of course, he would ask the most complicated question first.

Chapter 10

Darcy crossed his ankle over his knee and bounced his foot. His cousin had disliked Wickham since they were boys. Wickham's propensity to insinuate himself into the favour of Darcy's father as well as the cruel and selfish nature the miscreant had always possessed heightened Richard's distrust of the man as the years passed. That dislike blossomed into an intense hatred fuelled solely by Wickham's attacks on the remaining Darcys, in particular Georgiana's near elopement. That immovable abhorrence rendered Richard's insistence upon an answer to those questions first and foremost far from surprising.

"When I stayed in Hertfordshire with Bingley." Darcy set his cup and saucer on the side table. "Wickham was encamped with the militia in the nearby village of Meryton. In August of 1812, Wickham convinced the youngest Bennet sister to run away with him to Gretna Green. She was a year older than Georgiana when he attempted the same with her—but Miss Lydia did not have Georgiana's fortune, but a paltry one-thousand pounds upon her mother's death and fifty pounds per annum while her father lived."

Richard sucked in a breath through his teeth. "And this girl thought Wickham would marry her? He would sooner go to debtor's prison than commit himself to a life without wealth." His cousin's forehead crinkled and his coffee cup tipped a fraction as though forgotten. His eyes narrowed, and he stared at Darcy, making Darcy shift in his place. "Miss Elizabeth is insensible, yet she knew to beg your help with Wickham."

Three or four seconds passed before Richard pointed at
Darcy, his finger wagging as he stood. "That Easter... At
Rosings, when Miss Elizabeth visited Hunsford. You were out
of sorts that year. First, you insisted on remaining longer than
planned, then all of a sudden, you decided to depart for
London two days after you had extended our stay for a
fortnight." He set his cup on the mantel and again pointed at
Darcy, his eyes still wide. "You were courting her! I cannot
credit that I never noticed. You walked out more than you rode,
which I found odd but did not think much of at the time. You
had never singled out a lady before. I had no reason to believe
you would court a lady under our aunt's nose." He blinked
several times before he barked out a chuckle. "I do not know
how I never saw it before."

Darcy's gaze traced the pattern of the cushion beneath
him, avoiding his cousin's eye. "I was in love with her." The
words choked him. His contemptuous behaviour upon their
first acquaintance remained, to this day, his biggest regret. "I
fled Hertfordshire after Bingley's ball to distance myself. I
thought myself above her and feared I might reveal my feelings
if I remained."

"This is more the behaviour I would expect from you."
Richard turned towards the fire then in a swift motion rounded
back on Darcy. "Miss Bennet was the lady with unsuitable
connections. The one you took great pride in saving Bingley
from."

"I proposed, Richard." His words broke.

His cousin blanched. "I beg your pardon?"

He met his cousin's eye and glared. "I said I proposed
marriage. My foolish heart believed she was expecting my

addresses—that she desired my addresses. In my arrogance, I made my offer, and she refused me." Darcy shook his head before Richard could say a word. If his cousin continued to interrupt, he would never manage to recount the dreadful encounter. "She accused me of pride and of harming Wickham's prospects. He had, of course, told her his usual tale of woe. The morning we departed for London, I handed her a letter explaining myself. I had known Wickham was encamped in Meryton, but I had never told anyone of his habits."

"You could not do so. You had to protect Georgiana."

"In the letter, I told Elizabeth of Ramsgate." Richard's mouth opened and closed, so Darcy rushed to speak. "I would not have done so if I was not certain she would guard Georgiana's secret. After our departure, I did not see Elizabeth again until August at Pemberley. She was visiting Lambton with her aunt and uncle when the unfortunate situation with her youngest sister occurred. As soon as they discovered Miss Lydia's folly, they departed with haste for Hertfordshire. I rode to the inn that afternoon, believing I had perhaps opened Elizabeth's heart to my suit, but they were gone. I assumed I had misread the situation and returned to Pemberley to lick my wounds."

"Did you not return to Hertfordshire at all?"

"No," he said. "I penned a letter to Mr. Bennet, enquiring of his family and requesting permission to call upon Elizabeth. After the initial sting subsided, I had decided to ensure my assumption in Lambton was correct before trying to forget her. When I failed to receive a response, I thought Elizabeth had rejected my suit once again. Bingley, at the insistence of his sisters, had ended the lease of Netherfield, intending to spend the autumn in Scarborough."

Richard set a hand upon the mantel and watched him with an intensity that made his insides clench. "What truly happened?"

"I did not know until January of the next year that upon reading the note from the militia colonel detailing Miss Lydia's disappearance with Wickham, Mr. Bennet suffered a fatal apoplexy. Mr. Gardiner, Elizabeth's uncle, took it upon himself to locate the wayward couple. He failed in his search."

"Good God." Richard closed his eyes and swallowed hard. "But once you learned of Mr. Bennet's death, did you feel you could not offer for Miss Elizabeth while Georgiana remained unmarried?"

"By the time Georgiana and I learnt of the Bennets' tragedy from the Gardiners, I was too late." Darcy combed a hand through his hair. Elizabeth may have been, at that very moment, alive and in his home, but the recollection was too painful. His chest squeezed so tight breathing was a chore, causing him to rub the spot over his heart. Why would that ache not subside?

"What do you mean?"

"The Bennet's estate, Longbourn, passed to Lady Catherine's parson, Mr. Collins, so the Gardiners brought Miss Bennet and Miss Elizabeth to London to live with them. Miss Mary and Miss Kitty were to remain with their mother, who was to reside with Mrs. Bennet's sister in Meryton." His throat began to squeeze closed just as it always did when he relived these memories. "But Miss Bennet and Elizabeth disappeared soon after arriving at the Gardiners' home in Cheapside."

"Disappeared?" Richard's eyebrows drew down in the middle. "How do two gentlewomen vanish?"

"I have not asked them the particulars," said Darcy, his blasted voice hoarse once more. "I do know Mr. Gardiner searched and even hired detectives in an effort to find them. Nearly three months passed before they finally had word. The detectives Mr. Gardiner had hired had tracked the ladies to St. Giles—"

"St. Giles!" Richard's agape expression was a perfect illustration of Darcy's sentiments on their choice of neighbourhood. He could not blame him for his reaction. No lady should be exposed to such deplorable conditions.

"We believe the accommodations were all they could afford without resorting to working in a brothel."

"But how did they arrange a lease not to mention acquire the funds to live?"

"According to the Gardiners, the sisters often saved their pin money for their trips to London. When I aided Miss Bennet in bringing Elizabeth here, they were living in a small, shabby one-room hovel. They took in sewing to support themselves." He gulped hard. Thinking of Elizabeth in such squalor nauseated him. She deserved so much more.

"When Mr. Gardiner knocked upon the door, no one answered, but a man who lived next door, Mr. Cooke, informed their uncle they had both died of some plague. You are aware how those parts of town forever have some pestilence travelling from household to household. Mr. Cooke took Mr. Gardiner to the local churchyard where the ladies had been buried in pauper's graves, but the graves had been unearthed. Mr. Gardiner was led to believe resurrectionists had stolen the bodies."

Richard turned to the fire and stared into its depths. "Did they ever find Miss Lydia?"

After nodding, Darcy sipped his coffee. "Yes, I found Mrs. Younge, who told me of her fate. Wickham had abandoned her about a month after the elopement. The girl could not afford a room in Mrs. Younge's boarding-house, so the woman had turned her out into the street." His cousin growled and began to pace. No doubt, Richard would tear the miscreant limb from limb if afforded the opportunity. "Miss Lydia was unrecognizable she had grown so thin, not to mention she wore filthy, tattered clothes. Once bold as brass, she cowered when I approached. I had to send for Mrs. Northcott to help me persuade her into the carriage." Darcy dropped his head back.

Richard stopped and faced him. "Where is Miss Lydia now?"

"While I had left Georgiana safe at Pemberley with Mrs. Annesley, Lady Catherine was visiting me at the time and insisted on taking the girl as her companion. Miss Lydia lives at Rosings, though no one but myself and our aunt knows of where she is. She is known by a different name and wishes her whereabouts to remain a secret." He lifted his head, though he was weary of holding it up. "She was too timid from her ordeal to wed and save her reputation as Lydia Bennet. Fortunately, our aunt is no longer fond of dinners and balls and receives very few callers. Miss Lydia strolls the gardens and reads aloud to our aunt but does not remain when callers do arrive since strangers still prove too much for her." The image of Miss Lydia's condition when he found her came to the fore. His eyes slammed closed. Those memories needed to be shoved back to the dark recesses of his mind. Nothing could be done by dwelling on what could not be changed. "I cannot fathom the violence she endured. She bears scars that I am certain are more than skin deep."

"What happened to Wickham?" Richard's hard voice carried a dangerous tone he rarely used.

Darcy scratched the back of his neck and avoided his cousin's boring gaze. "I helped Mr. Gardiner discover his whereabouts. Once we managed to capture him, we locked him in a storeroom at Mr. Gardiner's warehouse until we could arrange passage for him."

"I cannot imagine Wickham went without a fight."

Darcy kneaded his neck, digging his fingers into the tense muscle without a shred of mercy. "We may have put laudanum in his ale before transporting him to the shipyard. One of Mr. Gardiner's associates imports goods from the East Indies. Wickham had to work during the voyage and was not to be allowed return passage." When Darcy allowed himself to hazard a glance at his cousin, Richard's blank expression had never altered. Was his cousin shocked? Would he censure them for their actions? He could not imagine so, but Richard's current behaviour was puzzling indeed. Darcy stood and threw up his hands before letting them fall to his sides. "Will you not say something?"

Richard snickered, then coughed and brought himself under better regulation. "Forgive me. I am horrified by what happened to Miss Elizabeth and her family, but I am astonished. *You* drugged Wickham and banished him to the

East Indies? I never would have thought you capable." He began to laugh once more.

"Richard—" He should have known his cousin would enjoy Wickham's fate.

"No." Richard held up his hand. "Wickham deserves every bit of what he has received. I told you for years you needed to banish him from Pemberley or see him put in debtor's prison, but you refused on each and every occasion." He shook his head. "I must say this is an infinitely better solution than any of my ideas. Mr. Gardiner is a good influence on you."

"You are nonsensical."

"No, relieved Wickham is no longer capable of harming you or Georgiana." He picked up his coffee and returned to his chair. "I shall not lie to you and tell you I understand how you feel. Your belief in Miss Elizabeth's death explains your melancholy these past years. Discovering her alive must have been an immense shock. I imagine their relations must be overjoyed to have them restored."

He winced. "Miss Bennet begged me not to inform the Gardiners."

"But why?" Richard's agape countenance mirrored Darcy's feelings on the matter.

Darcy returned to his seat and propped his elbows upon his knees. "I wish I knew. As I mentioned, we have been too busy with Elizabeth's care to discuss much else. I am certain they will refuse, but I will not let them return to that abysmal home." The idea of her in such squalor made him tap his fist on the cushion and tilt his head to the side in an effort to relieve the tension in his neck and shoulders. He could return them to the Gardiners first, but she would never speak to him again. Would he be willing to risk such an eventuality?

"I am certain I know the answer, but what are your intentions?" Richard took his cup to the tray and filled it to the top.

"Miss Bennet has given me reason to hope that I may have a chance at Elizabeth's acceptance. When she is well, I shall again make her the offer of my hand, then do all I can to gain her agreement."

Richard sipped his coffee and returned the cup to the saucer. "I know you do not require my approval, but I shall offer it anyhow. You have never considered yourself first, putting Pemberley, Georgiana, and even me before your own needs. You are due your own happiness, do you not think?"

"I pray she survives," said Darcy.

"You must have faith. She was a healthy sort of girl as I recall." One side of his lips quirked up. "I must say. Even without her hair, her sister is a handsome lady. Bingley was leather-headed to take your advice."

At a knock, Darcy leaned his head back. "Come!"

Acker entered, set his bag on the desk, and pointed at the tray. "May I?"

"Yes, of course."

Cook had included spare cups, one of which Acker began to fill. "She is doing as well as I can expect, considering her fever. The rattle in her chest is no worse—a blessing really." He stood beside the fire with his coffee cradled in his hands. "I told Miss Bennet to expect the cough to worsen. Her body will need to expel the congestion if she is to improve."

"What of the fever?" asked Richard.

Acker grimaced. "I have given Miss Bennet leave to be more aggressive. When I left, Miss Bennet and Mrs. Cooke were dampening a bedsheet and tucking it around Miss Elizabeth. All of you have done remarkably well to provide teas and nourishment when Miss Elizabeth has the wherewithal to receive it."

With a sigh, Darcy pinched the bridge of his nose. His head was beginning to ache. "I wish we could do more. I feel so helpless."

"Unfortunately, precious little can be done for Grippe." Acker cleared his throat. "The next few days will tell the tale, Darcy. Either her fever will break or continue to rage. If it does not break soon, you must prepare yourself for the inevitable. She will not survive."

She struggled to draw air into her lungs, but the weight of something pressed mercilessly upon her ribs, refusing to let them expand. Why was she so cold? Her flesh prickled painfully, her body shook, and her teeth chattered.

"Jane?" Try as she might, her eyelids refused to cooperate. When she finally managed to pry them apart, a blurry light surrounded her and stabbed through into her skull. Her eyes clamped shut and a high-pitched gasp burst from her throat. A paroxysm of coughing ripped through her chest, tearing painfully at her lungs. "Jane?" She could barely say her sister's name. What was wrong with her?

"I am here, dearest." An arm slipped behind her shoulders and lifted. "Gemma, we need to prop her up a bit more."

Another arm pressed against her back until her head dropped to someone's shoulder. "Can you open your eyes?"

"Too bright."

"Mrs. Northcott has drawn the draperies. Will you not try again?"

Through small slits, a crackling fire could be discerned through the haze. "I am so tired."

"I know, but I need you to drink this."

She wrapped her lips around what was brought to her mouth and a small amount of liquid hit her tongue. Ugh! She drew back with what little strength she could muster. Why was she so weak? "'Tis cold. I am so cold."

"I know cool broth must be unappetizing," said Gemma from her opposite side. "But your fever has been very high. Jane also feared burning your tongue." The cold china touched her bottom lip. "Lizzy, you must drink if you are to improve." Elizabeth whimpered and swallowed down every bit of what they gave her.

"Pray, no more. I cannot..." Her back met the coolness of the bedding, and she sank into the pillows, letting the darkness consume her once more.

Chapter 11

"Mr. Darcy!"

Darcy sat straight up and swayed, his entire body on edge from being awakened so abruptly. "What is it?"

"'Tis Miss Elizabeth, sir," said Elsie. She panted as though she had run a mile instead of from a few doors down. "Mrs. Northcott and Miss Bennet are trying to bring down the fever, but 'tis terribly high. Nothing is helping."

He swung his legs out of the bed and stood, padding down the corridor. As soon as he entered, he halted in place. The difference in Elizabeth! How hot had she become? When he had last checked her, she had been a bit pink, now her flushed complexion was red. The bedclothes were pulled down past her feet, and she was covered in no more than what appeared to be a wet sheet and her nightshift. She shook violently, and her teeth chattered. "Why did you not awaken me sooner?"

"She was not so bad as this," said Miss Bennet. "I do not know what could have happened. She woke for a minute or two when Gemma and I first put the wet sheet over her. She did not seem to be dreaming. When she woke again three hours ago, we gave her the willow bark tea and the tincture, but not long after she drifted off, her fever began to rise. She cried out in her sleep more than once, but even that has ceased. The silence from her is terrifying."

He steepled his hands in front of his chin. "I dare not ask how much more it could rise."

"I do not believe we want to know," said Mrs. Northcott.

Miss Bennet crossed her arms over her chest. "That gentleman who was here earlier today—Viscount Carlisle?"

"Yes, my cousin."

"He mentioned a rain barrel, did he not?"

Darcy backed against the door. She could not mean to...? "Acker feared the shock could kill her."

His housekeeper propped her hands on her hips. "The sheet warms too quickly. We must do something more, yet the excess water has proven difficult to wring from the fabric. That water must be removed to ensure we do not soak the rugs and mattress beneath her. But we cannot keep up. If she becomes any hotter, the heat of the fever alone will kill her."

"That barrel is sure to contain a layer of ice at this time of night." He glanced at Elizabeth then scratched the day's growth upon his cheek. A better solution had to be found. Her fever could not continue to rage, but what if the shock of the cold water? Acker had been adamant of the dangers of such a scheme. "How many pails of water did the footmen bring to the dressing room before they retired?"

Mrs. Northcott poked her head into the adjacent room. "Four," she said.

His foot tapped upon the floor as his gaze darted to each of the ladies. "Wake two footmen and have them bring the larger hip bath from the servants' wing to this dressing room." Elizabeth would not be able to sink in that size tub, but the level of water would be high enough to have an effect. "We shall use the water in the dressing room, which has been without a fire, so it should be cool enough. Also, have the footmen bring more cool water in the event we need it." He ran a hand across his mouth and frowned. "I understand you are desperate for something to prove a remedy, yet I cannot imagine how painful an ice-cold bath would be for her. I believe Acker would think this to be a better course as well."

Without question, Mrs. Northcott rushed from the room while Miss Bennet sat at her sister's side and pressed a fresh cloth to her sister's forehead. "I cannot lose her," she said on a sob.

He set a hand upon Miss Bennet's shoulder. "We are not done fighting yet, Miss Bennet. Do not give up hope." The words may have come from his mouth, but did he believe them? Elizabeth would be well—she had to be well. He could not lose hope!

Her fingers wiped at her cheeks. "Mr. Darcy, I believe you should call me Jane. Continuing with such formality at times such as these is more than we should have to manage. We are friends, are we not?"

"I would be honoured to be counted among your friends, Jane. I pray that one day, we shall be family too."

She took his hand in both of hers with a watery smile. "I pray for that too. I believe Lizzy would be truly happy as your wife. I desire nothing more for my dearest sister."

They remained at Elizabeth's bedside while she dragged in rattling breath after rattling breath. How long would she suffer so? She lay there unmoving, other than a fierce shivering as well as a periodic cough so deep one could believe it came from the tips of her toes, each punctuated by a grimace.

When Mrs. Northcott returned, Elsie followed her into the room. "The tub is in place, and we have plenty of water should we need it."

Jane stood and backed from the bed. Darcy scooped Elizabeth into his arms, leaving the damp sheet in place to preserve her modesty while he carried her to the tub.

One end of the hip bath slanted at an angle, and while an individual would usually bathe with their back to the opposite end, which was straight up and down, he placed Elizabeth backwards. She would be reclined and more comfortable in such a position. No one would need to support her.

"I believe that will work admirably, sir," said Mrs. Northcott as Elsie stepped beside her, pail in hand. When he gave a jerky nod, the maid slowly poured the water to Elizabeth's side. He crouched as close to Elizabeth as he could and held his breath while the tub began to fill. What would happen when the water penetrated the nightgown and touched bare flesh?

A second or two later, Elizabeth gasped, frowned, and as the second pail was poured, began to writhe and whimper. Darcy leaned his forehead against her temple. Dear Lord, he needed her to survive! They needed the water to cool her. He could not consider the alternative.

His hand slipped between her head and the unforgiving metal of the tub, lest she injure herself. Her teeth began to chatter with more force and the intensity of her shivers increased until she almost seemed to be convulsing.

Jane reached across him and pulled the cap from Elizabeth's head, soaking it in the water and draping it back over her sister's scalp. Elizabeth cried out and arched her back, almost removing the offending article, but he kept it in place with his fingers.

He looked from Jane, to Elsie, to Mrs. Northcott. "How long should this take?"

Jane shook her head, her eyes shiny with unshed tears. "I wish I knew."

"Until she cools," said the housekeeper. Despite her authoritative tone, she began to pace while Elizabeth suffered. Elsie did nothing more than stare and shake her head, her arms crossed tightly over her chest.

They remained for the next half-hour in an odd sort of vigil. Darcy remained near Elizabeth's head in the event she thrashed or made a sudden movement where she could harm herself, Jane continued to dampen the cap and sponge water from the tub onto her sister's neck and face, and Mrs. Northcott and Elsie both remained silent, Mrs. Northcott's hands steepled over her mouth.

Once Elizabeth's shaking had visibly lessened, Mrs. Northcott pressed a palm to her forehead. "I think she is improving. She is not so flushed, and her face is much cooler."

"Do we take her out?" Elsie looked back and forth between them.

Jane shrugged and sighed. "We could return her to the water should her fever return."

He needed no further permission to slip his arms into the water and bring Elizabeth to his chest. The bath helped. Why prolong her misery? Elsie began wrapping towels around Elizabeth. "Where do you want me to place her?"

"This way," said the housekeeper. Mrs. Northcott rushed ahead of him into the bedchamber. When he entered, a clean, thick rug had been placed over the bedding. The moment he withdrew, he turned his back so they could begin tending to her. "I shall find some dry clothing for myself. Open the door once she is changed so I may return."

"Yes, sir," said Mrs. Northcott as he closed the bedchamber door behind him.

He replaced his soaked lawn shirt but left his breeches. They had not absorbed a great deal of water and would dry soon enough.

As soon as the door to Elizabeth's bedchamber opened, he rushed inside and stood behind the chair at her bedside, gripping the back. She still frowned, though she did not shiver or squirm as she had. She was not so much as wiggling a finger. Why would she not move? The stillness thickened the air in the room until he struggled to draw breath.

Jane sat on the mattress at her sister's side. "I suppose we wait."

Mrs. Northcott and Elsie sat near the fire while he settled into the chair. They did not speak while they watched Elizabeth for any change. How he hoped she would open her eyes and smile, but she remained calm and still. Elsie replenished the fire when necessary, Jane ensured Elizabeth's fever remained manageable, and he and Mrs. Northcott remained in case they were needed. Tonight would surely be one of the longest nights of his life!

——————◆——————

Darcy bolted awake from a dreamless slumber. He lifted his head, though opening his eyes proved a challenge and his sluggish mind refused to cooperate. After forcing his eyelids wider, he glanced about him. One of his hands held Elizabeth's at her side, and he exhaled in relief at the steady rising and

falling of her chest. He pushed himself up from the edge of the
mattress where he had apparently fallen asleep sometime after
four in the morning. Was that not the last the clock had
chimed?

"I take it the night was difficult."

Darcy blinked up at Acker, who stood at his side with a
hand on his shoulder, and nodded. He rubbed his eyes and
glanced about the room. Mrs. Northcott slept, leaning against
the side of the Bergère chair, while Jane slept curled up at
Elizabeth's side, her fingers wrapped around her sister's arm.

Acker pointed to his patient, and Darcy rose, moving to
allow the physician to step to her side. After reaching for the
ceiling in a long stretch, he cracked the door. The footman who
stood against the opposite wall sprang to attention. "Sir!"

"Pray, have trays of coffee, tea, and breakfast brought to
this room. Mr. Acker, no doubt, knows the house well enough
to find his way when his examination is completed."

The footman executed a quick bow before hurrying off,
and Darcy closed the door. He yawned and stepped over to the
housekeeper. "Mrs. Northcott," he said with a hand to her
shoulder.

She flinched and her head jerked back and forth before
she exhaled and relaxed. "Forgive me, sir, I seem to have fallen
asleep after I sent Elsie to bed."

"Do not trouble yourself. We all did. I sent a footman to
the kitchen for tea and coffee." He required the coffee after
such a long and trying night.

"Of course." She stood and brushed off her skirt. "I should
go below stairs and ensure all is as it should be. Do ring if you

have need of me." After a curtsey, she bustled towards the servants' stairs.

"Tell me what happened during the night." Acker spoke just above a whisper as he stepped closer.

"She was burning up." He ran both hands over his head before crossing his arms over his chest. "The sheet, for the difficulty it required, was not efficient enough. I had footmen move a hip bath into the dressing room, and we bathed her in cool water for close to a half-hour. We did not want to remove her and have to repeat the process too soon. When her fever rose again, we put her back in the tub." They had not waited until Elizabeth was so poorly for the second bath. Thankfully, she had not needed to remain in the water for as long.

"What time was the last bath?"

He pressed the heel of his palm against his forehead. The long night made thinking a chore. "Close to three, I think."

"So, almost five hours since you removed her from the water? And she was changed into dry clothing?"

Darcy nodded. "Yes, of course." What was he about?

A wide grin overspread Acker's face, and he slapped Darcy on the shoulder. "She has sweated off the fever."

"What do you mean?" Darcy took four swift steps to the bedside and cupped her cheek. She was cool to the touch and no longer flushed. His pinkie finger brushed her damp neck when his hand withdrew. "She is wet."

"The bedclothes are as well. The bedding and nightgown will need to be changed as soon as can be."

Darcy leaned across and shook Jane's shoulder. "Jane." She blinked and her forehead crinkled as he straightened.

"Elizabeth's fever has broken. We can manage long enough for you to get some rest. Why do you not retire for a while?"

She kissed Elizabeth's forehead and gave a laughing sob. "Thank God." She covered her mouth with her hands and shook her head then placed both hands on her cheeks. "Thank you so much—both of you."

"She is not well yet," said Acker. "She may still suffer from a slight fever in the afternoons and evenings as she improves, and be warned that coughs from Grippe can linger."

Jane looked back and forth between them. "But there is hope."

Acker gave a knowledgeable dip of his chin. "She has endured the worst, I believe." Darcy sank into a chair, his legs weakened by the news. Elizabeth would be well.

After a knock, Elsie and another maid entered and bustled around as they set trays of tea, coffee, and some breakfast dishes upon the table near the fire.

"I requested tea and coffee should you wish for some before you retire." He bent forward and took Elizabeth's hand in his. He would sit with her forever if afforded the opportunity.

After Jane rose, she gazed at the breakfast the maids delivered with a smile. "Yes, I am famished. I hope you both will join me. I am of a mind to celebrate. This morning may be a small victory, but 'tis a victory nonetheless."

Chapter 12

Elizabeth blinked and raised an unsteady hand to her head. Lord, but her temples throbbed as though a blacksmith hammered at the inside of her skull. She groaned and squeezed her eyes shut, searching for a moment's respite from the incessant pounding.

"Miss Elizabeth, 'tis good to see you awake."

Whose voice was that? The person spoke in soft tones, so she shifted her head in its direction, opening her eyes slowly. Otherwise, the discomfort would be too much. When the room came into focus, two candles provided additional illumination to the lady sitting at her bedside. "Who are—" Coughs wracked her body, and she curled onto her side as the dull pain in her head and neck intensified. Would that the coughing would cease! Every bark threatened to rip her lungs from her chest and the pain travelled into her temples and behind her eyes, making her cradle her forehead and whimper.

"There, there," said the woman. "I believe you were going to ask me who I am." She gave a motherly smile while she arranged the coverlet. "My name is Mrs. Northcott, and I am the housekeeper."

Housekeeper? Elizabeth's stomach clenched, and her eyes darted about the room. The bedcurtain blocked the opposite side of the dim bedchamber, preventing her from seeing much. What she could make out, however, was far too fine for St. Giles or even her uncle's house. What had Jane done?

"I hope you will forgive me for having the presumption to care for you in your sister's stead, but we have insisted upon sitting with you some so she can rest. The poor dear was exhausted after last night. I believe those circles under her eyes were darker than when the two of you first arrived. I am pleased to report most of her colour has returned in the past week."

"Week?" Her eyes had threatened to close of their own accord, but at the woman's mention of time, Elizabeth wrenched them open.

"You were brought here five days ago. You have been quite ill." The woman lifted a cup with a spout. "I know this is bitter, but your fever has been more manageable today. We must keep it that way."

As soon as Elizabeth swallowed the last of the vile concoction, she shuddered and coughed several times, causing that same tearing pain through her chest with every heave. "Where?" She hacked in an effort to breathe.

"I know you have questions, but while you are awake, I need you to take some broth as well." The woman held another cup to Elizabeth's lips. "I promise this is the last, but I can see that you are fighting to remain awake and you desperately need nourishment."

After several swallows of the tepid liquid, Elizabeth wrenched her face away. "No more." She made to ask another question, but the darkness lingering around the edge of her vision swallowed her whole.

At three in the morning, Darcy sat up with a jolt and fought off the last vestiges of sleep while the clock in the sitting room finished chiming the hour. Still dressed in his breeches and shirt, he eyed the topcoat left on a chair while he tied a simple cravat and slipped on his waistcoat. He had no desire to be trussed up to sit at Elizabeth's bedside, so he left the topcoat, pulled on his boots, and stole down the hall.

When he entered, Mrs. Northcott rose and smiled. "She woke near midnight and took some willow bark tea and broth. I sent Elsie to bed since the young miss was not upset at my presence."

"She was lucid?" He could not help the eagerness of his voice.

"She did not speak much, but she was more wakeful than I have seen her thus far. Her dreadful cough kept her from saying much before she fell back asleep." She walked to the fireplace and replenished the fire. "I shall fetch some hot water for tea and bring more broth in the event she wakes again."

Mrs. Northcott disappeared into the servants' passages, and he settled into the chair his housekeeper had vacated. He took Elizabeth's hand and placed his fingers along her cheek. Thank goodness, her skin was cool to the touch. When she frowned and whimpered, he drew his hand away sharply.

She had yet to be truly awake in his presence, and how he longed for it and feared it all at the same time. Would she be angry with Jane for begging his help? Would she allow him to court her—to prove to her he would be fortunate to have such a wife? Her acceptance of him during her most feverish moments gave him reason to hope those tender feelings existed or she would not have called for him, trusted him when she was most vulnerable.

After Mrs. Northcott returned, she did not linger but completed her tasks with efficiency before leaving him to his vigil. He picked up a book he kept nearby for these quiet moments at Elizabeth's bedside, but instead of reading, he began to wool-gather, those long-held dreams he had relied upon of Elizabeth as his wife overtaking his mind.

His fingers caressed her knuckles before wrapping around her hand. For so long, he had imagined Elizabeth beside him, a spectre that could never be reality, or so he thought. He pressed his forehead to their joined hands and closed his eyes. Lord, but he was weary! Since being awake all night the day before, he had retired earlier than was his wont so he could wake to care for her this morning, yet even with the near sleepless night, he had trouble succumbing. His mind would not calm enough for Morpheus to take him.

———————◆———————

A low light lit the room, providing Elizabeth the ability to see more of her surroundings. She blinked and concentrated on what appeared to be an ornate canopy that decorated the ceiling above her. She could not discern the colour of the fabric, yet it appeared quite fine.

She closed her eyes to withstand the aching of her head and neck while she moved. When she opened her eyes once more, the opposite wall showed a stone fireplace where a fire burned low, the coals glowing in the dark recesses of the grate.

Something caught in her throat. She needed to be gentle while attempting to clear the tickle, lest she aggravate that incessant pounding that seemed to plague her during her waking moments. She clenched her hands, but her right wrapped around flesh and bone: another hand held in her own.

With great care, she turned her head and winced at the soreness of her neck. Could she not wake without hurting?

That woman during the night, the housekeeper... What was her name? She could not remember, but that lady had said Jane would return, had she not? Perhaps Jane could help her.

Once she faced the direction of the hand, she opened her eyes, but Jane's serene smile was nowhere to be found. Instead, a male crown of unruly mahogany curls rested upon the mattress. She frowned and tugged her hand free with care, her fingers pausing before they combed the hair away from his forehead.

Her eyes burned, and she squeezed them shut against the threat of tears. She had no need to see all of his face to know his identity. How often had she dreamt of him since Pemberley? Yet, if this was truly a dream, he would vanish before she could sink her fingers into the softness of his hair. She would never set eyes upon his beloved face, his eyes would not open and look upon her with a softness she craved, nor would he speak, his deep tones soothing her unease. If she could, she would shake off those useless thoughts. Her situation relegated her hopes and dreams to ash.

Her trembling hand crept closer until she touched his soft curls, moving them aside and revealing what had been hidden of his beloved face. She gasped, which induced a fit of coughing that startled him from his slumber.

Fitzwilliam jumped and moved beside her so he could wrap his arm around her shoulders. "When you can, drink this," he said near her ear. After one last huge bark, she shoved the cup away and collapsed back into the pillows. "Elizabeth, this will help."

A sob tore from her chest. "This *is* your house."

"Yes, but I beg you not to be angry. You needed more than your sister or the Cookes could provide." He took both of her hands and grasped them firmly. "You were so very ill. Jane feared for your life—I feared for you as well."

Hot tears coursed down her cheeks and dribbled down her neck. She opened her mouth, but wracking coughs prevented her from speaking.

He moved to help support her, and again placed the cup near her lips. "This is willow bark tea. It will help with the headache." As soon as her breathing allowed, she drank the entirety of the cup. Anything to help with the pain! He then gave her a spoonful of some foul concoction before pressing a teacup to her lips. "To help with the taste. 'Tis nothing more than weak tea with some sugar."

She swallowed the last gratefully and let her head rest back into the pillows. Was she wearing...? She placed a hand to her nape, her fingers slipping under the fine muslin to her scalp. Where was her hair?

Mr. Darcy tugged her hand away to hold in his own. "Your sister and Mrs. Northcott thought removing your hair would prevent continued problems with itching." She covered her face and let her tears fall as they came. How could he not be disgusted by her? How long had she been ill? The woman during the night had said a week. She had been thin before. After such an extended illness, she would be thinner. Now, without hair, how could he stand to look upon her?

He drew her hands from her face. "Pray, do not cry. I cannot bear it." With a soft touch, he dabbed at her cheeks with his handkerchief. "You are lovely."

"Liar," she said followed by a cough.

He cupped her face in his palms. "Elizabeth, these past two years, I have thought you dead. You cannot know how that pained me. Your illness and lack of hair do not matter to me. You are still the most handsome lady of my acquaintance. Do you understand?"

Her eyelids tried to flutter closed, but she forced them to remain open. "I am so tired."

"You should take some broth first." He rose and stepped over to the fireplace. When he returned, he helped her sip the rich stock until she pushed the dish away.

"Pray, no more."

His blue eyes watched her intently while he wiped her face with a damp cloth. "Is there anything I can do for you?"

She shook her head. "No, thank you. I am enough of an imposition as it is."

"No," he said in a firm tone. "Do not speak of yourself so. You could never be an imposition."

He was, no doubt, sincere, but before her father's death, she had been the daughter of a gentleman and had still been below him. By leaving her uncle's protection, she lowered herself further. Mr. Darcy wedding a lady from a small estate or Cheapside was one matter, but a woman from St. Giles? That situation was impossible—especially bearing in mind that he had Miss Darcy's future to consider.

How could Jane have brought her here? Her sister was too good to know Elizabeth's shameful thoughts—how often she had stopped herself from journeying to Fitzwilliam's doorstep and begging to be his mistress. She loved him that much. Her love for him had only grown during their time apart, and now she would be forced to leave him—again. How fleeing

Derbyshire had devastated her! Fleeing him now would rip away a part of her soul.

He picked up a book from beside her and began to read, his deep voice soothing the pain of the separation that would need to come. Her eyelids fluttered closed, and his beloved voice followed her into her dreams.

When next she woke, the room was brighter, allowing her to see its features in greater detail. The ornate canopy was a beautiful muted, pale green and ivory that complemented the wall coverings, which featured lush green bamboo with flowers in varying shades of pink as well as birds and butterflies that perched or flew among the branches.

A damp warmth on her shoulder made her flinch and turn her head with care. She refused to aggravate her neck or head by another sudden movement. Jane stood beside the bed, drawing a cloth down Elizabeth's arm to her hand. Her sister dipped it into the basin on the bedside table and wrung it out before bringing it to Elizabeth's neck. "Oh!" she said as she jumped. "You are awake."

After dropping the rag back into the basin, Jane brought a cup to Elizabeth's lips and assisted her by holding the back of her head. "You must drink."

Elizabeth grimaced as she wrapped her lips around the spout. They had her drink the bitter tea whenever she woke. What she would not give for something more! After two swallows, she pushed the cup away just in time to dissolve into a fit of coughs that doubled her over.

"There, there." Jane's hand rubbed up and down her back until the last of the hacking subsided, and Elizabeth dropped back into the pillows. Once she caught her breath, Jane held the cup before her. "Do you think you can manage the rest?" A small amount of the disgusting tea remained, but after the coughing, the foul liquid soothed Elizabeth's throat.

"I was beginning to be jealous," said Jane with a soft smile. "You have graced Mrs. Northcott and Mr. Darcy with your delightful conversation, but I have yet to partake in it."

Elizabeth's eyes drooped as she tried to smile at Jane's jest. "Hardly." She cleared her throat after rasping her response. Her palm pressed against her stomach as it growled. When had she eaten last—truly eaten? "Jane, I am hungry."

"Let me ring the bell. Elsie has not returned with fresh broth yet." When her sister again sat upon the bed, she finished wiping Elizabeth's arm. "Cook mentioned making some pap now that you are waking more."

"No," said Elizabeth. "Pray, no pap. I could never stomach it when Mama made me eat it. No possets either." Just the thought of pap or possets made her nauseous.

"Perhaps some soft vegetables in the broth or a bit of bread."

Jane turned all of a sudden, drawing Elizabeth's attention to a man who stood near the door. He was not much taller than Jane and handsome. He wore a pleasant smile that appeared somehow earnest, and held a small leather bag.

"Forgive me for surprising you. With Miss Elizabeth's disturbance at loud noise over the past few days, I did not knock."

"No, you need not apologize." Jane drew the coverlet up and moved to the side. "Lizzy, this is Mr. Acker, Mr. Darcy's physician."

The gentleman stepped forward. "I am pleased to make your acquaintance, Miss Elizabeth. I am also glad you have an appetite." Elizabeth's gaze followed Mr. Acker's hand as he placed it upon her forehead. "Your fever is much improved. Do you have any pain?"

"My head throbs." She swallowed and wet her lips with her tongue. "And my throat is sore."

"That is to be expected. I know the willow bark is not pleasant, but it will be of aid." He sat upon the chair beside the bed while Jane bustled to the other side of the room in response to a knock. "I hope you will forgive me for being presumptuous, but we need you well. I am tired of my good friend driving me to distraction over the state of your health. The sooner you marry him, the sooner I hope to be called for happier tidings."

Was he certain she no longer had a fever? Her face suddenly radiated enough heat to warm the entirety of Longbourn. "Mr. Darcy has not... I mean I cannot. I do not belong here."

Mr. Acker leaned closer, though not so close to be inappropriate. "I am certain Darcy would disagree with you—most vehemently. Do you not agree?"

She took a deep breath and allowed the physician to continue his examination. She could not dwell on what would happen when she was well. If she thought of the pain, she would never have the strength to leave him when the time came—and she had to leave him. No other choice existed. Since Lydia's folly, she was too far below him, and as much as she wished the past could be changed—altered so she could be the lady Fitzwilliam required, nothing could be done. The sooner those around her accepted that, the better.

Chapter 13

Darcy stood and reached his arms towards the ceiling. His muscles stretched in a satisfying manner and his joints clicked, releasing the tension of sitting so long in one attitude. He lifted the candle and raised it to the clock on the mantel. How had it been a mere two hours since he had relieved Mrs. Northcott? He would never forgo sitting with Elizabeth, though these early morning hours were the most difficult.

Three days ago, Elizabeth's fever seemed to break, only to return by late afternoon. Acker had predicted as much, yet his warning did not lessen the alarm. During the night, her fever broke once again while she slept with the cycle repeating itself on the following day though not as severe as before. Her improvement was steady, and he was thankful for every bit of progress, no matter how small.

He pulled aside a drapery panel and sighed as he released the heavy fabric to fall back into place. The sun would not rise for another two hours. How desperate he was for an occupation—any occupation. His eyes could not close lest he fall asleep, and Elizabeth needed him to remain awake. After a glance about the room, he stepped over to the fire, stoking and replenishing the fuel so the room stayed warm.

"Mr. Darcy?"

He spun around at Elizabeth's crackling voice and rushed to her bedside. "Good morning." His voice remained soft so as to not cause her head additional pain. "How are you feeling?"

She grimaced and licked her dry, cracked lips. "What I would not give for some toothpowder and a...a real bath." Her face held a pinkish hue in the dim candlelight.

"As soon as you take your draughts, I can arrange for some tooth powder." She swallowed the offending tea without complaint, though she frowned and crinkled her nose. After the dose of tincture, a search of the dressing room failed to produce toothpowder, so he retrieved some from his rooms for her use. The ever-prepared and efficient Morton never failed to have a spare hidden away in the event it was needed. A new container would likely appear on the morrow when the need arose.

"As for the bath, I shall leave that discussion for your sister and Acker. I am certain you must first regain enough strength for the endeavour before such an indulgence will be allowed. You do not want to overtax yourself to the point that you relapse."

She coughed and groaned, pressing her hand to her forehead. "I merely want this to disappear. I want to go home."

A sharp pang in his chest ripped the breath from his lungs without mercy. Was she so desperate to leave him? "You cannot be considering a return to St. Giles."

"We must live somewhere, sir. Our circumstances are not what they once were, and we cannot impose upon our uncle. He should not need to support us as well as his growing family. The burden is too much." Her hands pressed against her forehead as she coughed from deep in her chest. "We have learned to live with simple means. We do not require much."

His hands trembled and his heart beat in a heavy thump against his sternum, threatening to burst from his chest if the pounding became stronger. His legs itched to move, so he hopped up and pulled the bell to request more soup. Elizabeth would need to eat before she became too tired. "What of me?"

His breath caught in his chest. "I could never consider you a burden." The words were croaked out due to the lack of air. Why could he not speak as he wished?

Her head shook in a slow, controlled manner. "We cannot remain under your roof forever—two ladies, wholly unrelated to you, who live in your home with you and your younger sister. We would be a greater scandal than the Devonshires ever were."

He sat upon the edge of the mattress and took her hands, his fingers brushing over the calloused from the past two years of toiling over sewing in order to eat. How could she think of returning? "Not if you married me."

She withdrew her hands and crossed her arms over her chest. "You would grow to resent me as would Miss Darcy." A tear escaped one eye, falling to her cheek where it forged a slow trail towards her jaw.

He tilted her chin so she was forced to meet his gaze and leaned closer. "Elizabeth, my sister wed the Viscount Witney nearly a week before your sister arrived on my doorstep. Nothing I do can harm her."

"You cannot know that." She pulled his hands from her face and doubled over in a fit of coughing.

He prepared a glass of water mixed with wine and held it to her lips when she could manage to sit up. "Drink this." As soon as she swallowed the last, he offered her a handkerchief to dab her chin. "She would desire my happiness over all other concerns—"

"Her husband could resent the connection and insist she sever her ties with you." He opened his mouth to continue, but

Elizabeth's fingers pressed against his lips. "Pray, I cannot take any more. You must leave me be."

"Lizzy?" At her sister's voice, he turned. Jane stood just inside the door, her eyebrows drawn towards the middle. When had she arrived?

"I am well, Jane. Mr. Darcy and I were having a difference of opinion."

He shifted to the chair, but his eyes never left Elizabeth. She, however, avoided his gaze, watching Jane, who hastened to her sister's side. "You are looking much improved this morning."

"I hope so," said Elizabeth. "The sooner I improve, the sooner we can go home." He bristled inside. Why was she so eager to return to that filth?

Jane's eyes flicked to Darcy then back to her sister. "We must not rush matters. Mr. Acker will let us know when you are well enough." She sat beside Elizabeth and wrapped an arm around her shoulders. "Mr. Darcy, you mentioned my aunt and uncle on the evening we brought Elizabeth to your home. When did you see them last?"

He was caught unawares at the unexpectedness of the question. They had discussed her family, though that evening, Elizabeth's condition had weighed on him. Try as he might, the conversation with her elder sister was difficult to recall with any clarity. "The Gardiners attended my sister's wedding with Miss Mary a fortnight ago."

Elizabeth lifted a single eyebrow. "My aunt and uncle attended your sister's wedding?"

"Yes," he said with a nod. "The Gardiners and I have become friends and have dined together quite often. Miss

Mary is also the best of friends with Georgiana. The wedding is the last I saw of them. We have not corresponded since you arrived. I did not want to inadvertently reveal your presence."

"We understand," said Jane. "Lizzy and I appreciate you honouring our wishes. We know we ask a great deal." Elizabeth concentrated on the coverlet as though the fate of the world rested in the pattern. "Do we not, Lizzy?"

"Yes," she said. She dropped her head forward as coughs wracked her small frame.

Her sister rubbed her back and held the handkerchief Darcy had provided in the event Elizabeth had need of it. "Oh, my poor dear."

Darcy offered another glass of water mixed with wine, which Jane helped her sister sip.

The servants' door opened and Elsie bustled in with a tray she set on the bed. "I brought up soup for Miss Elizabeth." She looked to Miss Bennet. "Do you have a preference for breakfast, Miss?"

"Tea and toast would be lovely, thank you." Elsie curtseyed before she hurried out.

Darcy stood and scratched the stubble upon his cheek. Elizabeth surely desired his absence. "Morton will be in my dressing room, waiting upon me, and Elsie will bring a tray to my study soon after she delivers yours." His eyes met Elizabeth's. "If you require anything...anything at all, I shall be pleased to be of service to you. Truly."

<hr />

As soon as the door closed behind Mr. Darcy, Elizabeth trained her eyes on the canopy and breathed to keep herself from collapsing into a heap. She despised being angry with Jane, yet how could she prevent those words poised on the tip of her tongue from escaping? After Lydia's ruin, Fitzwilliam Darcy became an impossibility—a dream that would remain unfulfilled. How was she to face living in his home day after day? How could she keep from running mad?

Stupid, stupid Lydia! She tarnished more than her own virtue by running away with Wickham. She had cost them all their future happiness. Her youngest sister had never thought of anyone other than herself and her own entertainment. She hated Lydia. How the guilt ate at her for harbouring such an immovable dislike of someone—her sister in particular.

And here sat dear Jane while she ladled a hearty soup into Elizabeth's mouth. Her elder sister would never harm a fly. "What could you and Fitzwilliam have possibly been arguing about?"

After she swallowed, she rubbed the ache in her chest. "I do not wish to speak of it."

"He has done so much for us, and he cares for you a great deal." Elizabeth made to speak, but Jane shoved another spoonful into her mouth. "Chew that potato and listen. When he first saw me on his doorstep, he turned positively ashen. He was so stunned, I thought he might faint at my feet.

"And the manner in which he has tended you. He bathed your forehead and cheeks when you were most feverish, he assisted when you needed to take your draughts, and he calmed you when you begged for his aid in finding Lydia."

Elizabeth gulped down the last bite and fought down the sudden lump that threatened to burst through her throat. "What?"

"When you woke, you were often insensible, and Fitzwilliam was ever so generous. He would promise you all in his power while also seeing to your needs. He is every bit the gentleman." Jane looked down to the bowl with a shuddering breath. "He loves you, and I know you love him."

"I have never spoken of my feelings." She lifted her head to face Jane more directly. "And since when do you call him Fitzwilliam?"

One of Jane's shoulders lifted. "I invited him to address me in a more familiar manner while we cared for you. The formality made speaking with haste more difficult. Does our familiarity bother you?"

"No!" Elizabeth coughed, making her cradle her head in her hands.

"In regards to Fitzwilliam, I have suspected your feelings for some time. You have made comments—I suspect when you thought no one was listening. Then, you spoke of how much you love him during your illness."

Her hands trembled. "Not with him—"

"No," said Jane, "not with him in the room." Her elder sister's eyes shone. "I cannot imagine what it must be like to be the recipient of such devotion. He has not laid eyes upon you in over two years, yet he has not wed nor does he seem inclined to court any lady but you."

Elizabeth pulled up her legs and rested her forehead upon them, pressing her eyes closed. "How do you know this?"

"Mrs. Northcott, Elsie, and I have had conversations while tending to you. Mr. Acker has also said that he has never seen Mr. Darcy as anxious over anyone as he is over you—his sister is the sole person who has come close. As much as I could wish he had, Mr. Bingley never held such a strong attachment to me. Could you imagine Papa fussing over Mama the way Mr. Darcy worries over you? I envy you his devotion."

"He only *thinks* he wants to marry me." Her headache had intensified and now pulsed behind her eyes. She needed to rest, but she could not while Jane insisted upon this conversation. "But that does not mean we would find felicity in marriage. No one in the *ton* would accept me as his wife, and I do not desire an unequal alliance." At a knock, she lifted her head.

"Come in!"

"These just arrived for both of you ladies from the seamstress," said Mrs. Northcott as she and Elsie entered. They both held numerous parcels, which they set upon the foot of the bed. "The note said the remainder would be delivered by the end of next week.

Elizabeth eyed the packages. Dare she ask what was inside? "Remainder?" She clenched her teeth. What had Jane done?

Her sister's eyes widened. "I cannot imagine there are more."

The housekeeper smiled and clasped her hands together. "Since you will not be shopping any time soon, Miss Elizabeth, I shall send Elsie to the shops for some necessities when you feel like dressing. I also sent a note requesting the dressmaker to return for Miss Elizabeth's fittings. Hopefully, you will be well enough by the time she is free."

Shopping? Necessities? "I beg your pardon, but did you say dressmaker?" Her mind would not stop spinning. "Pray, tell me Mr. Darcy is not purchasing us clothing."

L.L. Diamond

Mrs. Northcott's eyebrows rose upon her forehead. "Indeed he is, miss. You are his guests. He can certainly provide more than what has been set aside for the ragman." She stepped around the bed. "I see you ate all of your soup."

"Yes, it was excellent, thank you."

"Cook will be pleased to hear it." Mrs. Northcott picked up the tray. "Do not hesitate to ring if you are in need of anything."

"Thank you," they both replied.

When she and Jane were alone, Elizabeth straightened. "Jane, we cannot accept all of this."

"You know as well as I do that our home in St. Giles was filthy and infested. We both had what we believed to be bug bites and our hair—well, I shall express my relief not to itch so. Mrs. Northcott was right to suggest burning our clothing and shaving our hair."

"I confess to being upset when I first realised my hair was gone," said Elizabeth, fiddling with the ribbon of the cap. She relaxed back, too fatigued to hold herself up any longer. "But I do understand why. I am not angry over it." She exhaled and closed her eyes against the persistent ache. "We had funds to purchase fabric and could have made our gowns ourselves. I hate to be indebted to Mr. Darcy."

Jane rushed forward and grasped Elizabeth's hands. "While I offered to sew everything myself, Fitzwilliam insisted upon hiring a seamstress. He knew I would not have the time since I would be caring for you. Mrs. Northcott gathered the gowns Miss Darcy set aside to be discarded, which are still serviceable and of far superior quality than we have ever owned. I have worn those until new could be made. I also told

Mrs. Northcott these would suit me well, but she appeared scandalized by the notion."

"I can imagine," said Elizabeth, with a hacking laugh.

"Oh, dearest." Jane offered her more water mixed with wine. "I believe this is the longest you have yet been awake. You must be exhausted."

"My head has begun to pain me dreadfully."

"Then you sleep." She picked up one of the parcels. "I shall await you to open these, and if you like, we can pretend it is Christmastide."

"You open them." Elizabeth's eyes closed despite her best efforts to keep them open a few moments more. "I want you to." Paper crinkled while Jane sang in soft tones. After several minutes, Jane's singing faded away as well.

Chapter 14

Elizabeth huffed. Four days had passed before Mr. Acker would allow her the luxury of a bath. First, the physician wanted the fever banished completely, then he wished to ensure she was hale enough so as to not become overly fatigued while in the water. She was not helpless, so why was she not even allowed to walk the handful of steps from the bed to the dressing room?

Her face radiated heat when Fitzwilliam entered, bowed, and lifted her with one arm under her knees and the other behind her back. "I am pleased to see you so well," he said as he carried her into the dressing room. She held herself stiff as an iron rod. Propriety would have a footman carry her, though she would never have preferred the arms of a stranger to those of Fitzwilliam. The tension began to leave her, and she began to soften in his embrace. Perhaps allowing this indulgence was a mistake? The knowledge of his embrace could be dangerous. Before, she could merely imagine, but now she knew the strength of his arms and the wholeness that accompanied them. The separation when he deposited her onto the stool was a shock. He did not linger but gave a slight bow and left her to the care of Jane and Elsie.

When she lowered herself into the fragrant bath, she let out a moan. The hot water was heaven itself! Her skin reddened and tingled while she relaxed back and inhaled the orange blossom scent of the oil Elsie had mixed into the hot water. Elizabeth held her breath and dropped her head under the surface, emerging to a loud "Lizzy!" from Jane.

"Forgive me, but this is glorious. I cannot remember the last time I had more than a bath from a basin."

Jane handed her a cake of soap. "Wash then, and if you like, I shall scrub your back when you are done."

As she ran the soap along her leg, Elizabeth sighed and melted a little further into the water. "Could I not sit in here all day? Elsie could put the lid on to keep the water warm and let me stew."

The maid laughed and placed the towelling on the stool. "You would wrinkle like a prune."

"I do not care." With a grin, Elizabeth lifted her other leg out of the water and began soaping. "The lid could also act as a table at mealtime."

"Such ridiculousness," said Jane with her arms crossed over her chest. When Elizabeth handed her the soap, Jane soaped up her hands and rubbed them over Elizabeth's head. "Your hair has grown. I confess I am envious." Jane's hair had always slipped through their maid's fingers like silk, which made it difficult to arrange and near impossible to curl.

With a shrug, Elizabeth toyed with some bubbles floating upon the water. "I do not require the cap since my scalp is covered, but it is hardly able to be arranged."

Jane shifted to face her and rolled her eyes. "Well, when your hair is blonde and fine, we shall discuss how long it takes to grow back. I still appear bald. I believe Sir William Lucas has more hair than I possess at this moment." Elizabeth laughed, but a slight rattle sent her into a fit of coughing.

"I am well," she said when she could speak once more.

Elsie returned from the bedroom, frowning. "That cough still sounds dreadful. I shall send for some tea."

After the maid hastened out, Elizabeth trailed her fingers through the water, the ripples spreading until they lapped against the sides. "We need to return home, Jane. We cannot stay any longer."

"Until that cough is gone, returning to the damp and dirt of that part of town will do you no favours. You do not want to undermine all the healing you have done."

Elizabeth pulled her legs up to her chest and rested her cheek on her knees. Jane had no idea the agony of living in Mr. Darcy's home day after day. Thankfully, two days ago, they ceased sitting at her bedside during the night, which meant other than instances where she was not allowed to walk and Mr. Darcy carried her, her care was mostly left to her sister and the female servants. Jane still slept beside her during the night. Thus far, Elizabeth had not required her presence, yet the dear soul that she was, Jane had insisted.

What an ungrateful wretch she was. Well, perhaps not quite ungrateful. She was quite thankful for all Fitzwilliam had done. Jane credited him with her survival, and her sister was not one to exaggerate. Would that she could avoid that inevitable moment he broached their future! The possibility of such an encounter made her stomach roil and her heart ache.

She was tired. How could she not be exhausted? Aside from her illness, she was fighting to protect him from the harm of an association with her. That fateful day could not be avoided without sneaking from the house in the middle of the night, never to return, yet Jane would never agree to such a scheme.

She was not insensible to the knowledge that she would break his heart. If he fought tooth and nail to have his way, regardless of her honour or pride, she would surrender. One day she would finally lack the strength to resist, and what a pitiful creature she would be then. Could he not understand that she had no desire to refuse him? Why could he not realise that she thought only of him?

Richard accepted a glass of port, lifting it a fraction in salute before settling into his favourite chair by the fire. "How are your guests?"

"Much improved," said Darcy. He sat in the matching chair across from his cousin and crossed his ankle over his knee. "Jane has regained her colour and once again has a healthy complexion."

"Jane?" His cousin raised those infernal eyebrows of his.

"We are nothing more than friends. She hopes one day to call me brother as I hope to call her sister, nothing more."

After studying Darcy for a moment, Richard tipped his head a hair to one side. "And Miss Elizabeth?"

"She no longer suffers from fevers, though she does struggle with a cough. Acker has indicated she will for a while yet." Little of his wakeful time had been spent with her of late, but her deep cough could be heard through the walls of the family apartments. The depth and rawness of that interminable hacking made his chest hurt for her.

"When will you ask her to marry you?"

He swallowed his sip of Port and sighed. "I broached the subject several days ago. She had expressed a wish to go home, and I suggested she could marry me and need never return to

St. Giles. She is convinced she will somehow harm
Georgiana—"

"You explained Georgiana is married?"

"Yes!" He nodded as though it needed emphasis. How
many times had he repeated their conversation in his head?
"She also insisted she had fallen too far—that I would grow to
resent her."

Richard swirled the tawny vintage around his glass with a
frown. "While I hope you disabused her of that notion, I must
admit your proposal was not the most romantic of declarations.
Would you be overwhelmed at the offer of, 'marry me and
escape your life of poverty?'" He said the last in a mocking
voice and exaggerated hand gestures before shaking his head.
"You are going to need to speak to her—discover why she fears
your resentment. As for the *ton*, the Bennet girls are
gentlewomen. Miss Mary is to wed a relation of Georgiana's
husband. Between the Darcy name, Viscount Witney, and the
Goodwins, they would have connections. My mother's support
would ensure Miss Elizabeth's acceptance, and she would be
pleased to sponsor Miss Elizabeth for your sake. Infuriating my
father would be a happy coincidence." He gave a one-
shouldered shrug. "Not that you have ever enjoyed the Season
or the *ton*. You would be well-satisfied to spend all your time at
Pemberley. If Miss Elizabeth is so concerned, no one will know
or care of her past in the north."

"I shall not allow her to depart before that cough subsides,
so I have time, but I do not see her as often since she has
improved." He dropped his head back and closed his eyes.
How often had he exhausted himself considering ways to
convince Elizabeth to accept him? Was this truly a fruitless

exercise? "She is sleeping when I attempt to visit her. I fear she is avoiding me."

"She cannot avoid you forever, Cousin."

At a knock on the door, Darcy lifted his head. "Come!"

"I beg your pardon, sir, but Mr. and Mrs. Cooke have called. One of the maids is escorting Mrs. Cooke and her son upstairs—"

Darcy jumped up and approached the door. "Mr. Cooke," he said as he bowed. "Welcome to Darcy House."

After Mr. Cooke bowed in return, he glanced about the hall. "I do not wish to disturb you, sir. My wife said you invited her to use the front door, but I am content to wait for her in the kitchen."

Darcy held out an arm towards the fire in his study. "You are not here as a delivery boy or servant but a welcome guest who has been invaluable to the survival of the Miss Bennets. I do not expect you to await your wife below stairs."

The man took hesitant steps into the study, constantly examining his surroundings until he stood before Darcy. "I thank you."

When Mr. Cooke stepped further into the room, Richard set down his glass and stood. He gave a slight lift of his brow.

"Richard Fitzwilliam, The Viscount Carlisle, may I present Mr. Erasmus Cooke? He and his wife were neighbours of the Miss Bennets in St. Giles." After they bowed, Darcy gestured for Mr. Cooke to sit. "We are drinking Port, but I also have brandy, or I can send for coffee or tea if you would prefer."

The tall man sat with slow movements upon the sofa. "I have never had either."

"I shall ring if we need anything further. Thank you," said Darcy with a nod to Watson. He poured small measures of Port and brandy and set them before his new guest. Mr. Cooke picked up the brandy and sniffed, recoiling a bit at the strong odour.

Richard grinned and leaned against the arm of his chair. "Do not feel obligated to drink them. Darcy will be pleased to provide whatever you like."

Mr. Cooke took a small sip and coughed. "'Tis strong." He tasted the Port and held up the glass. "I much prefer this. Thank you."

After Darcy filled the glass, he returned to his seat. "Thank you for escorting your wife to visit. I am certain her company does a great deal to lift the ladies' spirits."

"She has missed them." His guest frowned and exhaled. His knee began to bounce while his gaze seemed to flit about the room. "Sir, I do not wish to be intrusive, but may I ask you a question?"

Darcy shifted in his seat and nodded. What would he wish to know? "Yes, of course."

"Do you plan on marrying Miss Elizabeth?" His cousin snickered into his drink, prompting Mr. Cooke to glance back and forth between them. "What did I say?"

"Do not mind him." Darcy used a flat tone while flashing a look at Richard. "He was questioning me on the subject before you were shown in." He scratched the back of his neck. "Nothing would make me happier than obtaining Miss Elizabeth's acceptance of my hand, but thus far, she is insistent she cannot marry me."

Mr. Cooke held his glass in both hands, giving nothing away in his expression. "I do not mean to pry into your affairs. I... Perhaps I should explain." His forehead furrowed. "Since my wife and I wed, I have hoped to remove us from the city. I met a gentleman at the inn a fortnight ago, who offered me a job in the stables at his estate near Stapleford. I would assist the stable master." He opened and closed a fist several times in succession, his knee still bouncing without ceasing. "So, you see, we shall be departing London, and my wife and I are concerned for Miss Bennet and Miss Elizabeth should they return to St. Giles without protection."

"Quite understandable." Richard's earlier amusement had been wiped from his face in an instant.

Darcy stood and stepped to his desk, leaning against the edge. "Mr. Cooke, I can assure you I have no intention of allowing those ladies to return to...to St. Giles." He had almost called it a hovel. He understood the Cooke's home was not as small nor as shabby, but he still needed to be more careful. "I do hope Miss Elizabeth will become my wife, but if she refuses, my plan is to find them a home in the country."

"They will not accept without a struggle," said Mr. Cooke.

Richard sat up in his seat, and after a glance at Darcy, he held up a finger. "I beg your pardon, Mr. Cooke, but did you say Stapleford?"

The man's forehead furrowed. "Yes, why do you ask?"

With a lop-sided grin, he turned back to Darcy. "Did your father not inherit a small property near Derby some ten years ago?"

"Yes, a cousin of mine died childless, and the entailment made my father the heir. As he had no need of living there, he allowed the widow to remain at the estate until her death a few years later." He ran his fingers through his hair. The idea had merit. "How would I gain their acceptance of an estate?"

Richard chuckled. "I am not suggesting you give it to them, but you must admit the location is ideal. They would be close to the Cookes and have the means to visit, but they would also be close enough to Pemberley for you to ensure they are well. In time, you could also perhaps persuade Miss Elizabeth to accept you. I am certain you could devise some means to persuade them to stay."

"They would need to feel as though they are of use," said Mr. Cooke, who continued to sit stiff as a rod.

"I believe I understand." Darcy blinked and moved his wrist in a constant motion, the liquor swirling and coating the glass. A great deal would need to be accomplished. "I have two footmen at Pemberley who I employed for the sole purpose of protecting Georgiana. I had not yet decided upon a new task for them. They would be ideal to act as servants in that home." Darcy held out his glass. "Thank you for conspiring with me."

His cousin grinned and the others touched their glasses with his. "Anytime," said Richard.

Mr. Cooke's nod was tight as was his smile. "Thank you. My wife and I can be at ease, knowing they will not be on their own."

"I have not gained their acceptance yet." Darcy crossed his arms over his chest with his glass propped on his elbow. "When do you depart for Nottinghamshire?"

"Two days hence. We shall be following the master with three new horses he purchased at Tattersalls. He has moved us into the servants' quarters of his home on North Row until the journey."

Darcy stepped around his desk, withdrew a folio, and placed some paper inside, pausing for a moment. "I should ask if your wife knows how to read."

"Yes, sir."

He finished packing the paper, added sealing wax, and an unopened bottle of ink. Once he closed the packet, he offered it to Mr. Cooke. "So your wife can write to Miss Bennet and Miss Elizabeth."

"Sir," he said in a low and serious voice. "'Tis too much. We cannot accept."

"You helped them for nothing more than the sake of being of aid to those who needed it. I know the Miss Bennets would be upset not to hear word of you, so pray, accept this from them." Darcy shifted on his feet and again offered the folio. "I wish you and your wife well, but should you ever find yourself in need of another position, know I would be pleased to have you at Pemberley. Pray, understand that I am in earnest. I am always in need of honest and honourable men to work on the estate."

Mr. Cooke set his glass upon the table and accepted the gift with both hands. "Thank you, sir. Your offer is most appreciated."

"Capital!" Richard lifted his glass with a grin. "Now, let us raise a glass and celebrate the Cooke's new life in Nottinghamshire."

Darcy retrieved his Port from the table and held it aloft. "Hear, hear!"

Chapter 15

Jane exhaled heavily and propped her hands on her hips. "Lizzy, I gave the dressmaker your measurements when she came for my last fitting. I understand your hesitance to have Mr. Darcy spend his money on us, but I had not the time nor the patience to sew gowns while you were ill."

Elizabeth covered her face with her hands and prayed for composure. "I do not blame you. I simply detest the feeling of indebtedness I carry since waking in this house—even the use of Miss Darcy's cast-offs feels wrong." How would they ever repay Fitzwilliam for all he had purchased? The indebtedness ate at her gut and put a bitter taste in her mouth. The nightgowns that had arrived last week were made of quality fabrics with a delicate ruffle along the edging and pale pink ribbons for trim. They were even superior to the ones she wore as Miss Elizabeth Bennet of Longbourn. The chemises and stays were also lovely and beautifully constructed. The seamstress, though Mrs. Northcott denied it, was, no doubt, a Bond Street dressmaker. She would wager all she owned that they came from the shop of Madame Villers.

Jane sat at her side and clutched her hands. "You still sleep for several hours every day and should rest rather than toiling over clothing. Pray, let the seamstress do the fitting. I would be put at ease if you would. After all, the gowns are already made. They will go to waste if you refuse them."

Her eyes squeezed closed. "You do not play fair, Jane." She whipped the covers from her legs and stood. Once Jane helped her don her chemise, stays, and slippers, which were another delivery from the week prior, and brushed the tiny growth of hair on her head, Elizabeth pointed at her sister. "Do not dare call Mr. Darcy. I *can* walk." What little walking she had done thus far had been tiring, but she would do for herself as much as she could. She refused to accept aid unless the exhaustion proved to be too much. Being helpless was not in her nature.

Without argument, Jane followed behind as Elizabeth made her way into the sitting room where a well-dressed woman waited with a welcoming smile upon her face. Had she not spoken to her before? Gemma often made the enquiries. If she were here, she would know which of the shops the woman worked. "Good morning, Miss. I hope you are feeling better."

"Yes, thank you."

The soft gown slipped over her head and fastened the back, then they turned her towards a mirror placed near the door of the bedchamber. A gasp threatened to burst from her chest, but she swallowed it down. My goodness, how perfectly the pearl-coloured sprigged muslin fit around the chest before falling into soft folds to the floor. To finish the ensemble, a pearl-coloured satin ribbon wrapped around the waist, and the hem of the gown boasted of an exquisite, plum-coloured embroidered trim.

"How lovely." Jane's voice was tremulous. "The fabric and cut suits you."

"You did not select it?"

Her sister shook her head. "No, I did no more than furnish your measurements. I suspect Mrs. Northcott made the selections."

The dressmaker tugged at the sleeves and the skirt, stepping back after she was finished. "The fit is flawless. Do you have any changes you desire?"

Elizabeth swallowed back the lump in her throat. "No, thank you." The second gown was a pale green, long-sleeved day gown. She had never owned any clothing in that colour. Her mother had always reserved pale blues and greens for Jane, claiming they complemented her complexion better than Elizabeth's.

She smoothed the fabric down her stomach. "The work is beautiful. Thank you."

The seamstress bobbed a curtsey and held out a dark blue pelisse for Elizabeth to slip her arm into the sleeve. "I want to ensure it fits over the gown."

Her eyes traced over the trim, and when the seamstress requested she turn, Elizabeth peered as best she could over her shoulder. Were those pleats in a sunburst pattern? She cringed. How would she ever repay Mr. Darcy? The clothes he purchased cost significantly more than she and Jane had earned in the past two years sewing for the clothiers on Bond Street. They would be indebted to him for life.

"These do not require any alterations," the woman said to Elsie, who stood to one side of the room. The dressmaker helped remove the pelisse and handed the maid the clothing Elizabeth was not wearing. "I shall add the buttons today. I expect the remainder of the order to be completed in a se'nnight."

"Remainder of the order?" Elizabeth looked between them, then dropped into the chair behind her. This was too much.

Jane rushed over and pressed her palm to Elizabeth's forehead. "Lizzy, are you well?"

"Forgive me. I did not mean to frighten you." Elizabeth rose and walked through to the bedchamber where she stopped. How she longed to leave this room! She could not lay in that bed and rot for another moment. Before Jane could stop her, she hurried out of the room and glanced back and forth. The passageway to the right was shorter, so she bolted in that direction and nearly cried out at her success when she turned and the staircase stood before her. She took a quick peek over her shoulder. Jane had not caught up to her thus far. After a fortifying breath, she hitched up her skirts just enough to keep from falling and made her way to the bottom.

"Lizzy, what are you about?" When she turned, Jane appeared at the top of the stairs. "You should not be exerting yourself in this manner."

"I shall not overdo. I promise." Elizabeth pivoted in a complete circle, narrowing her eyes. Which one could it be? One of the doors was closed, so she straightened, squared her shoulders, and stepped forward to knock firmly.

———————◆———————

Darcy's head jerked up. "Come!" The door opened, and he shot up from his chair. When had Acker given Elizabeth permission to leave her rooms? His hands clenched tight against their sudden shaking. "Miss Elizabeth, I am overjoyed to see you so well."

She did indeed look well—very well indeed. Much of the colour had returned to her cheeks, her hair had grown, and she wore a fashionable pale green gown that complemented her eyes as well as her complexion. A flutter overtook his chest. Not only had she left her rooms, but she had also sought him out. Was she furious with him for some reason? He certainly hoped not.

"I need to speak with you." She clasped her hands in front of her, her knuckles white from the grip, and gave a slight lift of her chin. "I would prefer to do so in private. I understand being alone with you may damage my reputation further, but as you helped care for me during my illness, I do not see that my reputation has much further to fall."

If Elizabeth desired privacy, she would have it, but where was Jane? When he peered into the hall, Jane stood at the top of the stairs with one hand raised. "I am surprised Jane allowed you to walk so far." He pulled the heavy oak panel closed behind him.

"I am afraid I did not give her much choice."

His lips curved slightly. Some of the conceited independence Miss Bingley once accused Elizabeth of possessing had returned. He motioned towards a chair near the fire. "I hope you will sit. Shall I ring for some tea?"

Elizabeth shook her head in a jerky manner. "No, thank you."

"Is that one of your new gowns?" Perhaps he could distract her from whatever brought her to his study. He did not want her upset and did not wish to have her ire aimed at him. "You look lovely."

"I do not mean to sound ungrateful, Mr. Darcy—"

"Fitzwilliam," he said in a gentle tone. He could not bear to have her call him Mr. Darcy.

She straightened. "Pardon?"

"On several occasions while you were ill, you called me Fitzwilliam. I would prefer you continue." He would not crowd her by sitting on the sofa, but if he retreated behind his desk, he would be too far away. "Unless the familiarity makes you too uncomfortable." He sat upon the edge of his desk where she had no choice but to turn to face him.

"I know you and my sister brought me here with the best of intentions. Jane is certain I would have died without your intervention, so I can be nothing but grateful for all you have done to return me back to health."

He winced and shifted on his feet. He did not want her gratitude. He could have sent Acker to treat her in St. Giles, but once he set eyes upon the squalor, he never could have abandoned them. Elizabeth stood a better chance of survival in his home as opposed to that damp, one-roomed hole they inhabited; however, bringing them to his home was motivated by his own selfishness. He had believed her dead for so long. Was he dreadful to want her close while she recovered? "I assure you I was pleased to be of service."

She bit her bottom lip and tilted her head. "As much as I appreciate your help, this," she smoothed the front of the gown, "is too much." She took in a large breath. "We live modestly since Papa's death. I fear the expense of the fabrics, ribbons, and lace will go to waste. They are beautiful—the gowns and all you have purchased—but it is not possible for us to ever repay you."

He flinched inside and clasped his hands behind his back. Did she not understand he expected naught of her in return? "You need not provide funds or any service in return for what I have done." He spat the words. They were as bitter to his tongue as hers were painful to his ears. "When your sister appeared at my door with the news you were alive, I could not travel to St. Giles fast enough. I had to see you with my own eyes. Your survival was not a reality until I stood in front of you and touched your feverish cheek.

"You had need of me, and I have been pleased to provide all you required to heal from your illness. The necessities—and I consider what Mrs. Northcott has ordered necessary—were to replace all that we left behind and burned. You and your sister needed clothing." How could he forget the threadbare spencer and gown Jane wore that night? The weather that winter had been frigid. Such paltry garments could not have kept them protected from the cold. "What I have spent on you and Jane will not cause me a hardship. I am happy to provide you some much needed comfort, and your sister a bit of respite. Georgiana is married, and I have never spent my income freely. You will not break me."

He swallowed hard. "You do not know how lost I have been with you gone." He could not hold her eye so he stepped to the fireplace and watched the flames flicker and curl into fine points. "I regretted every prideful remark and arrogant statement made in your presence, I regretted not following you and the Gardiners to London when you received word of your sister, and I regretted not calling on the Gardiners sooner upon my return to town." He took the poker and jabbed at the coals. After he rested the tool back in its stand, he propped his arm upon the mantel and closed his eyes. "You cannot know how my words from Hunsford haunted me—how your rebuke haunted me.

"When the Gardiners informed me of your death, I decided I would never marry. I had no desire to feign intimacy with any woman for the sake of an heir, and I could not make an offer of a heart that was not mine to give." He turned his head, his eyes tracing over every detail of her beloved face. "I know you believe you cannot marry me, but you must know that I could never wed another. I do not know what scares you so—"

She shifted in her seat, and her eyes widened. "Why do you believe me frightened?"

"You said I would grow to resent you." He shook his head. "I assure you that is not possible. Nothing you nor anyone else could do would change my love for you."

"Mr. Darcy... Fitzwilliam, I do not know what to say."

He massaged the palm of one hand with the opposite thumb, concentrating on the task. "I do not expect you to respond as yet. Instead, I ask you to allow me to arrange a journey for you, me, and Jane to a small estate of mine in Derbyshire. You would have peace and country air for your recuperation, a well-stocked library for your entertainment, and as spring draws closer, a park where you can walk and regain your strength. I confess I would not object to spending more time with you, if you would grant me the privilege of your company, of course." He looked up and his gaze latched onto hers. "I have no expectations. I merely beg of you to afford me this opportunity. If, once I explain all, you are still set against me, I shall return you to London." He shuddered in a breath as he stepped forward and took her hand, cradling it in his own. "I love you. I want nothing more than the honour of being your husband—"

A cacophony of voices erupted in the hall as the door swung open, bouncing back when it hit the bookcase on the wall behind. He started at his aunt in the doorway, a hard expression upon her visage. Why was she in London? "I told you I can find my way." A harried Watson stood behind Lady Catherine, attempting to squeeze around her but to no avail.

In an instant, his aunt's eyes latched on to Elizabeth and narrowed. Elizabeth stood. "Miss..." She wagged her finger. "Miss Elizabeth Bennet."

Elizabeth curtseyed while his aunt studied her from head to toe. "Lady Catherine, I am pleased to see you. I hope you are well?"

"I am always well." She held her walking stick extended with a sniff. "I was informed you had died, but I suppose Mr. Collins must have been mistaken."

"Not exactly mistaken," said Elizabeth. "May enquire of Miss de Bourgh? I hope she was well when you left her."

Darcy winced, pressed his lips together, and studied the floor. Elizabeth could not have known, but how bad would his aunt's reaction be?

"Dead," said his aunt bluntly. He coughed to disguise a bark of a laugh. His aunt was far from predictable these days and never failed to shock him.

As she walked to the sofa, her walking stick tapped against the wood floor until she sat and began to remove her gloves. "Nephew! I require tea." Elizabeth all but collapsed back into her chair when Lady Catherine motioned for her to sit with a single finger. "Miss Elizabeth will join me."

After he pulled the bell, he crossed his arms over his chest. Did she mean to evict him from his own study? "I am sure you would be more comfortable in the drawing room."

"Nonsense," she said with a long look around the room. "This room has a fire. Since you did not expect me, the drawing rooms will be cold."

He bit his cheek. "Well, since I was not forewarned of your arrival, may I ask if you are to use your own home, or do you intend to stay here for the night?"

"Of course I intend to sleep here tonight. You know how I dislike opening my own home for such a short visit, and I refuse to stay with Richard!"

One of Elizabeth's eyebrows rose at the same time a slight smile appeared on her face. "The colonel has his own home?"

"You have been away far too long," said Lady Catherine. A maid bustled in with the tea service while Watson stood in the doorway. He must have rushed to the kitchen to notify Mrs. Northcott of their unexpected visitor.

Darcy sidled over to Watson. "Pray, have Mrs. Northcott prepare a room for Lady Catherine, and apologise to Cook for the inconvenience."

"Mrs. Northcott has already sent maids up to Lady Catherine's usual rooms to ensure all is in readiness for when she wishes to refresh herself. She is also conferring with Cook over tonight's dinner. Will the Miss Bennets be eating in the dining room?"

"Set places for both of them. If Miss Elizabeth is too fatigued, she can request a tray and retire early."

"Very good, sir." Watson hastened away while Darcy took in a deep breath, fortifying himself for the unexpected pleasure of an evening spent in the company of Lady Catherine de Bourgh.

"Nephew!" His head whipped in the direction of his aunt, jarring his brain in the process. "Leave us!" She waved him away. "I wish to speak to Miss Bennet."

"Miss Elizabeth," he said. "Her elder sister is upstairs."

"Well, she is not in the room, is she? Miss Elizabeth's last name is Bennet. Without her sister present, she is still Miss Bennet." His aunt handed Elizabeth a cup of tea. "Now leave us."

As he was closing the door, Elizabeth's head gave a subtle shake, her eyes wide. He hated leaving her thus, but what was he to do? The door clicked and his shoulders dropped. Elizabeth was never going to agree to marry him after he abandoned her to the whims of his aunt. If she did not flee the house before their trip to Derbyshire, it would be a miracle.

Chapter 16

Elizabeth's heart sank as her sole route of escape closed before her eyes. First, he told her of his plans to take her to Derbyshire, then before she could enquire further, he abandoned her to the whims of his aunt. He made mention of a small estate. He could not mean Pemberley, could he? After all, Pemberley was not a modest estate. She steadied her hands, cradled her cup, and shifted as far back as she could into the chair so as not to spill the hot liquid onto her gown. If she had the energy for it, she could be very put out with him.

Despite her questions, she needed to disregard Fitzwilliam for the time being and consider the situation before her. Why did Lady Catherine want to speak to her in private? What if she intended to scold her for enquiring after Miss de Bourgh? Perhaps Lady Catherine objected to Fitzwilliam's interest in her? All of her questions were possibilities. Elizabeth gripped the saucer and steeled her resolve. "May I enquire of the Collinses? I think of Mrs. Collins quite often."

The lady finished making her own tea and straightened. "They are well. I receive a letter from Mr. Collins when he has news of importance. Mrs. Collins and I are frequent correspondents. She is a sensible woman. You will be relieved to know she controls much of what occurs with your father's estate. Out of fear for the future of the property, the steward enlisted her aid not long after they took possession."

She had been about to take a sip of tea, but lowered the cup. Hopefully, her chin was not resting in her lap. "And Mr. Collins is in agreement with this?"

"No," said Lady Catherine. Her response was accompanied by what resembled an abrupt giggle. "Mrs. Collins is intelligent enough to let her husband believe he is master, and Mr. Collins is dim-witted enough to remain in peaceful oblivion."

Elizabeth laughed. "I am glad to know she is happy."

The grand lady sniffed and shrugged. "She has never been one to complain, so I suppose she is content. Her letters contain news of the estate and their daughter...Catherine Anne."

She pressed her lips together. Mr. Collins surely selected the name, and Charlotte would be practical enough to accept his decision with grace, particularly if she wished to distract his attention from her own doings.

Lady Catherine shifted her walking stick against the arm of the sofa. "Why have you allowed your family and friends to believe you dead?"

So, she was to be interrogated in a similar fashion to dinner at Rosings—during which Lady Catherine questioned her incessantly. "My sister and I have no desire to be burdens upon them."

"Hmm," said the lady. Elizabeth waited. Lady Catherine would not withhold her opinion and would at some time speak regardless of what Elizabeth said or did. "What of their grief? Do you believe the ease you have created in their life justifies their suffering?"

"I beg your pardon?" Was Lady Catherine taking her to task? "Perhaps you are not aware of my youngest sister's ruin?"

"Mr. Collins informed me of what happened with your family. He is a miserable little man." She shuddered. "Upon learning of your father's death, he hastened to Rosings to gloat over his inheritance and the terrible circumstances of his 'poor dear cousins.'"

Elizabeth stiffened and dug her fingernails into her palm. "If he is so miserable, then why did you offer him the living? How well does that speak of you?"

"Insolence!" Lady Catherine retrieved her walking stick and struck the floor. "You and your sister have survived these past few years on your own. How did you tolerate the manner in which you were treated by men?"

"Our landlady was a widow, who cared not if we could sign a legal contract. If we did not pay, her sons would have removed us from the building without an ounce of remorse. Our good fortune carried into our friendship with a married neighbour. We searched for work together from dressmakers and housekeepers."

The lady's sole reaction was a lift of her eyebrows. "I see." Lady Catherine set down her cup and saucer and poured herself another serving of tea. "Despite my title and circumstances as a wealthy widow, solicitors, peers, and the like all spoke to me as if I lacked a sound mind and the ability to reason. After Sir Lewis died, Fitzwilliam's family remained at Rosings for a month complete. His father helped me hire a new steward as well as a new solicitor who did not speak to me as though I were an errant child. Mr. Collins was the first appointment I made after the death of the previous rector. I confess to enjoying the deference Mr. Collins showed—at first."

"At first?" Elizabeth pressed her lips lest she laugh. She could imagine how tiresome Mr. Collins proved to be.

"The grovelling began to grate. I sent him to your family in the hopes of bringing tolerable company to the vicarage. Anne and I were thankful he married a sensible woman. I invited them to dine at Rosings for Mrs. Collins's conversation, just as I invited you along with them for your conversation."

Elizabeth froze for a moment, her cup suspended just below her chin. "Forgive me, but did you just say you enjoyed my conversation?"

"You responded to my intrusive questions with wit and humour. Anne and I were excessively diverted."

Her jaw went lax while she stared at Lady Catherine. Who was this lady? She was not the Lady Catherine Elizabeth had met in Kent.

"Pray, stop gaping at me like a fish."

"You played a game."

The lady flinched, her chin doubling as she hitched it back. "What? I do not play games." Her voice resembled more the imperious tone she had used in the past.

Elizabeth narrowed her eyes. "You did. You baited me at dinner for my reaction. You wanted to know what I would say—"

"This is not why I requested an audience with you," said Lady Catherine with a lift of her nose. "Indeed, you must know why I wish to speak to you."

"I do not." Would that she had some clue.

The lady huffed and rolled her eyes. "When I entered this room and found you with Fitzwilliam, I confess to being surprised. I knew of your supposed death from Mr. Collins, of course, but I did not know you were on such intimate terms with my nephew."

Elizabeth used her handkerchief to cover her mouth while she coughed. "Forgive me, but I cannot claim any particular intimacy with Mr. Darcy."

"Nearly two years ago, my nephew changed. I am not aware of the precise timing since he was not at Rosings when the change occurred. I know grief when I see it, and now that I have found you here in his house, I realise he has mourned for you. The letter from Mr. Collins revealing your death arrived approximately a month before Fitzwilliam and Georgiana visited. I noted the difference in his demeanour then, but I never intruded so much as to ask of his loss."

The tickle in Elizabeth's throat intensified. "You would not enquire of his feelings, yet you have no qualms about intruding upon mine."

"I envy you his devotion, but I wish to know if you reciprocate his love." Lady Catherine's knobby fingers brushed along the dainty handle of her cup while she stared as though she could see past the surface—as though she could read Elizabeth's thoughts.

"Lady Catherine—"

Lady Catherine huffed. "His feelings are a different matter entirely. While you hid yourself away, you knew he lived and could determine his whereabouts with little effort— or you would not be residing in his home as you are now. I merely wish to know if you share his attachment. Do you love him as he loves you?"

After clearing her throat, Elizabeth dug her fingernails into the arm of the chair. "You may desire to know my heart, but I can choose not to answer. Whether I love your nephew and agree to marry him is a matter to be discussed between the two of us. You do not have a say in the decision." Elizabeth pressed a hand against her chest and coughed while Lady Catherine set down her cup with a clatter.

"I am almost the nearest relation he has in the world and am entitled to know all his dearest concerns."

"But you are not entitled to know mine." Elizabeth had not even finished speaking when the words ripped at her chest, sending her into a barrage of coughs that doubled her over. As she recovered, soothing words crooned in her ear, and she dropped her head against the back of the chair and turned. When had Fitzwilliam entered?

"Better?" The man she adored knelt beside her chair, his hands supporting her tea. The hot liquid would have spilled all over her gown without his aid.

"Yes, thank you."

"Have you been ill?" Lady Catherine stood in front of her, holding her walking stick so it stood centred to her body.

"Miss Bennet begged my help when Miss Elizabeth became ill with a severe case of Grippe. I brought both ladies into my home until Miss Elizabeth could regain her health. She is much improved, though she still suffers from a cough and some fatigue."

Elizabeth accepted the return of her tea from Fitzwilliam and sipped the warm brew, relaxing as the sting subsided. "I am suddenly tired." He helped her to stand. "Lady Catherine, I hope you will forgive me, but I must retire. This is the first opportunity I have had to spend time outside of my bedchamber since my arrival. I fear I do not have the stamina to remain as long as I would prefer."

"I hope I did not tax you too greatly," said Lady Catherine, her brow wrinkled.

"I merely want for some sleep." She smiled as much as she could manage. Was Lady Catherine truly concerned? She had never witnessed such an expression on the older lady's countenance.

"Aunt, I shall escort Miss Elizabeth to her rooms and speak to you when I return."

His aunt retrieved her shawl and draped it over her arm. "Nonsense. Your servants have had enough time to prepare my usual rooms. I shall refresh myself from the journey and rest before dinner."

Lady Catherine proceeded through the door with them following behind. When they reached the stairs, Elizabeth looked up and sighed. How would she make it to the top?

"Are you well?"

"The distance was not so far when I came downstairs."

He held his arms before him. "I would be happy to carry you, should you require the aid."

"I am sure you would," she said with an easy laugh. He lifted her as though she were made of the lightest, most delicate crystal and held her securely to his chest, watching her with an intent expression. How much younger and carefree he appeared in that moment. She should remain rigid and not take comfort in his embrace, but how could she muster the strength? Instead, she closed her eyes and rested her head against his shoulder, inhaling his cologne, which only made her burrow closer. She would nuzzle her face into that spot between his chin and shoulder if she allowed herself to become any closer to that spot. She had attempted to be strong and resist her love for him but was she too far gone? She had to leave. She had to remove herself from his constant society or she would succumb.

How could she travel with him to Derbyshire? The idea of time in the country appealed to her, but the idyllic scenery of the Peaks would, no doubt, render St. Giles dreary and bleak when they were forced to return to their former lives. What purpose would that serve? Her agreement to his scheme would accomplish nothing but further heartbreak.

When he laid her on the bed, his fingers trailed down her cheek before he stepped back. "I apologise for my aunt's interruption and interference. I hope she said nothing disturbing." He took her hand and caressed the top with his thumbs. "You know my wishes, but do understand that what I desire most is your happiness." He stood and stepped back, the loss of contact between them tearing at her equanimity. "Pray, think on what I said before my aunt's arrival. If you agree, we can talk more before the journey, or when we arrive at our destination."

She blinked and sat up, hugging her knees. "When would we travel?"

He perked up at her words. "So you will come?"

"I am still unsure. You have told me little yet expect a great deal. Where exactly in Derbyshire do you wish to take me? How long would we be away? I assume you are to remain at this estate with us since you said you hope to spend time with me. I also would like to know how long I have to make a decision?"

He clasped his hands behind his back and furrowed his brow. "I shall do my best to answer your questions, but I hope you will allow me a bit of mystery." He stretched his shoulders back then reset them. "I hoped to depart in a few days, but at any time, I shall ensure you safe travel should you decide to return to town. As I said earlier, I have a small estate south of Pemberley. The house is well-kept and the park picturesque. The Cookes are not far away, near Stapleford, if you should wish to visit. And yes, I had planned to remain, but if my presence disturbs your equanimity, I could remove myself to Pemberley. Of course, I would prefer to be in your company, but I shall not force myself upon you. Eventually, we shall need to have a discussion of the future—of all your options should you be set against me. I have an idea—"

"You cannot speak to me of your idea here?" She spoke the words slow and even.

"I could, but I feel I could explain my scheme better should we be at our destination."

What could be so complicated? Her eyes roved over his features. "May I take a bit of time to consider it?"

He blinked two or three times before he nodded. "Yes, of course. May I say how much I hope you will accept? I shall always desire your presence by my side."

His words created a fluttering in her chest. She could not speak. She would not cry. With a deep breath, she gave him a slight smile before he departed her bedchamber. Then, Jane entered and fussed over her until she fell asleep.

Chapter 17

"Nephew!" Darcy's shoulders sagged at his aunt's demanding tone. Drawing in a deep inhalation through his nose, he made a slow pivot on his heel to face her. "You will attend me." She stood in the open doorway of her sitting room, her eyebrows raised. Why had she employed that look—the one where she conveyed, without words, that the encounter would not be avoided?

His aunt's arrival today was without doubt unexpected. Why had she come, and without warning? Elizabeth's presence would demand an explanation, which, of course, he had no wish to provide—not at this time. He withheld a groan. He would have no choice.

As soon as the door swung closed, she sat near the fire while he clasped his hands behind his back and rocked on his feet. "Oh, for goodness' sakes. Sit down. You look as if I am forcing you to the gallows."

He measured his breathing lest she discompose him. "Thank you, Aunt, but I prefer to remain standing." Sitting appeared a less defensive posture, but was there an advantage to his current position? His aunt was intimidated by few—and certainly not by him.

"An unexpected report reached me two days ago, and I came to London to determine its legitimacy and warn you of its existence." She held her walking stick upright with both of her hands resting on top.

"You travelled to London due to an idle rumour?"

"An idle rumour?" She pointed at him with a crooked finger and wagged it in his direction. "If you knew what I have heard as well as the source of the report, you would not be so quick to dismiss it."

"Very well, Aunt. Tell me of this gossip that disturbed your peace of mind to the extent you felt the need to make a day's journey to see it contradicted."

"Insolent boy," she said in a mutter. "I received a letter from Lady Chester. She had been shopping at Madame Villers' establishment on Bond Street when she overheard two of the assistants gossiping about an order from Mr. Darcy. The two girls were all in titters about the dressmaker coming to *this* home to measure and fit your mistresses."

He gasped, taking in more than air, and began to choke. One hand went to his chest while the other covered his mouth. When he managed to regain control, he panted to catch his breath.

"Do you still believe the report to be idle?"

"I never specified to Madame Villers the identity of the ladies, but when I spoke to her upon her first visit, I did mention the Miss Bennets were sisters." He attempted to clear the hoarseness from his voice. "Mrs. Northcott selected a great deal of their purchases as I did not want the Miss Bennets to know I was using Madame Villers. Miss Bennet was adamant I not go to such a great expense."

His aunt relaxed from her rigid posture. "Yet, you did anyway. Why?"

"I already possessed an account with the woman and refused to force Mrs. Northcott spend her valuable time searching for a seamstress more to Miss Bennet's specification." He squeezed the bridge of his nose between his fingers. "The squalid condition of where they lived necessitated burning their clothing. From what Miss Bennet has told me, they kept the place as tidy as they could, but that part of town—"

"What part of town?"

"St. Giles," he said plainly.

"St. Giles!" Lady Catherine gulped and shuddered. "Those girls lived in St. Giles! No wonder Miss Elizabeth's hair is gone, and she is so weak. I can only imagine the disease rampant in those streets."

"Miss Bennet appeared at my door in a threadbare gown and spencer with a filth-stained hem. They had worn the gowns they had brought with them two years ago, which were now barely serviceable. Burning them was necessary and provided me the ability to ensure they were well-clothed. At first, Mrs. Northcott gave them garments Georgiana had left behind for the ragman. Much to our dismay, Miss Bennet insisted they were adequate and wanted to make them over for herself. They have both protested the purchase of what I deem essential, though Miss Bennet has now admitted she would never have had the time to sew all they required while caring for her sister."

His aunt stared at the carpet while tapping a finger on the top of her cane. "What are your intentions?"

"I have told Miss Elizabeth of my desire to make her my wife. She is resistant for fear of harming Georgiana as well as me."

She shook her head. "Georgiana is married and married well. I doubt she would suffer any ill-effects from you marrying Miss Elizabeth, and she would be pleased to see you happy. As for you, you are as active in the *ton* as I am. You would not feel that loss."

"I have said as much to her."

His aunt lifted her head and faced him once more. "So, what are your plans to secure her?"

"You would support me?"

Lady Catherine shifted and reset her shoulders. "There was a time when I hoped for an alliance between you and Anne. I never made a secret of my hopes. Anne and I spoke a great deal as her energy waned. She never wished to marry and wanted you to find someone who gave you joy. She was dismayed to see your sadness during your last visit." His aunt closed her eyes and shook her head. "Anne would want nothing more than your felicity, and so I can do naught but wish for the same. The Miss Bennets are the daughters of a gentleman. No one need know where they spent the past two years, and a sanction of your marriage by myself and Lady Fitzwilliam would do a great deal to ensure some measure of acceptance."

As she opened her eyes, she rocked her walking stick away from her then back to its original place. "Do not concern yourself with Lady Chester. I shall pen her a letter before dinner."

"What will you tell her?" He cared not for the opinion of the *ton*, but could they mitigate the gossip? A possible scandal would do naught to aid in making Elizabeth his wife.

"How successful do you think you will be with your suit?"

"I do not know. Her sister has hinted that Miss Elizabeth's feelings match mine, though I have yet to persuade her to admit it. I need to assure her of my constancy so she lets go of the fears holding her back. I have asked her to travel to my estate near Derby in three days. I hope to plead my case there."

Lady Catherine's lips flattened and her nostrils flared. "I would prefer more confidence, but I shall wager on your success." She stood and moved to the escritoire, removing a sheet of paper and setting it upon the surface. "I intend to inform Lady Chester that the ladies residing here are your betrothed and her sister. They travelled to London to purchase her wedding clothes and have been guests of yours while in town." She pivoted in the chair and leaned an arm on top of the paper. "How long have the Miss Bennets been in residence?"

He furrowed his brow. "Since five days after Georgiana's wedding. Why?"

"So I can claim to have been living here during that time. I have not received callers at Rosings since my return, and no one of consequence attends services at Hunsford. I rarely correspond with Lady Chester, so she will be none the wiser."

"But you did not attend the Miss Bennets' fittings."

His aunt drew herself up and waved him off with a huff. "Why would I want to shop with two young ladies? They have a different sense of fashion and would not give one whit for my say. Besides, your betrothed became ill during the trip, did she not? She has been recovering since, which is why she has not been seen on Bond Street." She tipped the pen in his direction. "We must make it seem as though you have nothing to hide by Madame Villers attending the ladies here as opposed to her shop. I shall also pen a note to Lady Fitzwilliam since her support will be of more consequence than mine in garnering Miss Elizabeth's acceptance. Before I forget, Mrs. Smith sends her regards. I hoped to tempt her to accompany me, but she is still too frightened." She turned her back to him and began to write. "Now, leave me. I have a great deal to accomplish before dinner."

He was stunned at her abrupt dismissal. Why did his aunt's abrupt behaviour surprise him? Rather than argue, he departed and returned to his study. As he passed Elizabeth's bedchamber, he paused and placed a hand upon the door. Would she be angry at his aunt's presumption? He hoped not, though he would never tell her before such a confession was necessary. Her acceptance of his suit should be due to the contents of her heart rather than his aunt's machinations. He would accept nothing less.

———————◆———————

"Will there be anything else, sir?" Morton stood to the side of the pier glass while Darcy straightened his topcoat. He had not dressed for dinner since Georgiana wed. Some semblance of the ordinary was a welcome change.

"No, thank you." His valet bowed and disappeared through the servants' door as Darcy made his way downstairs. Upon reaching the hall, voices carried from a nearby drawing room. He stopped and frowned. Had his butler admitted a caller, but not informed him?

"Sir, your guests await you in the rose drawing room."

Darcy rounded on his heel to Watson, who stood behind him, his eyes wide. "Guests?"

"Yes, sir. Lady Catherine received Lord Carlisle and Lady Fitzwilliam a half-hour ago. She notified Mrs. Northcott of the dinner arrangements after her tea with Miss Elizabeth."

Why had Mrs. Northcott not notified him of the changes to the dinner plans? Had he lost control of his own home? He rolled his tight shoulders and strode through the door Watson scurried to open.

"Nephew!" said Lady Catherine, holding her dainty glass of sherry aloft. "'Tis past time you arrived."

"If I had known I was to have guests for dinner—other than yourself that is—I would have been dressed prior to their arrival."

"Oh, Fitzwilliam, do not be cross." Lady Fitzwilliam sat upon the sofa with her hands in her lap. "You should have enlisted my help with these ladies long ago. I could have arranged for Madame Villers, which would have kept vicious little tongues from spreading their lies. A wedding will nullify any gossip that Miss Elizabeth is your mistress, but my preference would have been avoiding the necessity to overcome that gossip."

"You beg him not to be cross, but you were angry with me over keeping his confidence," said Richard. He gulped a measure of brandy and bared his teeth as he swallowed.

"Do not pout, son. You are not a child."

"You slapped me!" His tone was high-pitched as he set down his glass on the tray.

Darcy pressed his lips together and tried without success to keep his shoulders from shaking. "You slapped him?" His voice cracked with his chuckles.

"Yes, I slapped him. He should have told me." Lady Fitzwilliam rolled her eyes with her arms crossed over her chest. "You had two ladies, not of your relation, in this house. The elder Miss Bennet could have been considered a chaperone, yet you purchased her clothing as well. The two girls at Madame Villers should not have spoken as they did, but my presence during Madame's call could have prevented any hint of impropriety as well as imply their acceptance by the family."

He sighed and leaned against the closest chair. "When I brought the Miss Bennets here and arranged for their care, I tried to respect that they would not want their names bandied about town because their London relations believe them dead." He held up a hand. "I hope to persuade them to contact the Gardiners, but I did not want to pressure either of them while Miss Elizabeth was so ill. Mrs. Northcott arranged everything."

Lady Catherine lifted her eyebrows at Lady Fitzwilliam. "Well?"

Lady Fitzwilliam tilted her head up at him. "I understand you are to travel to Pemberley. Have you applied for a special license?"

"We do not away to Pemberley." Darcy frowned. "We go to Drayton."

"Whether you are to go to Pemberley or Drayton is of no consequence." She waved off his correction. "You still require a special license."

He shrugged and shook his head. "What use would that serve? I can purchase a common license from the bishop in Derby if I have need of one."

"I shall send a note to my cousin at Doctors' Commons this evening after dinner," said Lady Fitzwilliam. "I am certain he can arrange one before you depart."

"Aunt—"

She leaned forward and rested her hands on the cushion. "Fitzwilliam, marrying away from the prying eyes of London would be best, but regardless of where you wed, the inclusion of 'special license' into the wedding announcement will go a long way to making this arrangement appear planned."

Darcy held out a hand. "Pray, remember that the Miss Bennets' aunt and uncle do not know they are alive. I have promised them—"

"Really, Fitzwilliam." Lady Fitzwilliam glared at him as though he was a small child who put a frog in her reticule. "You would think I am not circumspect. I would never blather your business about without your approval."

"Forgive me, but the gossip thus far seems to omit their identities. If that knowledge were to get out, it could ruin everything. Miss Elizabeth must trust me if I am to succeed."

The door opened, prompting those seated to stand, while Watson showed Elizabeth and Jane into the room. As soon as they noted the number of people, the sisters made an abrupt halt and looked to him. "I apologise," said Darcy. "Lady Catherine invited my aunt and cousin to dinner. I was unaware of her plans until I came downstairs myself."

"Fitzwilliam," said Lady Fitzwilliam. "Do introduce us."

He cleared his throat. "Aunts, may I present Miss Jane Bennet and Miss Elizabeth Bennet." He held out an arm to ensure his aunts knew who was whom. "Miss Bennet, Miss Elizabeth, I present Lady Evelyn Fitzwilliam, Countess Fitzwilliam and Lady Catherine de Bourgh. You have both met my cousin Richard Fitzwilliam, Viscount Carlisle. Miss Elizabeth, you would remember him as a colonel in the Regulars, but last year he became the heir of his brother's estate and title."

"I am sorry to hear of your loss," said Elizabeth.

As Jane echoed Elizabeth's condolences, she brushed her hands down the front of her skirt. "I am pleased to make the acquaintance of Mr. Darcy's family. He has been a godsend to us."

"Miss Elizabeth, you should sit," said Lady Catherine. She raised her walking stick, pointing at the chair closest to the fire. "You will fatigue before dinner if you continue to stand as you are."

Richard stepped beside Jane and offered his elbow. "Miss Bennet, you are lovely this evening."

His mother laughed as she resumed her seat. "For goodness' sakes, Richard, the girl can make it to the sofa without your arm."

Jane took his cousin's arm and allowed him to steer her to the seat closest to Elizabeth's where she sat primly with her hands clasped in her lap.

"My son is correct that you look lovely Miss Bennet," said Lady Fitzwilliam. Her gaze traced over both ladies. "That ivory silk is quite becoming, Miss Elizabeth. The Brussels lace is an elegant touch."

"Thank you. Jane was kind enough to lend me her new gown for dinner." Elizabeth tugged at her butter-coloured, long gloves. "Mr. Darcy has been very generous. We shall never be able to repay him."

Richard handed each lady a glass of sherry. "My cousin takes prodigious care of those he holds in high regard. I can assure you, he does so with no thought of recompense. He desires no more than your comfort." Darcy's cheeks burned. If only his cousin were mute.

"He is a true gentleman." His gaze shifted to Elizabeth, who looked upon him with soft eyes, a slight smile gracing her lips. She wore that same expression sitting beside Georgiana at the pianoforte at Pemberley. That moment, when their eyes had met, his heart had beat like a hammer against his ribs and his mind had swam with images of their future. He shook off the memory. He would not relive that heartbreak in company.

His cousin sat beside Miss Bennet and grinned. "I am pleased we are in company once again. We had no opportunity to become acquainted when we first met." Elizabeth lifted that one eyebrow and relaxed back into her chair, her eyes remaining fixed upon his cousin. "Now that your sister is recovered, I should be happy to escort you to Hyde Park or perhaps Vauxhall."

Jane peered around the room. "I thank you for the invitation, my lord, but I believe we are to journey to Derbyshire soon. I do not expect we shall have the time before we leave. The weather has also been too cold and too poor for the pleasure gardens and promenading." His mother coughed in an obvious attempt to disguise her mirth while Lady Catherine did not attempt to conceal her laughter. Elizabeth covered her mouth.

"I say," said Richard who looked to Darcy with a frown. "We planned to away to Pemberley together. Why was I not informed of the change?"

Darcy clasped his hands behind his back. "We do not journey to Pemberley. I thought to remove Miss Elizabeth from the filth of town to aid in her recovery. She is sure to benefit from the fresh air of the country. I did not assume you would want to accompany us. We are hardly a house party."

With an affected gasp, Richard pressed his hand to his chest. "Cousin, I am insulted." A melodic laugh came from Elizabeth, attracting Richard's attention. "What amuses you so, Miss Elizabeth?"

"You." She made the statement simply and without apology. Darcy had missed her frank manner. "While I shall not presume to claim I knew you well when I visited Hunsford, we did enjoy a number of pleasurable conversations. I find your manner now to be markedly altered—amusing but altered."

Richard crossed his ankle over his knee and rested his elbow against the back of the sofa.

"Dinner is served."

Thank goodness for Watson, whose appearance in the door brought a halt to their discourse. If his butler had been but a moment later, Richard would, no doubt, have enquired of Elizabeth's observations. Lady Catherine and Lady Fitzwilliam would have found humour in the exchange, but would Richard have taken offence?

When he rose, he made to offer his arm to Lady Catherine, assuming Richard would escort his mother, but she and Lady Fitzwilliam walked arm in arm towards the door, their heads close together while they spoke in quiet tones. Their sharing of confidences was never a good sign. Their pairing, however, allowed him to offer his arm to Elizabeth, which was a more desirable match in his view. "May I?"

When she set her small hand along the inside of his elbow, a frisson of current shot through the layers of his clothing. His heart skipped a beat or two but a certain restlessness calmed at the sensation.

She drew his arm back a fraction while watching his cousin step around them with Jane. "I hope you and your family can forgive me for being rude to your cousin. I am unsure of the pointed attention he gives Jane. He stared at her from the moment of our entrance until he approached and behaved as he did. His manner is not genuine, as it once was, and unsettles me. I do not want my sister's hopes raised by an insincere flirtation. She has suffered one such disappointment, as you know."

"Do not distress yourself. My aunt has chastised him for how he has changed since inheriting his brother's title, so she will not hold your observation against you. In essentials, he is much the same, and the manner you witnessed does not carry over to his private interactions. He never desired to be the heir of the earldom and has not enjoyed the increased attention he has gained with his elevation in rank." Richard and Jane spoke quietly, with Richard leaning closer to Jane's ear, while they walked ahead of them. "If he appears to commence in her pursuit, I shall speak to him. I shall not allow him to trifle with her."

Elizabeth looked up at him in a fashion that set his blood racing. "Thank you, Fitzwilliam."

Chapter 18

Elizabeth sighed and walked the perimeter of the library, running a finger along the books arranged in perfect alignment upon the shelf. How thankful she was to escape the confines of her bedchamber, if only for a half-hour! She loved Jane, but her incessant mothering was beginning to wear. Elizabeth still tired without much effort, but to lie abed all day was about as appealing as drinking a posset!

After dinner with Lady Catherine and Lady Fitzwilliam, Fitzwilliam had been excited to show her this room. The moment she stepped through the doorway, she had fallen in love. The space was not large but well-used, with a ladder required to reach the highest shelves. Light streamed into the fanlight window near the ceiling at the far end, bathing the room with afternoon sunshine that provided a welcoming glow during certain times of the day.

She removed a volume of poetry and opened the cover. "Lord Byron?" She grinned. "How scandalous, Mr. Darcy."

"Have you read Lord Byron?"

Her head shot up, and she pressed her hand over her heart. When had he entered? "You frightened me."

"I apologise. I had not intended to do so."

Elizabeth snapped the book shut. "No. I have not."

"No?" he asked. He tilted his head and his forehead crinkled in the most adorable way. Her fingers itched to smooth those lines and comb his curls from his face. She shook off those thoughts. They did her no favours.

"I have not read his work," she said, cradling the book to her chest. "My father considered him rather infamous."

He leaned against the door frame with a crooked smile. "The man or his work?"

She laughed lightly. "I would wager both." When she lived at Longbourn, she had read a little of the well-known poet's escapades in the gossip columns. Her father found the man's supposed antics amusing when her mother made mention of him, though she was certain a copy of one of Lord Byron's works resided on a top shelf in her father's book room.

His gaze followed her as she made to return the book. "You may read it if you wish. As I said before, you are welcome to borrow the entire contents if you so desire."

While turning in a full circle, she perused the room. "That would take a long time."

"Perhaps an entire lifetime."

Her stomach twisted while her heart quickened a bit. Would that she could!

"I said, I shall see him now!"

Fitzwilliam looked over his shoulder, and his back stiffened, a frown marring his handsome countenance. He held up a hand and departed the room, closing the door behind him.

She frowned. "Who could cause such a distinct reaction?"

With careful steps, she approached the door and opened it. This particular entrance was not the one she had used earlier, but it led to Fitzwilliam's study. She tiptoed a foot or so inside. The voices gained in volume as she neared the hall. Would Fitzwilliam be angry with her for disobeying his wishes and following?

"Have you so little respect, boy?" a man's voice growled.

Elizabeth's head hitched back a hairsbreadth. Who could be addressing Fitzwilliam so? When she had the first opportunity, she peeked around the doorframe and into the hall. Watson flanked Fitzwilliam before the entrance. Both master and butler stood almost toe to toe with a tall, rather unattractive man whose red visage and sweating brow made him appear as if he might explode at any moment. Meanwhile, Fitzwilliam held himself straight as a rod with an unyielding expression, his jaw working in a near constant motion while he stared down at the man.

"I fail to understand why you are here, Lord Fitzwilliam. I gave explicit instructions to my servants that you are not to be admitted. I believe I did so with you present. So, why are you making a scene on my doorstep?"

"Why?" The man hissed spraying spittle in the process. "You should know why? You should know what is being spread about London—what is being said at your club! For years, I brought you suitable candidates to be your wife." He ground his teeth and held out a finger, jabbing it at Fitzwilliam as he spoke. "You refused them, each and every one. You said you would choose your own wife, yet you have yet to wed or even court a lady of standing or wealth. And now," he said, his voice rising with the last. "Everyone is saying you have brought courtesans into this home—my sister's home! You have made me a laughing stock!"

Fitzwilliam stepped forward and the man stepped back. "This has been my home for some time—"

The man's head turned in Elizabeth's direction, but he did not acknowledge her presence. Instead, he began to face Fitzwilliam before he jerked back and sneered. "Is this one of those chits?" His eyes raked over Elizabeth as though she were covered in filth. Was this man Fitzwilliam's uncle? She smothered a gasp. This was Colonel Fitzwilliam's father—no, Lord Carlisle's father! Lady Fitzwilliam had made a shocking comment about him at dinner, yet who could have believed the man was so disagreeable.

"Have you forgotten what you owe your family?" Lord Fitzwilliam's voice had become a growl. "What you owe me?"

Fitzwilliam inched further forward, making his uncle stumble backwards. "I told you years ago I would not agree to your marriage schemes. I shall one day wed my wife with nothing but my own happiness and that of hers in mind. I owe you nothing." Her eyes stung, and she crept forward into the doorway. The man had noticed her presence. She had no reason to hide any longer.

"What of—?"

"No more!" Fitzwilliam spoke with a firmness that made his uncle clamp his mouth shut. "I have told no one of the breach between our houses, but your display of ill-temper today, in full view of those on the streets and the neighbouring houses, should have tongues wagging for weeks. Do you wish all and sundry to know why I have broken with you? By this afternoon, I am certain all of London will know you were denied entry to my home." The volume of his hard voice must have carried into Hyde Park.

Elizabeth glanced over her shoulder through the windows behind Fitzwilliam's desk. A gentleman and a lady stood upon the pavement, watching the drama unfold upon the doorstep of Darcy House. Fitzwilliam was correct. The gossip could not be contained.

His uncle peered behind him in both directions. "This is not over, Darcy."

Darcy chuckled and leaned closer to the earl. "This is indeed over. You tend to your house, and I shall tend to mine. While you are doing so, you might spend less time at the club playing cards. I believe you have enough of your late son's and his wife's gambling debts to pay."

Lord Fitzwilliam turned almost purple before he spun around right into Lord Carlisle's chest.

"You," said the earl in a jeer.

Fitzwilliam's cousin gave no indication of disquiet nor did he bow. "My Lord, I am here to call upon my cousin and his guests." He gave a crooked smile. "Have you met the Miss Bennets? They are quite beautiful are they not—in particular, Miss Bennet. A man would be fortunate to find such a lady for a wife."

"You will not marry that trollop! I forbid it!"

Lord Carlisle snickered. "I made the acquaintance of Miss Bennet two days ago. If I were to make a lady the offer of my hand, I would prefer to know more of her before my proposal, yet I assure you, I shall marry a lady of my choosing. You can forbid me if you wish, but you will not stop me. In that, Darcy and I are of precisely the same mind. You have attempted to twist and bend the will of your family until we act as you desire. By joining the Regulars, I removed myself from your machinations long ago, and while I am now your heir, I refuse to be controlled by you." Richard stepped around his father and walked inside, presenting his back to the man.

As soon as the door closed on his uncle, Fitzwilliam brushed his hands against one another. "I apologise for Lord Fitzwilliam's spectacle."

"You have nothing to apologise for," said Elizabeth in hushed tones. She lifted her eyebrows at Lord Carlisle. "Will you be well, my Lord?"

He shrugged while Watson helped him remove his great coat. "Pray, do not concern yourself with me. My father and I shall never see eye to eye. Darcy's excellent father took me in when I left home, and Pemberley was where I returned from Cambridge as well as where I resided when I had leave from the military. Darcy, Georgiana, and my mother are my family."

She rubbed her arms as though she were cold. "He sounds a very lonely and bitter man."

"That he is," said Fitzwilliam. He glanced at her hands. "Did you not select a book?"

"No, I admit to being curious about the disturbance."

Fitzwilliam scratched the back of his neck. "Forgive me, Richard, but would you mind if I spoke to Miss Elizabeth for a moment?"

His cousin gave a dramatic sigh. "Do not mind me. I shall settle myself into the drawing room with a brandy and wait."

Fitzwilliam held out an arm, motioning for her to enter his study. When they were alone, she clasped her hands in front of her. "Is something amiss?"

He strode around his desk and propped his elbows onto the back of his chair. "I have delayed as much as I can. I need to know whether you and Jane will journey to Derbyshire with me. As much as I do not want to press you, I must make arrangements if we are to travel. As it is, I have delayed far too long for when I hoped to depart."

This conversation was inevitable, no matter how she wished to avoid it; however, Jane refused to hear of their return to St. Giles as of yet. Her sister insisted the persistent cough needed to heal completely, and Elizabeth regain all of her strength before they so much as considered being on their own. "I cannot." The words rasped out at a whisper, and her stare locked onto the floor where it remained. She could not bear to witness the heartbreak on his dear face.

"Is this all the answer I am to receive?"

She squeezed her eyes closed. "I do not know what else to say. I believe this is best for all concerned. I am sorry if it brings you pain." Did he not understand how much she wanted to go? How she never wanted to leave him? Telling him no shattered her heart as well.

"Pain?" His footfalls moved back and forth while she traced the pattern of the carpet. "Pain is what I have endured these past two years. I cannot return to that place. I cannot continue to live what was no more than a mere existence. Can you not understand that I love you, that I want none but you?" He took her face by the cheeks and drew her eyes up to his. "I have endured the deepest agony, only to be shown a hope so bright I cannot but yearn for it." He released her to rake his fingers through his hair. "I cannot fathom why you do not admit to feeling the same—why you will not consent to be my wife. I requested no more than you away with me to Derbyshire. You would not be alone. Your sister would accompany us. We do not even go to Pemberley since I feared you may feel pressured by residing in that home, by the expectations of the servants and those who may call upon us there. We would be more isolated at my smaller estate." He took in a deep breath, his eyes pleading with her. "Do you not love me as I do you?"

Her eyes stung and her heart raced. As much as a part of her screamed to lie to him—to release him once and for all—that selfish part of her soul rebelled. "I do. I do love you, which is why I should return to St. Giles. Do you not see it is best that way?"

He stepped back from her, and his eyes narrowed. "No, I do not see." He studied her in such a way she wrapped her arms around herself. "Unless..."

"Unless what?"

"You are scared." He gave an incredulous bark. "You would rather live in that hovel than be with me, and because you are terrified of what? Being happy? Of having all you ever desired—a home, a husband you love, children?" He pointed his finger directly at her chest. "You are afraid."

Her breathing changed, coming in pants. "I am not."

"What else would you have me think?" With every word from his mouth, his voice raised in volume.

She began to shake, and her hands fell to her sides in fists. "That I want you to be happy, even if it is not with me."

"That is impossible without you!"

"I do not want you estranged from your sister—from those you care about. I do not want you to one day come to the realization that you hate me!" Why could he not understand? While he may be pained now, the injury she inflicted would pass. She could not be the means of hurting him for a lifetime.

"I have reassured you of the impossibility of such a thing— my aunts both dined with you in this home, confirming their acceptance of you, but your fear prevents you from trusting me as I do you! If you wish to return to St. Giles and live with your cowardice, then go. I shall call my carriage to take you."

She gasped and her fingernails dug crescents into the tender flesh of her palms. "I am not a coward!" Her chest protested at the force of her cry, prompting her to clear her throat in the hopes of preventing a coughing fit.

"Only a coward would flee back to the slums of London to lick her wounds! If she were brave, she would put her health and happiness first. She would travel with me to Derbyshire!"

"I am not a coward!"

He angled forward and pointed. "You *are* a coward!"

She trembled in her spot. How dare he! Her insides coiled like a snake about to strike. "Very well! I will go!" She flinched. Had she just agreed to his scheme? Oh no! What had she done?

"Good! I shall make the arrangements!" He paused, blinked, and sank back onto his heels. He opened his mouth. Without waiting for him to speak, she spun around and rushed through the hall, not stopping until she reached the top of the stairs. The exertion created such a pressure in her chest that she dissolved into a deep hacking that scratched as it tore through her windpipe. She sank to her hands and knees, pulling his handkerchief from her pocket and covering her mouth.

Gentle arms embraced her and lifted her. "Forgive me," said Fitzwilliam close to her ear. "I should not have become so intemperate." His breath caressed near her ear, causing gooseflesh to erupt along her neck and back. Her head collapsed against his shoulder as the cough subsided, and she closed her eyes.

"I do not want to quarrel with you."

He rested his cheek against her head. "I have no wish to quarrel with you either. I know I shall regret much of what I have said, but I cannot let you go without first fighting for our future." His voice cracked and shredded her heart, letting all of what was inside come oozing to the fore. If she continued, she would lose his love, his friendship, his faithfulness—all those small bits of him that made her feel more than she had with any other person. The hole left behind when they were apart was greater than even that left by her father's death. How could she leave without losing a vital part of herself forever?

Tears began to stream in warm paths down her face. "I am sorry." She took one last inhale of his woodsy scent before he set her upon the mattress. Unable to meet his eye, she rolled away from him and curled into a ball. She could not say when Jane came in and began to fuss over her, but she refused tea and food then cried until she fell asleep.

Chapter 19

Darcy sank back into the squabs and let his eyes flutter closed. The pounding in his head, which had begun with a slight throb but had progressed to an incessant hammering against his temples, needed to subside, and soon. He shifted at the press of a knee against his leg. Blast, Richard! He peered across the carriage and frowned at his cousin. The addlepate slept against the side of the coach, spreading his legs as if he were the sole occupant of the equipage. What was to be next? Snoring?

Why had Richard even come? Darcy had groaned aloud when his cousin appeared on the doorstep of Darcy House before sunrise the day prior. The servants from Carlisle House had even delivered his trunk to the mews in advance of his arrival, which had joined their luggage on the accompanying carriage. Since their departure, Darcy had given Richard's company an unusual amount of thought, but no matter how hard he tried, he could not understand Richard's desire to join their journey. They were not partaking of a house party at Pemberley, and they could be making a swift return to London if all went badly. Where was the entertainment in this for him?

At Elizabeth's soft laugh, he rubbed his eyes and let his gaze roam over her sweet face. She had been quiet since their argument two days ago, and her reserve unnerved him, making sleep all but impossible. Her behaviour since their disagreement resembled more of what he remembered of Jane from Netherfield. "What amuses you so?"

"You." Jane slept against Elizabeth's shoulder, and she spoke in a low tone. "You allowed him to come rather than argue. Now you glower at him."

"When the two of us travel together, he spreads his long legs and big feet around the coach, but we have enough room so he does so without intruding upon my comfort."

"Oh, so your sour expression is due to our presence?"

"No, not at all," he said in a rush. "I—" Her light laugh brought a smile unbidden to his lips. "You are teasing me."

"Am I?"

His heart lightened and the weight that had been pressing on him since their argument halved. How he regretted upsetting her so! The evening of that disagreement, Elizabeth had requested a tray and retired early, even though Jane had joined him and Richard at dinner. Jane had not said more than Elizabeth was well, only fatigued, but due to the lack of further information, he bristled. Richard had complained of his boorish attitude when they removed to the study for brandy, but of course, he had overheard what was said between Darcy and Elizabeth. With their voices raised, his cousin's hearing would have been poor indeed if he had not.

"I hope your accommodations last night were acceptable?" The inn was one he used often. He found the rooms comfortable and the food always exceeded his expectations, but he did not want to assume Elizabeth and Jane's experience matched his own.

"Yes, thank you. The meal impressed me, and the room was very comfortable. I assure you my sister commented much the same." Her tongue peeked out to lick her lips, and he struggled to keep his attention on her eyes. "So, we are no longer in London. I can hardly flee when I have no money and no willing companion. Will you not tell me our destination?"

He bit his cheek and tilted his head. Should he reveal his plan so soon or wait until he could present the entire scheme at once? He shrugged and kept his voice easy. "Derbyshire."

"You have said as much. Will you not tell me more? Are you taking us to Pemberley?"

"We are not travelling to Pemberley. While the park is larger, the house itself is slightly more grand than Longbourn. We shall be rather close to Derby."

She gave an overly dramatic sigh and crossed her arms over her chest. "I should be very put out with you, Mr. Darcy."

"And I should be put out with the both of you," said Richard who sat up. Blessedly, he pulled his enormous boot back to his own side of the coach and crossed his arms over his chest, mirroring Elizabeth's position. "Am I really so altered from Hunsford?"

"Not since we departed, but at dinner with your mother and Lady Catherine, indeed your behaviour was quite affected."

"Ah!" He lifted his eyebrows. "Not an improvement, then?"

Elizabeth glanced at him for a second then shook her head. "Forgive me, but no. I would not say it is—"

"Lizzy!" Jane lifted her head from Elizabeth's shoulder. "Really?"

Elizabeth moved closer to the window. "Would you prefer me to lie?"

"No," said Richard. "I always prefer the truth." Jane pressed her lips together and turned her attention to the passing scenery.

"May I ask how much longer until we change horses?"

Darcy nearly jumped when Elizabeth addressed him once again. He peered out of the window and consulted his watch. "A half-hour at the most."

She stretched her arms in front of her. "Good. I dearly wish to walk for a bit."

Elizabeth closed the book and held it upon her lap while she turned her attention to the man seated across from her. Fitzwilliam's eyes were closed as he relaxed into the squabs, providing the perfect opportunity to observe him without his notice. What could he have planned that necessitated travel to Derbyshire? They were indeed in Derbyshire, so he was not absconding with her to Gretna Green.

She peeked around the carriage. Though the hour was yet early, Lord Carlisle and Jane slept while leaning against the side of the carriage. Jane had always preferred to pass the time travelling asleep. Elizabeth could not understand how she still slept during the night. She would be wide awake if she did the same.

With no one to criticise her, Elizabeth's greedy gaze returned to the object of her reverie. She traced the straight line of his nose, the curve of his closed eyes, and finally, his lush, full lips. His sizeable hands rested upon his thighs, his breeches revealing his legs to be long and muscular. He was a beautiful man, but his handsome exterior held a generous heart she loved with her entire being.

As much as she had tried to resist, she had grown quite attached to his presence and his solicitous care of her and her dearest sister. Her eyes burned and her vision blurred. How would she return to London without him? She had loved him before, but her feelings had only deepened during her recent time with him. Why had she not insisted upon returning to St. Giles as soon as her health permitted? Giving him up then would have been terrible, but prolonging their separation would just make things worse once the inevitable day arrived.

"What makes you so sad?" When she looked up, he was watching her, his brows drawn together in the middle.

"I believe I am fatigued at being so long in one attitude. I long to walk and take the air rather than be confined in a carriage."

He shifted to look through the window, withdrew his pocket watch, and flipped the lid. "We should be nearing our destination. You will have ample opportunity to ramble if you desire."

As though the driver could hear their conversation, the equipage slowed, rousing Lord Carlisle and Jane, who proceeded to put themselves to rights, speaking of the favourable weather during the journey as well as their good fortune in the repair of the roads. Elizabeth had to agree with them. With no rain to contend with, their journey had been easy indeed!

The specifics of their conversation gradually became lost to Elizabeth, who instead returned her gaze to the forest as they turned and passed through a gate. Soon after, they crossed an old stone bridge where water rushed over ancient rocks towards some unknown end. A doe bolted into the woods. Had their carriage frightened her away from grazing along the roadside? No other reason for the deer's escape was evident, so Elizabeth turned her attention back to the passing view.

As they cleared the trees, a hunting lodge of sorts sat near the top of a heavily wooded hill, and the river they crossed moments ago emerged from the base to wind through a vast pastureland dotted with white and black sheep. Everything was so lovely. How she wished to ramble through it all!

When the carriage came to a halt, Elizabeth bent forward to look past Jane. A grey stone house constructed of a similar rock to the bridge stood proudly against the cloudless azure sky. "Where are we?"

Darcy adjusted his gloves, lacing his fingers and pressing them together. "Drayton Abbey."

The door opened and the step was set, which allowed for Mr. Darcy and Lord Carlisle to alight. Mr. Darcy helped Elizabeth down and offered her his arm. As they approached the house, she took in everything from the natural appearance of the park to the rock that formed the barriers and pathways through the gardens. At the entrance, a cheerful, portly woman stood beside an imposing man, who appeared happy with no one and nothing.

"Welcome to Drayton, Mr. Darcy," said the woman with a bob.

"Welcome, sir," said the man in a voice lower than any she had ever heard.

"Thank you, Mrs. Deering, Mr. Haggard. I hope you had no difficulties readying the house. I do apologise for the late notice, but our travel plans were not fixed until the evening before our departure."

"'Twas no problem, sir, none at all." Mrs. Deering clasped her hands and led them into the great hall. "All is as you requested, sir. We have hot water prepared for you to refresh yourselves and fires have been lit in the bedchambers as well as the rooms we thought you most likely to use. With the clear skies and sun, I planned luncheon to be served in the breakfast parlour. The wall of windows on the north side of the house has a brilliant view of the park and the hills today."

"Thank you."

A maid, Mrs. Deering, and Mr. Haggard helped them remove their coats and hats before they were escorted upstairs. Elizabeth all but ignored Jane's admiration of the home as the portraits lining their way and the simple elegance of the furnishings held her attention. When the bedchamber door closed behind her, she exhaled and leaned against the solid panel. Though not as grand as Darcy House, the well-appointed bedchamber suited her tastes. The pale floral of the wallcoverings and more distinct print of the canopy brought to mind the out of doors in spring. The footboard boasted a matching fabric to the canopy, and a chaise of deep crimson sat at the foot of the bed, welcoming someone to sit and pen a letter at the small table before it. The room was not too large, but boasted of comfortable furnishings with luxurious fabrics.

She stepped over to the window and gasped at the prospect. The view was stunning. The river she had espied as they arrived wound around the side of the house through the gardens. A stone footbridge, a short distance from the wall, led a possible walker to the unfettered park surrounding them.

How she wished to change her gown and explore, but if she wished to enjoy a good ramble, she would need to rest first. She sighed. When would this fatigue end?

She jumped at a knock. "Yes?"

Elsie hurried in from an entrance to the side of the room, wearing a bright smile. "I have hot water for you to wash and your pale green gown pressed should you wish to change from your travelling clothes." The day before they departed London, the dressmaker had delivered a celestial blue travelling gown with a medium blue redingote, which Elsie had ensured she wore for the trip. Elizabeth had been thankful for the consideration of Mrs. Northcott, who had requested those two items before the other parts of the order. The bricks and rugs planned by Fitzwilliam had been helpful when the weather necessitated them, but the addition of the warmer gown and coat had been most welcome.

"I would appreciate removing the dust of the road, thank you." Elizabeth followed the maid into the dressing room. After she washed, she curled into the luxurious mattress and promptly fell asleep.

When Elizabeth woke, she dressed with Elsie's help. Her maid's selection of the long-sleeved day gown was perfect. Though the day was not warm by any means, the sun prevented a hard chill from permeating the air.

When she entered the hall, she caught a glimpse through the window of a couple walking in the garden near the house. Was that Jane and Lord Carlisle? She made to join them, but a throat cleared, preventing her escape. "Miss, the master wishes to see you in the library."

"Of course he does," she said in a mutter as the butler led her through the passage. She did not object to seeing more of the house, yet she had said how she desired to walk when the opportunity arose. Could she not stretch her legs first?

Fitzwilliam stood staring out of a window when she entered, making her smile. How many times had he stood in a similar attitude while visiting Meryton? She glanced over her shoulder to Mr. Haggard. "Thank you."

Once Mr. Haggard departed and they were assured of their privacy, Fitzwilliam faced her. "What think you of Drayton?"

"What I have seen, I like very much. The park is lovely in its wildness. Did you select my room or did the housekeeper?"

One side of his lips quirked upward. "I remembered the prospect from my first visit. If you prefer a different suite, you may select one. I shall not mind."

"No," she said quickly. "The room is perfect."

His forehead furrowed as he clasped his hands behind his back. "I expect that you are wondering why I have brought you here." He shifted in his place. "You have spoken of your reservations in regards to marrying me." He cleared his throat and adjusted his shoulders before his eyes met hers. "I still hope I can convince you to accept me, yet I realise the choice is yours and yours alone. If you are definitely set against me, then I am aware of my obligation to release you. My request, should you refuse my hand, is for you to live here so I can be assured of your safety and well-being. The Cookes are not far away. I believe I mentioned before, they live near Stapleford, so you would be close enough to visit them should you wish it. Pemberley is also an easy distance in the event you have need of aid." Jane had mentioned the Cookes had moved to Stapleford, but to have the ability to visit would be a luxury she had not considered possible. Fitzwilliam pulled his shoulders back a little then released them. "I could not bear it if you returned to St. Giles or another neighbourhood of a similar reputation.

"The steward in place here is young. Jane has mentioned that you helped your father with Longbourn, so I thought you could, in effect, run the estate with the help of the steward. You would have a place to live and keep a portion of the income for your time. If you increase the yield, you will keep any additional profit for your use." All she could do was stare at him agape. He could not be serious. "No one in this home beyond Mrs. Deering, Mr. Haggard, and the steward would know the particulars of our arrangement—and Jane, of course. I cannot imagine you would neglect to tell her."

"You wish Jane and me to live here?" She could not prevent the high pitch of the words when they burst from her lips. How could this ever be arranged so they were not taking advantage of his generosity? He was, for all intents and purposes, giving them a place to live and money to boot!

"My father inherited this property from a childless cousin due to an entailment. The widow remained until she died."

"Your father was kind to allow her to stay. I am certain she must have appreciated the gesture."

He nodded. "She did. Unfortunately, she did not survive long after her husband passed. The house has remained empty since. I have long left it uninhabited in the event Richard was injured on the Peninsula and returned, unable to continue in the Regulars. He would never accept an estate outright, but I had a scheme for such an eventuality."

When his eyes met hers once more, he had an obvious difficulty holding her gaze. "I thought if you and your sister wished to remain, we could claim Jane a widow of some means who leased the estate and lives with her sister as her companion."

She tilted her head and frowned. "Why would Jane be the widow?"

He shrugged while lifting his hands then let them drop at his sides. "I thought as she is two years your senior, she would make more sense. You can be the widow if you choose. Who feigns their circumstances makes no difference to me."

She pressed her lips together then covered her mouth with her hand to keep from laughing.

"Am I amusing?"

"Forgive me." She bit the tip of her finger but could not help her smile. "I do not believe I have ever seen you exasperated. Aside from when you proposed at Hunsford and that night before we departed London, you are always so composed. Even when we argued at Netherfield, your temper never seemed to get the better of you."

"Miss Elizabeth!" Elizabeth whipped around to the former Georgiana Darcy standing in the doorway. As the young lady ran towards her, Elizabeth stiffened. What was Miss Darcy called now? She was a viscountess, was she not? Lady... Lady... What was it? Witney! That was her name! Lady Witney!

The lady rushed before Elizabeth and threw her arms around her. "You are alive!" When Lady Witney drew back, she cupped Elizabeth's face in her hands while Elizabeth gaped and blinked. The young lady then whirled around to face Fitzwilliam, hands propped on her hips. "Brother, why did you not tell me of finding Miss Elizabeth?"

He stared with his jaw lax. "How did you know we were here?"

"Lady Catherine! I had to hear from our aunt, Fitzwilliam!"

Elizabeth pursed her lips. "She does like to be of use." Fitzwilliam's head dropped and his shoulders began to shake, prompting Elizabeth to drop her gaze the floor. Laughing would have been rude, would it not?

"I cannot credit the two of you finding humour in this." Lady Witney stepped back and turned her head back and forth between them. "The remaining Bennets as well as the Gardiners have thought Miss Bennet and Miss Elizabeth dead, and you are finding humour in the situation?"

"Georgiana," said Darcy, who was all of a sudden serious. "Neither of us enjoys keeping this secret from family and friends."

Elizabeth grabbed Lady Witney's hands. "Forgive me. Jane and I had no desire to bring pain to our relations. We knew they would never permit us to take responsibility for ourselves, and we saw no other option. I beg you not to tell anyone of our presence since we have not yet decided our future plans."

"I do not understand what you need to decide. The Gardiners would be ecstatic to welcome you and your sister back into their home." She gasped and pointed at them both.

"If you wed Fitzwilliam, you need not live with the Gardiners, and we would be sisters."

"Georgiana!"

Elizabeth covered her face and shook her head. The more people who knew of them, the more their survival had the possibility of becoming common knowledge. "Lady Witney—"

"Fitzwilliam, leave us," said his sister sternly. "I want to speak with Miss Elizabeth."

He pinched the bridge of his nose. "You will not force Elizabeth's hand."

"No, but I can force yours. I can pen a letter to our uncle to tell him of Miss Elizabeth."

He narrowed his eyes and glared. "He saw her the day before we departed London and insulted her. You know what he would say."

Lady Witney crossed her arms over her chest and tilted her head. "Does our uncle know Miss Elizabeth is why you have refused all his attempts at matching you with one of his political allies' daughters?"

Her brother mirrored her stance and levelled a fierce expression in Lady Witney's direction. "You would not dare."

Lady Witney gave a crooked smile, resembling more her cousin than her brother in that moment. "Would I not?"

Chapter 20

After Lady Witney's threat, Fitzwilliam had not persisted in arguing. Lord Fitzwilliam's fit of anger had shown the earl to be arrogant and unfeeling, which made Lady Witney's threat all the more shocking.

Lady Witney rang for tea while Elizabeth sat in a chair near a panelled window, overlooking the front lawn. The view was delightful. Wild hedgerows and a small dry-stone wall separated the garden near the house from the fields that extended into the distance. Sheep grazed in the pastureland, oblivious to any turmoil within the house. Meanwhile, Elizabeth's stomach turned somersaults, making her nauseous. Why could none of this be simple?

The young lady sat across from her. "Now we can discuss Fitzwilliam without his interference."

"My lady, I—"

"I had hoped to call you sister when you visited Pemberley nearly three years ago, and I must confess I still hope to call you sister in the future. Pray, call me Georgiana."

Elizabeth traced the design on the upholstery with her fingernail and shifted in her seat. "I do not believe marrying your brother is possible."

"Do you not care for him? The manner in which you looked at him at Pemberley led me to believe you both were at least on your way to falling in love. Was I mistaken?"

Elizabeth fidgeted with the handkerchief she withdrew from her pocket. "No, you were not mistaken. I did... I do love Fitzwilliam." She spread the fabric and touched the embroidery, fingering the stitches with gentle strokes. "When he proposed at Rosings, I was a gentleman's daughter with no connections and no fortune. I do not know what he told you of why we departed Lambton."

"The Gardiners informed us of what happened to Miss Lydia."

Elizabeth blinked back tears and shook her head. "Stupid Lydia. Her selfish actions did more than damage our marriageability. As much as I wished I could run to Fitzwilliam and marry him, I feared he would not have me as much as I feared he would."

Mrs. Deering entered with the tea. She placed it on a table near Georgiana, curtseyed, and departed, closing the door behind her. "I do not understand," said Georgiana as she began spooning the crushed leaves into the teapot. "Why would you fear he *would* have you?"

"I did not want Lydia's folly to harm your prospects as it had ours. Her fall brought shame upon our family. What if her fall brought shame to your brother? I could not bear it. I could not endure his resentment." She had witnessed how damaging that particular attitude could be to a marriage.

"Who did you know...?"

"My parents," said Elizabeth. "My father fell in love with my mother not long after he returned to Longbourn from Oxford. According to my aunt, my mother was beautiful, amiable, and well-known for her cheerful disposition. My father was instantly charmed. He did not care that she was the local solicitor's daughter. He began to call, and after two months, he made her the offer of his hand."

"Nothing sounds bothersome thus far." Georgiana poured a cup of tea and passed it to her. "Do help yourself to the milk and sugar if you care for some."

Elizabeth placed her cup on the table and added a bit of milk. "No, by all appearances, their love story was nothing unusual. What was concealed was the opinion of my grandparents. They were furious, you see. They had intended for Papa to wed a young lady from an estate near Potters Bar, but he had defied them. My grandfather instituted the entail on the estate soon after. With the birth of each daughter, my mother became flightier and more panicked about her future while my father retreated into his book room to escape her antics and moaning."

"And he grew to resent your mother?" Georgiana stirred her tea. "His father could be considered to blame more than your mother."

"I suppose, but he often belittled Mama's complaints of her nerves. I always felt as though he resented her for not remaining the lady who captured his heart. He may have resented them both. I never asked."

"No, I would not expect you to." Georgiana relaxed into her chair. "You do recognize that your situation is strikingly different from your parents. When your grandfather instituted the entail, he stole away your mother's security, which without a son, altered her personality. Albeit indirect, your grandfather robbed your mother and father of something vital to each of them. I do understand your fears, but if the *ton* has a problem with your family's history, my brother will not care."

"He cannot claim indifference when he cannot know—" She shook her head and gulped down the nerves rising in her chest.

"Elizabeth," said Georgiana, leaning forward and taking her hands. "He may not know what people could say, but I can assure you, those who do not accept you will not matter to him. My aunt said you were ill upon your arrival to Darcy house, so you must have met Mr. Acker. He is what you can expect of my brother's true friends, who are few though loyal to a fault. You have also met my aunts, who accepted you and your sister without reservation. You see, those important to him will not abandon him. They will support both of you."

"And your husband? What if he demanded you sever ties with your brother?"

"My husband would never do such a thing. He knows the value of a love match and would never be so cruel as to demand I forsake Fitzwilliam. You must believe me. The two of you can be together at last."

A warm tear dropped to Elizabeth's cheek and began a steady track towards her jaw. With a trembling hand, she brushed it away. Georgiana had said nothing thus far that her brother had failed to mention, but could she put aside her apprehension and accept Fitzwilliam? Was it truly possible?

Georgiana set down her tea then removed Elizabeth's cup from her grip. After placing it on the tray, the young lady took her hands. "I accompanied him to the Gardiner's the evening he learnt of your death. You must understand. He had been sad before, but that night, a part of him died. For the past two years, he has mourned—has walked through life seeing little and feeling less. Because I love my husband dearly, I cannot imagine the joy my brother must have felt at learning you lived. You must trust that he knows his own heart."

A sob tore from Elizabeth's throat, and she heaved as she struggled to breathe through her weeping. Georgiana sat beside her and wrapped an arm around her shoulders while Elizabeth struggled to regain some semblance of control. She had swallowed her pain and disappointment when they had departed Lambton. Since that fateful letter from Jane, her survival resembled Georgiana's description of Fitzwilliam: seeing little and feeling less. She could not dwell on her loss. What would that have achieved? How would existing in a perpetual state of anguish benefit anyone?

Instead, she had pushed all of those messy feelings down until they became a hollow ache that had consumed her. She convinced herself that Fitzwilliam would continue without her. He would marry a woman of fortune and standing, have children, and ensure Pemberley prospered for the next generation. The knowledge that he existed in much the same fashion was agony. She had never wanted such an existence for him.

"Elizabeth?"

Georgiana's words pushed and pulled at her until her heart splintered apart. No more! She could take no more! With an abruptness that must have shocked Georgiana, she jumped to her feet and began to pace back and forth while her mind spun in a thousand different directions. What had she done? Her hands were unable to remain idle. Instead, they punished the poor handkerchief in her grip, twisting and tugging in a futile attempt to release the turmoil that wracked every fibre of her being. Georgiana watched, eyes wide, yet silent. What must she think of her?

On her next pass of the grand window, a latch, not quite concealed behind the drapery, came into focus. The door opened with ease and she rushed down the path away from the house. She had to escape—to breathe before she suffocated on the thickness of the air inside the house.

The cold stung the damp on her cheeks while she ran to the edge of the lawn then continued in the direction of the river. Wetness soaked through her slippers to the soles of her feet, creating an icy discomfort with every step, but she pressed forward until she stood upon the footbridge she had first seen from her bedchamber window. At that moment, she grasped the stone wall and drew in great gulps of bracing air, sucking the breeze into her lungs with the desperation of a starving child.

"Elizabeth?"

She spun on her heel and teetered as she lost her balance on the damp earth covering the surface of the bridge. Fitzwilliam grasped her elbows and steadied her, keeping her from falling into a heap at his feet.

"Thank you," she said. Her fingers dug into his great coat for added security while her gaze concentrated on her hands. The last thing she wanted was to release him.

"I apologise for Georgiana—"

"No!" She shook her head and gulped down a sob. "I should be the one apologising. When your letter reached us at Longbourn, I thought I was being noble—that by sacrificing you, I was preserving your honour and allowing you a life of happiness. I stupidly believed I would be the one who suffered the most, while our time at Pemberley would allow you to remember me with more fondness than disappointment. My selfish pride preferred that ending to that of Rosings.

"I never considered you had loved longer and when all hope had been lost. If I had allowed myself to truly acknowledge your pain, I never would have survived. I would have had no will to go on."

He appeared as though slapped. "You read my letter to your father?"

She inhaled deeply and nodded. "We remained at Longbourn for two months after my father's death. Mr. Collins felt the time was suitable for us to make other arrangements. Your letter arrived four days before Jane and I departed for London with my aunt and uncle."

He drew away and stepped to the opposite side of the footbridge, his back to her while he stared out at the pastureland. "I suppose I imagined Mr. Collins tossing it into the fire."

"I still have it, tucked away with the first letter you gave me, in one of my father's books. I could not bear to part with either." She opened the handkerchief she had clutched since fleeing the house, tracing over Fitzwilliam's initials with trembling fingers. He had pressed it into her hand that morning she begged for tooth powder and a bath. He had wanted to marry her then. How many times had he humbled himself since her illness? She covered her face and shook her head. If she desired happiness—desired him, her fears and insecurities would need to be banished forever. She would need to be braver than she had ever been in her life.

She pressed a hand between his shoulder blades. "Fitzwilliam?" He stiffened and his arms pushed further into the pockets of his great coat. He took in a shuddering breath that he released on the breeze. How he had suffered. The knowledge that she knew of his letter and had not responded was another agony to join the rest—she had known his intentions and still fled to one of the most squalid parts of London. Would he despise her now that he knew?

Her other hand joined the first, and she pressed them against his back, smoothing out from the centre until she could rest her head between them. "You were correct when you called me a coward. I am not proud I let fear and shame control my actions, but I do hope you can forgive me. I have no excuse other than the one I have told you before—that I wished to protect you from myself. I know how utterly naïve my assumptions were, and how much you have suffered." Tears dropped from her eyes and fell to the surface of the bridge. "Can you forgive me?"

He turned, which forced her to straighten and take his hands. She kissed his knuckles. "I knew upon reading the express from Jane detailing Colonel Forster's letter and Papa's death what I had lost." She brushed a tear from her cheek then clutched his hand once more. "Since waking in your home, I have hidden behind my own insecurities, and done naught but cause you more anguish, yet you have been charity itself—"

"Do you truly fear me so?" His voice broke, and her heart squeezed mercilessly.

"Fear you?" She enveloped his hands in hers and held his eyes. "No, I was more terrified of the unknown, those consequences no one but God could predict. As I explained to your sister, my father resented my mother for circumstances beyond her control. Over time, she became sillier, and his resentment grew. When I read the letter to my father, I was unsure if you knew of Lydia, and I could not bear to see your countenance when I told you. I did not want your pity. I was also certain we could never marry, and I was frightened of what I might do, what I might accept or even offer in order to be with you." Her cheeks heated while she concentrated on the buttons of his coat.

A moment later, his body gave a slight flinch. "Oh!" Her eyes lifted to his, and his gaze softened.

"Until that moment, I had never known myself," she said, tears pooling in her eyes. "I never understood how deeply I loved you—how deeply I still love you."

His palms cupped her cheeks, his thumbs caressing away her tears. "Elizabeth—"

"No." She pressed a finger to his lips. "You should not need to humble yourself again, not when I have been obstinate, headstrong, and completely undeserving of your devotion."

He opened his mouth to speak, but she shook her head. "Shh, let me finish." Her hand slid down over his heart. "Fitzwilliam Darcy, will you do me the honour of becoming my husband?" He stood stock-still, mouth agape. Of course, tradition held that men offered for ladies, yet could he truly be so shocked? "Will you not say something?"

A grin spread across his face, and she lifted one eyebrow as he began to chuckle. He grabbed her around the waist and spun them in a circle. When he set her feet back upon the grass, he pressed his forehead against hers. "Yes!" He laughed like a madman. "Yes, Elizabeth Bennet, I shall marry you."

She gasped as he lifted her once more. "You will render me dizzy and unable to stand if you continue."

"Then I shall carry you." He brought her fingers to his lips and bestowed pecks to the tips of each. "You are cold. How could I not have noticed your lack of coat and gloves?" He opened his great coat and drew her inside, wrapping it around her so it covered them both. The warmth of his body and the scent of his cologne enveloped her.

"I failed to consider my attire when I left the house." She peeled his coat back from her skirt. Her hem did not appear dirt-stained. "I do not believe I damaged the gown, but," she lifted the skirt enough to reveal the bottom of one foot. "I am afraid these are ruined."

He shook his head then kissed her forehead. "I do not care. The gown and slippers can be replaced." The tips of his fingers traced along her jaw. "You cannot. No one else will suffice." His eyes dropped to her lips and the heat of his stare made her lips dry. "May I?" She gave a barely perceptible nod.

Her body warmed as he leaned in ever so slowly and let his lips graze hers with the softest of touches. When she opened her eyes, the heartfelt delight upon his face prompted her to close the distance and press her lips against his once more. How long she had waited to know the feel of his kiss. This time, he cradled her upper lip before teasing the bottom. His palms, though in his coat pockets, pressed against her lower back and drew her flush to the heat of his body.

"Darcy! I say, man, that position is most improper!"

Fitzwilliam groaned and dropped his forehead to her shoulder. "I am going to murder Richard in his sleep."

Chapter 21

Despite Elizabeth's protests that her shoes could not be
ruined further by returning to the house on foot, Darcy had
carried her back and left her in Elsie's capable hands to put her
to rights. As he returned downstairs, he caught a glimpse of his
ridiculous grin in a gilded mirror along the wall. Was that why
his face ached? When was the last time he had reason to smile
for such an extended period of time?

A glass of brandy was shoved into his hand upon his
entrance to the library, and after a forceful slap to his back,
Richard held his own glass aloft. "I believe I should be
extending my congratulations. I am pleased she has accepted
you at last."

"Actually, I accepted her." Darcy laughed then took a sip
of the strong spirits, enjoying the slight sting on his tongue. He
had either been numb or miserable for so long. With the
discovery of Elizabeth, some of the numbness had dissipated,
and everything had a new life—everything was more vibrant
than before.

"Wait! You accepted her?"

He turned in the direction of Georgiana's voice, no doubt
grinning like a fool. Georgiana covered her mouth with her
hands, giggling, and rushed to throw her arms around his neck.
"Oh, I am so happy for you, Brother. I need to send a servant to
fetch James." Jane, who had been standing in the doorway with
his sister, approached at a more sedate pace, though wearing a
teary smile.

At the mention of James, Darcy jerked back and stared at his sister. "Witney is here with you? Why have I not seen him?"

Georgiana once again giggled and shrugged one shoulder. "He remained in our rooms. I knew you might be upset at my unexpected presence, so I asked him to wait until either all was well or we had need of a hasty departure. He will be relieved we are not forced to the latter."

As his sister rang the bell, Jane took his free hand in both of hers. "I must admit while I was terrified at the severity of Lizzy's illness, a part of me hoped this would be the result of requesting your aid. I have long known my sister held deeper feelings for you than she was willing to admit. Thank you for your patience with her." With shiny eyes, she kissed his cheek. "I shall be very proud to call you my brother."

The gravelly sensation in his throat necessitated that he swallow. "I do hope you will make your home with us. Whether for a month or the rest of your life, you will be welcome."

Jane smiled and patted his hand. "Thank you, Fitzwilliam. Mary and Lizzy have given me reason to hope I still may have a husband and a family one day, but I shall be honoured to be a part of your household until then."

His eyes darted to Richard, who stood not far behind her. She had not mentioned a name, but had she meant his cousin or a possible husband in general terms? While Elizabeth conversed with Georgiana, Richard and Jane had walked in the gardens. The pair had also walked and spoken during several of their stops to change horses. He shook off the speculation. He had no desire to consider Richard's intentions at this moment.

Today was for celebration and his own happy thoughts. He squeezed Jane's hand. "Any man would be fortunate to have such a wife."

"I did not know you possessed the skill of flattery, Mr. Darcy," said Jane, her cheeks pink.

His cousin barked a chuckle while he passed a glass of sherry to Jane. "I doubt he did either."

When Witney entered, he shook Darcy's hand while clasping his shoulder. "I wish you great joy, Darcy."

He choked back the squeezing of his throat and nodded. "Thank you. I am only sorry you have been sequestered in your chambers for so long a time."

Witney stepped back and took his wife's hand. "After Lady Catherine's correspondence and speaking with Georgiana, I understood the necessity. I was not bothered by an hour or two's solitude."

When Elizabeth joined them moments later, her long-sleeved gown had been swapped for a sprigged muslin that suited her well, and fresh house slippers. She entered the room, and unable to resist her pull, he stepped away to greet her, kissing her knuckles and the inside of her wrist. When he straightened, she took his brandy and brought it to her lips, watching him boldly while she sipped.

"You drink brandy?"

"My father drank Port more often since it is less expensive than brandy, but once in a while, we partook of a small glass. Uncle procured him a bottle for Christmas the year you came to Netherfield."

He clenched his hands as she took one more taste. Her lips caressed the crystal in a seductive manner, and her tongue peeked out to savour a stray drop that lingered along the corner of her mouth. How could she madden him in such a way? He had done no more than barely touch those lips, and he could imagine them, with vivid detail, as they entwined with his own, brushed his neck, caressed his—" He tugged at his cravat and coughed. Regulation! He needed regulation.

"When will you wed?" called Georgiana from near the window.

Elizabeth passed the glass back and rested her hand in the crook of his arm. "We have yet to discuss the matter. I am unaware of Fitzwilliam's wishes, but I would prefer sooner rather than later. We have waited too long as it is."

He moved to pour a touch more brandy in his glass and handed it to Elizabeth. "I have no objections to an immediate ceremony." She lifted her eyebrow and took a sip while he poured another for himself.

Georgiana clasped her hands with wide eyes. "What if we travel to Pemberley so you can marry there?"

"We need a license or to have the banns read," said Elizabeth.

"I have a license." He trained his eyes on his drink. Would Elizabeth be pleased or find his aunts' insistence officious? "My aunts insisted I acquire a special license before we departed London."

A light laugh bubbled from her lips. "Well, they have been wonderfully meddlesome, but at the moment, I cannot find fault with their scheming." She took his arm and held it close. "But what of my aunt and uncle? If we wed in haste at Pemberley, they would be unable to attend. Could we perhaps return to London? Jane and I could inform our aunt and uncle of our well-being and then, regardless of what occurs, we could wed the next day."

Jane gasped and looped an arm through Elizabeth's. "Yes, we should speak to Aunt and Uncle, but can we return to London so soon?"

"The journey is possible." Darcy glanced around at their family. "I could send my messenger tonight to arrange the inns as well as a letter to Mrs. Northcott. We should give the horses another day of rest, but we could leave the day following. I am certain my aunts could arrange a vicar to perform the ceremony." He searched her expression for any reluctance to such a swift wedding.

Her hand slipped down into his, she laced their fingers, and pressed against his arm. "As soon as we tell Aunt and Uncle, we wed. I have no wish to wait."

He dropped a kiss to the back of her hand. "I shall pen the letters without delay." With a slight smile, she moistened her lips before he walked away. He suppressed a groan and forced himself to put foot in front of foot until he reached the desk. He had never had a more uncomfortable experience while attending his correspondence. Elizabeth Bennet would be the death of him!

⸻◆⸻

The remainder of the day passed with the speed of a waddling hedgehog. Though Elizabeth loved the time spent with family, past and future, she desired naught but time alone with Fitzwilliam, which would come either by them marrying or stealing away—and no one would allow them to steal away today.

Fitzwilliam's low laugh rumbled from across the room. What had Witney said to him to elicit such a merry sound? She sat between Jane and Georgiana, who prevented her from hearing the men's discourse since there was never a moment's silence between them. For two rather reticent ladies, they chatted more together than she could have ever imagined. Nevertheless, the sound of his chuckle touched her as though he held her close at that very moment. She glanced from her lap to his face, wreathed in a brilliant smile. Her breath caught in her chest, hitching just so. He was a beautiful man.

"Lizzy?"

She was wrenched from her reverie to face Jane. "You seem fatigued, and Georgiana and I wish to retire. Shall we leave the men to their drinks and conversation?"

"Oh, of course." Upon rising, she stood with Georgiana while Jane announced their intention to depart.

In an instant, Fitzwilliam was at her side, his lips pressed to her knuckles. "You have made me very happy."

Her entire body heated at the intimacy of his tone. "I am pleased to hear it since I am quite content to be marrying you as soon as may be." Hopefully, her aunt and uncle would agree to a dinner not long after their arrival in London. They had been apart for too long. She would be Mrs. Fitzwilliam Darcy at their first opportunity. She sighed and smiled. "Goodnight, Fitzwilliam."

His steady eyes followed her. Even when she peered over her shoulder, he watched her. Georgiana excused herself at the top of the stairs, but when they reached Elizabeth's bedchamber, Jane held up a finger. "I need to give you something. Pray, allow me to fetch it."

Her sister's room was two doors down, so no more than a minute passed before she returned, bearing a bundle of fabric tied with an ivory silk ribbon. "While you were ill, Mrs. Northcott brought me this gown. She suspected with Mr. Darcy's obvious attachment to you that he would propose but was concerned that ordering a gown fine enough for a wedding would be too presumptuous. When you began to improve, she brought me this and asked if I would remake it for you. She found it in a trunk of Mrs. Darcy's gowns that had been packed away after her death."

Elizabeth took the bundle and entered her room, waving for Jane to follow. After she untied the ribbon, she let the fabric fall before her and stepped to the mirror. "Jane!" Her eyes bulged at the pearl-coloured silk with a shot sarsnet overlay that glowed in the candlelight. Seed pearls dotted the bodice and formed a trim at the top edge. She bit her lip and ran a fingertip along the finery. The gown was stunning.

"Mrs. Northcott searched several trunks in the attics. A number of the old gowns stored away were in disrepair due to age. We scavenged the pearls from them. She also set a few maids to work with what was left. You should have pearls, crystals, and other gems waiting for you upon your return to town."

She hugged the gown to her. "'Tis beautiful. Thank you. I shall have to thank Mrs. Northcott when I next see her." She pivoted on her heel to face her sister, then shifted on her feet. "I did not ask Georgiana if she was to travel to London with us.

"She is. She and her husband have their own carriage, but I believe they will follow." Her dearest sister kissed her cheek.

"Forgive me, but I am tired. We shall talk more at breakfast. Good night."

"Good night," said Elizabeth as Jane departed. When Elsie bustled in, she grinned as she took the gown. "Miss Bennet's work is wonderful, is it not? Mrs. Northcott and Miss Bennet searched through *La Belle Assemblée* for ideas so it more resembles the latest fashions."

"I like it very much."

"Your sister is very skilled with a needle. She taught me a few of her techniques while you slept during the fever." The maid draped the silk over her arm. "I shall pack it well for our return," said Elsie while she followed Elizabeth into the dressing room.

As Elizabeth prepared for bed, the girl chattered, speaking of how much Elizabeth would adore Pemberley. Finally, Elizabeth turned and pressed her palms together in front of her. "Elsie, I was wondering if you would care to be my lady's maid."

The girl blinked and set the brush upon the dressing table. "I did help Lady Witney's abigail and learnt a great deal from her, but I have never been one myself. Are you certain you do not want a more fashionable maid? Lady Fitzwilliam and Lady Catherine de Bourgh employ French abigails."

"I am pleased with your work thus far and see no reason to hire someone new. Your inexperience is not important to me since even established abigails must learn new hairstyles and habits over time. If you are willing and should like the position, I shall inform Mr. Darcy. We shall need to make Mrs. Northcott aware of the change." Would Fitzwilliam be unhappy with her choosing her own maid? He would wish her happy. Though she had not known Elsie long, she trusted her.

Elsie nodded with a giggle. "Then my answer is yes. Thank you, Miss Bennet."

"Good," said Elizabeth. Elsie started for the door, but Elizabeth called her name. "What is your surname?"

"Oh! I am Elsie Taylor."

"Thank you, Taylor. I shall see you in the morning." The girl offered a cheerful curtsey before she hurried out.

Elizabeth stood, made a circuit of the bedchamber, and stared into the darkness outside the window. With Georgiana and Jane retiring, she could not have been the sole lady to remain with the gentlemen, but after today's excitement, she was not tired. If only she could take a long ramble about the park. A walk would be ideal. Too bad the dark would keep her inside.

After cracking the door, careful not to cause a creaking, she peered into the hallway. No one lingered about, so she donned her dressing gown and tiptoed along the corridor, down the stairs, and into the library. The room was empty, so she began skimming through the shelves. Reading always helped her sleep, but what should she read? When she reached a section of poetry, she stopped and studied the books more intently.

"I thought you had retired."

With a small cry, she spun around, dropped the book, and pressed her hand to her chest. "I thought the room empty."

Fitzwilliam's eyes roved over her attire, the intense look in his eyes making her clutch the bookcase behind her. "I needed to speak to Mr. Haggard and Mrs. Deering."

"I have seen just one servant besides the two of them and Elsie all day."

"Mrs. Deering and Mr. Haggard are the only permanent household servants besides the cook."

She crossed her arms over her chest. "I hope you do not mind, but I asked Elsie to be my lady's maid."

One side of his lips quirked up. "I do not object in the slightest. She showed interest in the endeavour before Georgiana wed and took her own abigail with her. We should find a maid for Jane as well."

"I do not mind sharing."

His hand reached out, a finger trailing down her cheek. "You should each have your own." His head tilted a fraction as he caressed her jaw. "What brought you to the library?"

The air in her chest became heavy and difficult to move and gooseflesh erupted down her back. "I was not tired." He stepped closer. Had the warmth of him somehow penetrated the layers of her dressing gown and shift to caress her bare flesh? "What of you?"

He took her hand and tugged so he could slip an arm around her middle. "So much happened today, and my mind is too absorbed by you."

"You are full of pretty words." The words emerged tremulous and low. What was wrong with her voice?

He pressed his forehead to hers. "Are we truly to be married?"

"You have claimed it to be so." She lifted her eyebrow and smiled. "I cannot think of an objection to the arrangement. You will do, I suppose."

His low, rich laugh sent a heated shiver through her, and his eyes dipped to her lips.

"Do you know how much I love you?"

She wrapped her hands around the back of his neck, weaving her fingers into the curls at his nape and pressing herself to him. "Hopefully, as much as I love you."

Her eyes fluttered closed as his face drew closer until his lips claimed hers. Her body trembled from head to toe, and her heart stuttered in an uneven rhythm in her chest. His tongue caressed along the seam of her lips, and she allowed him entrance, gasping into his mouth when his tongue tangled with her own.

With a moan, his arms tightened about her and his fingers gripped at the back of her dressing gown. What began during the afternoon with a chaste press of their lips had progressed into a conflagrating, all-consuming need. No rational thought existed in her mind, just the softness of his locks against her fingers, the heat of his body that radiated through her nightclothes, and the laboured sound of his breathing.

"Fitzwilliam," she murmured as he kissed the corner of her mouth.

He flinched, stepped back, and ran a hand through his hair. "Forgive me."

"For what do you ask forgiveness?" Her skin prickled with the sudden chill of his departure.

"I swore to myself I would not rush you. We have been apart for over two years. I thought you might wish for time to adjust to your new circumstances. After what you confided today, about why you did not seek me out years ago, I also do not want to anticipate our vows. I do not want to show you anything less than the utmost respect."

She took his face in her hands. "I did not say your name because I felt rushed or wanted you to stop."

He took her in his arms and rested his cheek on the crown of her head. "We have waited so long to be together. I feel as though I am living in a dream." He tugged her over to the sofa near the fire and drew her into his lap. "If I make you uncomfortable—"

She rested a finger over his mouth. "I have spoken my mind since we first met. You must cease this fretting. I shall scream if you infuriate me or make me ill-at-ease."

With a smile, he brushed his knuckle down her nose. "You need not scream." He took her hand and bestowed a kiss upon each of her fingers while she rested her cheek upon his shoulder. "I find I am beside myself with joy. I had become so accustomed to dreaming of you as my wife, to have you vanish every morning with the daylight. This time, I know you will not disappear again, and that knowledge alone overwhelms."

"Soon," she said leaning up to bestow a kiss to his jaw. How could she convey the strength of her feelings without anticipating their vows? "Our wedding will be soon, then we never need be parted again."

Chapter 22

Elizabeth took in her reflection while Taylor finished fastening the back of her gown. She had to laugh when, upon their return to Darcy house, a plethora of packages from Madame Villers's establishment as well as the cobbler and milliner had awaited her and Jane. As much as she had attempted to rein in Mrs. Northcott and Fitzwilliam's enthusiasm for seeing her and Jane suitably attired, the duo had ignored the both of them. This evening, she wore a new primrose coloured silk creation featuring sleeves with detailed insets that she would have despised sewing as they required considerable time. A necklace of yellow topaz beads adorned her neck with matching ear-drops dangling from her earlobes. She hardly recognised herself dressed in such finery. At a knock, Taylor bustled to open the door, allowing Jane into the room.

Her sister fingered the layers of fabric on the sleeve. "You look lovely. I do like the sheer, detachable long sleeves, though I notice you are not wearing them tonight."

"No, I do not want to ruin them at dinner. Remember when you pricked your finger sewing a gauze overlay?"

Jane sucked air through her teeth with a grimace. "I do. I was terrified we would have to replace the fabric."

"I beg your pardon," said Taylor, "but will you be needing anything further, Miss?"

"No, thank you."

With a curtsey, the girl stepped back into the dressing room while Elizabeth picked up her arm-length, cream gloves. "Do you think Aunt and Uncle will forgive us?"

"I prefer to believe they will." Jane turned to the mirror and straightened the silver ribbon around her waist. Her gown was an elegant celestial blue with silver embroidery and gauzy mameluke sleeves that suited her well. Jane never failed to look well in blue. "We have always been close to the both of them. I hope they will be happy to know we are alive and you are to be so advantageously wed."

"I hope so too." Elizabeth plastered on a smile. "Shall we await them in the drawing room? Fitzwilliam had some business to attend before dinner, so he is sure to still be in his study."

They made their way to the drawing room Mrs. Northcott had explained was most used for company. Once they were settled into chairs before the fire, Jane rubbed her palm with the thumb of her opposite hand. "Are the arrangements completed for the morrow?"

Her chest fluttered at the mere thought of Fitzwilliam finally being her husband. For years such bliss seemed an impossibility—that too much had happened to keep them apart. Ignoring her fears would take time, but she would be content. They would be the happiest couple in the world.

"Yes, I believe so. Lady Fitzwilliam sent a note confirming that her cousin, the bishop, would arrive at half-ten. Lady Catherine will not be coming. She expressed that she had travelled enough and did not wish to leave her companion. Apparently, the lady has had a difficult time. Lady Catherine mothers her a bit."

Jane smiled. "Lady Catherine is not at all what I expected from your descriptions after your visit to Charlotte."

"She is altered since her daughter's death. I was surprised by one or two of her confessions when we spoke."

"You two were friendly when she visited here."

"We were." The rapping of the knocker caused them both to sit up and jerk their heads to the door. Elizabeth's stomach twisted into a knot so tight it all but bent her in two. The tension would make her sick if she did not calm. She trained her eyes on the floor and breathed while Watson greeted a guest. The voice was too low to distinguish. Was the knock her aunt and uncle? Her hands wrung and she chewed upon her cheek. When Richard strode into the room, her body sagged back to the sofa.

"They have yet to arrive," said Jane.

"That is good. I feared I was late." He bowed over Jane's then Elizabeth's hands. "Where is Darcy?"

———◆———

"Sir, Lord Carlisle has arrived. Miss Bennet, Miss Elizabeth, and the viscount await you in the blue drawing room.

Darcy set the letter he had just finished to the side of his desk. "Thank you." Without delay, he made to join his betrothed until their guests arrived. Elizabeth's nervousness over this evening had grown by leaps and bounds since their departure from Drayton, and no matter how he tried to soothe her, he could not completely distract his betrothed from the upset tonight could bring. She needed to see this through to be truly free of the ghosts of her past, but how would she cope if the Gardiners could not forgive her?

As he approached the room, Richard's voice carried into the hall, enquiring of his whereabouts. "I am here," he said as he entered.

One glance at Elizabeth was enough to reveal her distress. Her usually healthy complexion was too pale, like those ladies who used Gowland's lotion and other such creams to make themselves a pasty hue. He had never preferred society's preference for a sickly colouring. Elizabeth's appearance after walking three miles to Netherfield was one of his favourite memories. The manner in which her curls attempted to spring from their pins, the pink blush of her cheeks, and her eyes bright and alive from the exercise. He kissed Elizabeth's hand and pulled her to the sofa to sit beside him. He took her cold hands in his and rubbed them to return the circulation.

Richard leaned against Jane's chair. "You are certain they are coming?"

"We have received no word to the contrary." Darcy pulled out his watch and verified the time. "They are not late as of yet. The children may have protested at their leaving, or Mrs. Gardiner or Miss Mary could have taken more time to prepare than was expected."

"They are nothing like Mama," said Jane. She rested an elbow on the arm of the chair so she could look up to address Richard. "Other than a similarity in hair colour and eyes, my uncle is an intelligent man of good humour."

On their return from Drayton, they had stopped in Meryton to call upon Mrs. Bennet. Not twenty minutes had passed before Elizabeth requested they depart, mortified by her mother's reaction to their betrothal and the presence of an eligible viscount. They had not even stayed for tea.

"The Gardiners are welcome company," said Darcy. Elizabeth's hands trembled in his, and he brought them to his lips to bestow another kiss.

Richard sighed and tapped the toe of his boot on the floor. "Perhaps we should pour drinks? A sizeable brandy for each of the ladies would do a great deal for their disposition."

Voices in the hall halted all further conversation. Elizabeth and Jane both shot out of their seats, but stood stock-still. Elizabeth wrung her hands and stared at Jane, who had Richard gripping one of her hands for support.

Darcy took a deep breath. He would ignore Richard and Jane's position at that moment. This was not the time to inquire as to his intentions. Instead, he strode into the hall, made a quick bow, and shook Gardiner's proffered hand. "Welcome to Darcy House."

With a wide smile, Gardiner offered his wife his arm. "You mentioned something you needed to tell us, and I must admit to being curious."

"You will discover soon enough. I hope you will forgive me for being so secretive, but we felt the news we have to impart was best said in person."

Mrs. Gardiner's brows drew together. "We?"

"Lizzy!"

They all jumped at Miss Mary's cry. Blast! Miss Mary's penchant for wandering the hall had slipped his mind. She always studied the artwork and the ornate ceiling while he chatted with her aunt and uncle. She had requested permission during their first call, and he had been pleased to allow her the small freedom. How could he have forgotten!

The Gardiners gasped before rushing through the doorway of the drawing room where they came to an abrupt halt. He entered in time to see Miss Mary with her arms thrown around Elizabeth, sobs wracking her frame as she clung fiercely to her sister's neck. Meanwhile, Elizabeth embraced her younger sister with her eyes closed, their temples touching. When they separated enough to be face to face, Elizabeth cradled Miss Mary's cheeks. "My, you have become such a lady." Her sister gave a laughing sob and embraced her once more before running over to Jane.

After Jane kissed Miss Mary's cheek and hugged her, she kept hold of one of her younger sister's hands while she took several hesitant steps in the direction of her aunt and uncle. Meanwhile, Elizabeth wrapped an arm around Mary as they approached their relations who stood agape.

Mrs. Gardiner lowered her hands from her mouth. "You are alive."

"We are," said Elizabeth, wiping her damp cheeks.

Jane held one of Miss Mary's hands in both of hers. "We know we must have caused you tremendous pain and vexation. We are so sorry."

The red of their uncle's face extended from the top of his cravat to the hair upon his nearly bald head. "I would like to know why?" was all he said in a hard voice.

Elizabeth's hands clenched together while she stood rigid. What he would not give for the privilege of taking her in his arms and relieving her anxiety. "I heard you speaking to my aunt after Papa's funeral. You spoke of Lydia, of how unlikely it was any of us would marry and what you could afford. You said short of a miracle, you would never be able to support us

all for our entire lives. Jane and I knew we would be a burden—
"

"No!" Their aunt rushed forward and took Elizabeth's hand as well as Jane's. "You would never be a burden."

Jane sniffed and took a step closer. "But, we were. Before we left Longbourn, we sent out inquiries searching for positions as companions. As you know, we had uncle enquire as to positions, but naught came of any of it."

Their aunt's shoulders rose and fell with a heaving breath. "I wish you had come to us."

"We decided to do the only thing we could to help," said Jane. "We collected the pin money we had saved for the previous year and considered what we could afford. Lizzy also found twenty pounds in Papa's desk drawer that we added to our savings. Then one day while you both were out, we packed our clothing tightly into two small valises and sneaked into the mews."

"And you went to St. Giles," said Gardiner, his voice softer. He had, of course, known from the investigators where they had gone.

Elizabeth swallowed and nodded. "We walked to a boarding house, not far from Seven Dials, and spoke to the widow who owned it. We told her Jane was also a widow and I her sister, but the woman cared not for who we were, only if we had the money to pay. We possessed the ten pounds required to pay the year's lease of a small place a few doors away, which we paid then and there."

Mrs. Gardiner's eyes were shiny and bright with a line of tears along her bottom lashes. "I cannot think of what could have happened. The stories in the paper of what occurs at

Seven Dials." Darcy gritted his teeth. He had a similar reaction when he and Elizabeth spoke of the day they departed Gracechurch Street and obtained their home in St. Giles. They had been fortunate Mr. Cooke and his wife were what they seemed.

"But nothing happened, Aunt," said Jane. We had neighbours who took us under their wing. The Cookes lived in a larger home next door. We looked for sewing work with Gemma, Mrs. Cooke, while her husband ensured those who were up to mischief knew we were friends of his wife so under his protection." Jane swallowed hard and turned to her uncle. "Mr. Cooke was who you met when you searched for us. He took you to the churchyard."

Gardiner paled. "Do you mean you were there?"

"I was with his wife," said Jane. "That day, we returned the sewing we had completed to Bond Street then searched for more work. Lizzy sat with the Cooke's young son, Michael, while her husband worked at the inn."

Gardiner turned to Darcy. "But how did you find them?"

"Perhaps we should sit while the ladies finish their tale?"

At Richard's interruption, their aunt and uncle took notice of Richard's presence. Their uncle frowned. "Forgive me for intruding," said his cousin. "Darcy, would you introduce us?"

Darcy clasped his hands behind his back. "Richard Fitzwilliam, the Viscount Carlisle may I present Mr. and Mrs. Edward Gardiner, and Miss Mary Bennet. Mr. Gardiner, Mrs. Gardiner, Lord Carlisle is my cousin."

After the men bowed and the ladies curtseyed, Gardiner nodded and led his wife to the sofa. "Your cousin's suggestion has merit."

"Would you care for a drink?" Richard stepped over to the table, poured a glass of brandy, and offered it to Gardiner. "I have no experience to compare, but I am certain were I in a similar situation, I would require a restorative."

Gardiner's shoulders jumped with his single burst of laughter. "Thank you." He took a sip but remained stiff in his seat. "Jane, Lizzy, you were going to tell us how you came to be with Mr. Darcy."

Jane began the tale of the hackney ride to Park Lane with Darcy recounting bits and pieces when he had the opportunity. They spoke of Elizabeth's illness and recovery until Gardiner held up a hand.

"Though we are greatly appreciative for all Mr. Darcy has done thus far, you must return with us to Gracechurch Street. We cannot trespass on Mr. Darcy's kindness any further." He looked to Darcy, who stood beside Elizabeth's chair. "If you would provide me with the bills from the shops, I shall be glad to reimburse you for what you have spent for clothing and Lizzy's care."

"Uncle, we shall not be returning to Gracechurch Street— at least not to live." Darcy rested his hand upon Elizabeth's shoulder.

"Lizzy," said her uncle tersely, "you cannot remain—"

Darcy cleared his throat. "Mr. Gardiner, Elizabeth and I are to be wed on the morrow. My aunt, Lady Fitzwilliam, has arranged for the bishop to marry us by special license here at Darcy House. We thought to have the ceremony at Pemberley, but the ladies wished to return to London to inform you of their good health. We also hoped you would wish to be present when we exchange our vows."

"Do say you will come," said Elizabeth. "We broke our journey in Meryton three days ago to acquaint Mama with the happy news. I am afraid her reaction was everything horrifying."

"With the time we have spent in a carriage of late, we intend to remain at the very least through Easter before returning to Derbyshire," said Darcy. He squeezed Elizabeth's shoulder with a smile. "You are welcome to visit us here or at Pemberley as you wish. We would be pleased to receive you and your children should you want to leave the city during the summer."

Their uncle's eyes, which had been on Darcy, dropped to Elizabeth then flitted back to Darcy. "You are betrothed." Mrs. Gardiner rested her hand on her husband's forearm but said not a word.

"I can imagine Mama's reaction," said Mary before sliding her hand over her mouth.

Elizabeth gave a weak smile. "She was dreadful." She then told their uncle of Darcy's proposal at Rosings, her feelings two years ago, at Pemberley, then their trip to Drayton. He added a few words here and there when he could, but she spoke with feeling and her remembrance of their past encounters was similar to his. Several tears dropped to her cheeks when she spoke of Drayton. He could not blame her. His recollection of those days caused him no less emotion than she showed. "Pray, believe me when I say how much I love him. He is the best of men, and once I decided I would no longer stand in the way of my own happiness, I became determined. I do not want to wait. I hope you can understand."

Her aunt rose and stepped before Elizabeth, cradling her cheeks in her palms. "Dear girl, all we ever wanted for you was felicity and security, regardless of whether you wed or not. If you love Mr. Darcy, then we could not be more pleased."

Elizabeth sprang from her seat to embrace her aunt. Tears streamed down her face when Gardiner approached and hugged her as well. "Lord Carlisle," she said. "You have neglected to pour a brandy for me, and I could sorely use one at this moment." Darcy bit back a grin, and waved off Richard, stepping to the decanters to pour his betrothed a modest tumbler.

"Mr. Gardiner, I would like to request your permission to court Miss Bennet."

At Richard's request, Darcy nearly spilled brandy all over the tray. When had this happened? After a large gulp, he passed the glass to Elizabeth.

Gardiner held up a finger, swallowed the last of his drink, then handed the glass to Darcy. "I believe I could use a bit more." Gardiner chuckled. "After this, are there any more shocks I must endure? If so, I fear I may be in my cups by the end of the evening."

"Not as far as I am aware," said Elizabeth, her wide eyes staring at her sister. Had Jane neglected to speak to her sister of her plans?

As Darcy returned the filled glass, Richard laughed under his breath. "Miss Elizabeth, you should warn him of your mother's suspicions."

"All assumptions," said Darcy. "I set her to rights." Elizabeth took his arm and barely leaned into him. As he covered her hand with his, his chest swelled. How he loved being allowed the simple gesture of affection before her family.

She peered up at him. "Mama is not one to listen. The worst part of her gossip is how she embellishes the stories she tells. They are never what someone said to her in the first place." She tipped her glass towards his cousin. "Your cousin is correct."

"We do know better than to listen to your mother's tittle-tattle," said Mrs. Gardiner.

Miss Mary sat in a prim manner beside her aunt. "Mama's stories are just that—stories. They have been for as long as I can remember."

"She implied our disappearance and supposed deaths were so I could be Fitzwilliam's mistress. He is marrying me because I was clever enough to fall with child—his heir."

Gardiner's shoulders shook and he held up a hand. "Forgive me. I should not laugh, nor should I be surprised." He patted Elizabeth's shoulder. "Do not fret. I must travel to Hertfordshire next week to fetch Kitty. I shall speak to your mother. Even if she does not believe me, when no child is born six months hence, she cannot continue to spread such claims."

"I suppose not," said Elizabeth.

With an arm outstretched to shake hands, Gardiner clapped Darcy on the back. "We shall be here tomorrow. I shall be happy to take the day from work to attend." He glanced over his shoulder at his wife. "I must admit my wife and I had our suspicions at Pemberley, and we are pleased you found each other again. I can think of no one better for our Lizzy. I know she will be well cared for." He sighed as his gaze returned to his niece. "Lizzy, I do regret you overhearing our conversation, but I thought you would have spoken to me before committing to so rash a scheme as living in St. Giles. But, the past is done and behind us, and I believe we have much to anticipate in the future." He kissed Elizabeth's cheek then Jane's. "Lord Carlisle, if my niece has deemed you worthy, I shall not stand in your way, but I do ask you to respect her and treat her with kindness."

Richard gave a slight bow. "Thank you, sir, though you need not call me Lord Carlisle. Through Darcy's marriage, we shall be family. Family addresses me as Richard."

Elizabeth's uncle furrowed his brow. "You do not care for Carlisle?"

"No," said Richard. "The title belonged to my elder brother. I am forced to use the name when in society, but I have yet to feel comfortable with the appellation."

Gardiner winced and nodded. "I understand. I am sorry for your loss."

"Forgive me." Mrs. Northcott stood in the doorway. "Dinner is ready to be served."

Chapter 23

Darcy fidgeted with his cuffs while Morton brushed his topcoat. "Well?"

His cousin, who leaned against a nearby wall with one leg crossed over the other, glanced up from studying his fingernails. "You are breath-taking. Stunning. She will faint the moment she sets eyes upon you." Morton made a strangled noise. Had his valet laughed?

He rolled his eyes and stepped back from the pier glass, levelling his cousin with what he hoped was a stern stare. "Since I shall be Jane Bennet's brother before the end of the day, I want to know when you decided to court her and whether you are serious. You conversed during our stops to change horses, which I assumed was the two of you passing the time. When we were at Drayton, I suspected an interest, but I convinced myself you were being friendly."

"She is unlike the ladies my mother or father promote. Mother's choices are infinitely better than my father's but still maintain that practised air I cannot abide. After my brother's withdrawal from town and the rumours that abounded about his health, I began to receive more attention and soon, better understood your reticence in those settings. None of those ladies cared when I began to speak in the way the Miss Bennets found objectionable."

Darcy frowned. "I do not remember Jane objecting."

"After Miss Elizabeth censored me, I spoke to Miss Bennet as I would you or my mother—perhaps a combination of both. Before I departed, she told me she preferred the man she conversed with throughout the evening to the man who arrived. She was honest but polite." Richard began to pace. "I cannot deny I find her beautiful, but I also enjoy her company and find her easy to be with. I want to know her better."

Darcy crossed his arms over his chest with a crooked grin while Richard continued to pace, his hands moving while he spoke. "I never thought to see the day. You know you will need to burn your copy of Harris's List of Covent Garden Ladies."

Morton began to snicker while he brushed Darcy's topcoat one last time. "I beg your pardon, sirs."

After he rolled his eyes, Richard stepped forward so he stood with one foot thrown out in front of him. "The copy at Carlisle House is over twenty years old, and I showed it to you as nothing more than a lark. I have never actually used the book for more than a laugh since the descriptions of some ladies are horrible to the point of humour."

Darcy clapped his hands upon Richard's shoulders. "Relax. I was teasing."

His cousin slapped his arms away. "Darcy, you never tease." He wagged his finger at Darcy's chest. "This is Miss Elizabeth's doing. I am not certain I care for the change."

"Morton?" Darcy shifted to face his valet, who was over ten years his senior. "What do you know of Harris's List?"

The always proper servant started, and his face reddened darker than Darcy had ever seen. "I should not have laughed, sir. I apologise."

"I am not angry at your amusement. I just wondered at how you knew of the book."

The servant coughed and made a point of setting the brush down slowly. "During my first trip to London, not long after I became your valet, a group of footmen and I were curious of the book's contents. We all contributed to purchase a copy."

This time, Richard was the one to snicker. "I wonder if the men working at Carlisle House ever read the copy my brother owned."

"With its age, the book's original owner could have been your father," said Darcy. Richard swallowed hard, his complexion turning a greenish hue. "You never considered to whom the book first belonged, did you?"

"No," he said, "and I plan on relegating it to the fire as soon as I return."

"Sir, do you require anything further?"

"No, thank you."

"Very good." Morton bowed. "I wish you and Mrs. Darcy great joy."

"They are not wed yet." Richard rubbed his hands together with a grin. "She could still say 'no.'"

"She will not say no." Darcy refused to let Richard disturb his equanimity on such an important day.

"She could." Richard practically sang the words as if he were a little girl who had to be correct.

"You are ridiculous." Darcy opened the top drawer of his dresser and withdrew the ring he had removed from the safe.

"I am not."

After imparting a quick but distinct glare, Darcy turned his back on his cousin and strode through the door.

———◆———

Elizabeth fingered the necklace Fitzwilliam sent for her to wear: emeralds set between two gold chains with a single teardrop stone that rested in the hollow of her neck. She had never owned anything so fine, and the expense of such a piece rendered her terrified of losing it.

With a sigh, her gaze in the mirror shifted to her head, and she smoothed her hand over her short hair, which was now a thick layer that was beginning to curl at the very tips. Her hair had grown, but why could it not grow in a swifter fashion? This was not what she had ever envisioned for her wedding day.

"He loves you. He does not care."

Her gaze met Jane's in the mirror while Taylor finished the last fastening. "I know, but I can still wish I had a lovely fringe to curl in front of the bonnet in a becoming manner."

"Nonsense," said Aunt Gardiner. "Your hair will return soon enough, and you may just wish you could rid yourself of it once it does." Jane's nose wrinkled while Georgiana and Mary laughed from the chaise. "In particular, during the summer months when the heat becomes too much." Her aunt touched a bit near her ear. "Besides, the style does become you. I remember your hair when you were a little girl before you had such long tresses. Soon it will be a mass of curls your maid will need to style once more."

Her dearest sister pulled her around and set the bonnet upon her head. Another creation of Jane's, the bonnet boasted of the same pearl silk as the gown and was trimmed with shot sarsnet and ribbon. When Elizabeth turned back to the mirror, she tilted her head as she looked over the effect of the entire costume. "Mama would bemoan the lack of lace." Jane laughed and hugged her from behind. "I am so very happy for you. He cannot love you by halves; he loves you with his entire being. I never before witnessed a man so overcome as he was when he saw me that night, and the first thought he had was of you. He deserves you."

"I agree," said her aunt. "I remember his shock and dismay when we told him you were gone. He paled until he looked positively ashen. The smile he wore last night I have not seen since we visited Pemberley, and even then, his smiles were all for you."

When Georgiana stepped forward, she took the ribbons from the bonnet and began to tie them. "He has not truly lived since then. I am so happy he will have someone to love, and I know you will care for him as well. He needs you more than he has ever needed anyone." She stood back and looked Elizabeth over from head to toe. "You look exquisite. My brother will be speechless when he sets eyes on you."

"I hope you do not mind Jane reworking your mother's gown."

After stepping forward to take Elizabeth's hands, Georgiana leaned a bit closer. "I am taller than my mother was, so I could never alter one of her gowns for my own use. I am thrilled Mrs. Northcott thought to search the trunks. As far as I am concerned, any serviceable fabric or trim is yours. Do with it as you like."

The nerves wiggling around in Elizabeth's stomach left her with a large exhale. Though Georgiana had never used her mother's belongings and not taken them upon her marriage, Elizabeth could not help but fret that the young lady might still feel an attachment to them.

"In fact, I thought you could use these." A pair of elbow-length, fingerless lace gloves in the perfect shade to complement her gown dangled from one of her hands.

"Oh! Those are perfect." Elizabeth slipped one up an arm and reached for the second. "I shall return them before you depart. Thank you."

"Pray, do not trouble yourself to return them. I purchased them yesterday for you. I did not know if you would make it to the shops." At Mrs. Northcott entering from the servants' entrance, Georgiana began bouncing on her toes and rubbing her hands together. "I hope you are ready to marry my brother."

Mrs. Northcott grinned. "The bishop has arrived, and they are awaiting you."

"I wish you and the master great joy, Mrs. Darcy," said Taylor.

"I am not Mrs. Darcy yet." Elizabeth took her aunt's and Jane's arms as her stomach erupted into a million butterflies all attempting to escape their confines.

"As good as, Miss. Besides, I should become accustomed to addressing you as such." Taylor curtseyed and departed.

They followed Georgiana down the hallway towards the stairs. "Lizzy, are you well?" Jane spoke softly near her ear.

"I am well." She hugged Jane's arm to her. "I believe I am relieved to be marrying Fitzwilliam at last. For so long I thought it would never happen." She had no doubts about him, so why was she all aflutter?

When Georgiana pushed open the door of the drawing room, Elizabeth's eyes met Fitzwilliam's and her nerves vanished altogether. Lady Fitzwilliam's presence to one side of the room even went unnoticed. Elizabeth was where she was supposed to be. She was home.

In the end, the ceremony was blessedly short, particularly considering that the bishop had bound them together for the remainder of their days. Tears covered Elizabeth's cheeks when they were pronounced man and wife, and she covered her mouth and gave a laughing sob.

As soon as they had signed the register, Jane took her hand. "The ring is beautiful." She pulled Elizabeth into a tight embrace. "I am delighted for you, Lizzy. You will finally be happy—truly happy. We both deserve a bit of that, do you not think?"

Before she could respond, Georgiana squealed. "I am thrilled for you both!" She bounced forward and hugged her brother then grabbed Elizabeth. Witney and Richard clapped Fitzwilliam on the back and shook his hand.

Aunt Gardiner embraced her and wiped a tear as she stepped back. "I hope you will be exceedingly happy, my dear." Her uncle stepped forward and kissed her cheek. Were those tears in his eyes as well?

"Congratulations," said Mary. Her younger sister hugged her and kissed her cheek before shyly approaching Fitzwilliam.

"I wish you happy, Mrs. Darcy," said Lady Fitzwilliam in a dignified manner. A slight smile graced the lady's features at the unreserved behaviour of the rest of the family. "Should you require any help at all, do not hesitate to ask—particularly with the *ton*."

"Thank you, Lady Fitzwilliam." When she eventually managed to return to her new husband's side, she itched to touch him, so she wrapped a hand around his arm, which he covered with his own. "Are you well, Mrs. Darcy?" His eyes held an unusual sparkle and his voice was somehow richer.

"I am very well, Mr. Darcy."

"I wish you great joy, Mr. Darcy, Mrs. Darcy." Mrs. Northcott stepped before them and dabbed her eyes with a handkerchief. "Cook has prepared a breakfast we plan to serve in the dining room, if that is agreeable." Fitzwilliam tapped her hand with his finger.

"Very agreeable," said Elizabeth. "Pray, thank Cook for her hard work. We do appreciate what is certain to be a delightful meal."

The housekeeper dipped her chin and glanced between the two of them. "Thank you, ma'am. When you are ready, we shall begin."

The dining room was bedecked in flowers and candles that added a celebratory air to the opulent room. Fitzwilliam shooed away the footman and helped Elizabeth with her chair before he sat beside her. While their party dined on Cook's delectable feast, his steady presence overwhelmed. She did not have to look at him to know he was close, his proximity prickled at her flesh. When his knee touched hers under the table, she shivered, and her breathing quickened at the continuous frisson that radiated through her from that point.

When they stood to remove to the drawing room, Fitzwilliam placed a hand to the small of her back. "You hardly touched your food." The low whisper near her ear caused gooseflesh to erupt from where his breath caressed near her neck and lower. She almost closed her eyes to cope with the effect he had upon her.

"Perhaps 'tis the excitement of the day. I was not very hungry."

"If the food was not to your liking—"

"No!" She spoke forcefully, but soft so as not to disturb their guests who walked ahead of them. "I was impressed by the menu and the quality of the food."

Lord Carlisle leaned upon the back of a chair once they entered the drawing room. "Mrs. Darcy—"

"We are family now, my Lord. If you would prefer, you may call me Elizabeth, or Lizzy as my family addresses me."

He gave a brief bow. "Then you must cease calling me 'my lord.' Your husband addresses me as Richard to avoid confusion between us. You may do the same if you are so inclined."

Georgiana took Elizabeth's hands and kissed her cheek. "James has requested our carriage be brought around. We came so I could ensure my brother did not ruin his second chance with you, so now that you are wed, we shall return home."

"Why thank you, Sister," said Fitzwilliam in a dry tone.

Georgiana took his hands with shiny eyes. "I am so thrilled for you, Brother. I shall have to write to Lady Catherine and let her know she has been of great use. Besides, I would have been devastated to have missed your wedding, particularly considering I know how happy you are to be." A teary Fitzwilliam hugged his sister and kissed her cheek as her husband returned to drag her away. Once the couple said their farewells, the Gardiners and Mary, as well as Lady Fitzwilliam, also departed, leaving the remaining foursome to their celebrations.

Richard poured wine and brandy for the four of them, and they relaxed in the library, conversing for a time. "Shall we play Cassino?" asked Richard.

After several rounds of cards, Elizabeth waved her hands in front of her. "Enough. I have no interest in another round. Pray, let us sit before the fire."

No more than five minutes or so passed before Jane stood and shifted in an awkward fashion. "I believe I would like to rest for a while. All of the travelling has me quite fatigued." She covered her mouth with the back of her hand and gave an affected yawn. Elizabeth narrowed her eyes. What was she about?

Since the bishop had concluded the ceremony, Elizabeth had craved to be alone with her husband, but of course, her wishes remained mere wishes. Cook had toiled to create a special wedding feast they were obliged to partake of, and now they could not leave Jane alone with Richard—even without his apparent interest in her, it would be improper.

Jane looked to Richard, who sat with one leg kicked out to the side and slumped a bit in his chair. "Did you not mention a desire to ride this afternoon?"

Elizabeth leaned to peer through the window at the forbidding grey clouds that had since covered the morning's brilliant blue sky. "I did?" asked Richard.

"Yes, you did," said Jane. The side of her face to Elizabeth's side moved in an odd fashion. Was she winking at Richard? Since when did Jane heed Francine Bennet's lessons on manners and deportment?

"Oh! Yes, I did."

Fitzwilliam frowned, and he stared. "You intend to ride?"

"Why not?" Richard shrugged and rose, straightening his topcoat. "I am certain I have a horse in my stables who requires exercise. If you will excuse me, Rotten Row awaits."

Jane kissed Elizabeth's cheek. "Do not fret for me. I shall request a tray for dinner from Mrs. Northcott. Good night."

Her husband did not appear at all disturbed by the swift exit of her sister and his cousin. Instead, he took her hand and kissed the back, his eyes holding hers steadily. "What would you like to do, Mrs. Darcy? We can sit and read together in the library for a time, or we could spend the rest of the day alone in our sitting room."

She licked her impossibly dry lips. "I would prefer to be alone... I mean, to go upstairs." Her cheeks burned, and she rested her forehead against his arm while his shoulders shook.

"I would prefer to retire to our rooms as well." His voice washed over her with a warmth that consumed her to the tips of her toes. He took her hand and pulled her from the sofa, leading her up the stairs until they stood before the door of a room she had never seen.

"Where are we?"

"Your chambers. Mrs. Northcott placed you in Georgiana's bedchamber when you first arrived from St. Giles, and she returned you to those rooms again when we returned from Derbyshire since the mistress's chambers would not be proper because they connect to mine." He opened the door and drew her inside. The fabrics appeared new, and were very much to her liking. The pale greens and roses stood out against a pearl coloured background. The fabrics were pristine. Had the room just been redone?

"'Tis lovely."

"Do you like it?"

She smiled and nodded. "I do. The colours and fabrics are beautiful."

Fitzwilliam drew her into his arms and caressed the backs of his fingers along her cheek. "I had hoped you would. The redecoration was how I occupied much of my time while you were ill. Mrs. Northcott brought me bits of fabric from the warehouses so I could make the final selections. Between your rooms and the fabric for yours and Jane's gowns, she spent a prodigious amount of time at the warehouses."

"You did this?" Her vision blurred as she stepped into his embrace and took a long gaze around the room. "I am overwhelmed. You put all your hope into this."

"I believe I had a certain amount of hope, even in my deepest agony." His fingertips traced the line of her necklace. "After Georgiana was wed and I was all alone, I walked down Piccadilly to Hatchard's then down Bond Street until I reached my mother's favourite jeweller. I could not have told you at the time why I purchased this, other than I thought of nothing but you and how the colour of the stones would complement your eyes."

She rose on her tiptoes and wrapped her arms around his neck. "Fitzwilliam Darcy, you are the most sentimental man... I love you so much."

He pressed his lips to hers, claiming her mouth in a kiss unlike any they had shared thus far. Elizabeth followed his lead as his tongue tangled with hers, making her mind empty of coherent thought and causing gooseflesh to spread down the back of her neck.

With a groan, he buried his face into her neck. "With every day, I love you more."

"Flatterer," she said with a light laugh.

"No," he said lifting his head. He cradled her cheeks in his hands. "I am nothing more than hopelessly in love, and I always will be."

Chapter 24

June 1820

Elizabeth kissed the crown of young Emmeline's downy head and set her into the cot. "I must meet Lady Catherine when she arrives, and you must nap, young lady." She smiled at little Emme's toothy grin before she turned to the nurse. "If you have any problems, do not hesitate to send for me. I think the fever was naught but teething, but I do not want to dismiss it too easily."

"Yes, Mrs. Darcy," said the nursemaid, who bobbed a curtsey.

After leaving the nursery, she stepped two doors down and poked her head inside her son's room. When she noticed her mistress's presence, the nursemaid pressed a finger over her lips before she crept over to the door and spoke in hushed tones. "He just fell asleep."

Elizabeth stepped over to the bed, and with a gentle finger, shifted a curl from Hugh's eyes. He was so peaceful and sweet while he slept. In looks, their eldest child greatly resembled Fitzwilliam, but his mischievous grin and love for the out of doors resembled her father's descriptions of her as a child. His inquisitive nature also meant he had his own nursemaid instead of sharing with his eight-month-old sister. She and Fitzwilliam would be fit for Bedlam if Hugh wandered off when the nurse was busy with Emme. Their son also had his own rooms. If Emme woke her brother during the night, the two of them would see to it no one slept.

"You will wake him." She spun around to Fitzwilliam, who stood behind her, his face at her shoulder.

She pressed him back by his chest, took his hand, and led him into the corridor. "I was careful. Besides, he is adorable when he sleeps. He does not appear so grown and more the baby I carried all over Pemberley." They had not returned to London the Season after his birth, but remained in Derbyshire. The *ton* and town held little interest, and the solitude and comfort of Pemberley beckoned to them. They were quite content to be together as a family.

Fitzwilliam squeezed her hand and bestowed a feather-light kiss to her knuckles. "Lady Catherine should soon arrive. Is everything prepared?"

"Yes, I spoke to Mrs. Reynolds. She has Lady Catherine's and Lady Fitzwilliam's preferred rooms cleaned and aired as well as rooms for Richard, Jane, and the children when they arrive on the morrow." Since her marriage to Richard, Jane had given birth to three boys in succession. When they grew enough to play out of doors with Hugh, Pemberley would be in grave danger of being shaken to its foundations. Richard's older sons would not stop running from the moment they woke until they fell asleep at night. Their youngest was two months younger than Emme and was already showing a tendency towards his brothers' stamina.

Elizabeth leaned her head upon her husband's shoulder until they descended the stairs. As soon as they reached the bottom, he drew her into his arms and held her close. She did so love his spontaneous gestures of affection.

"I noticed you also received correspondence from Lady Fitzwilliam this morning."

"I did," she said. "I am glad she will arrive before Richard. She should be the one to tell him of his father's death. I have no desire for the chore." After the bluster and mayhem the earl had created during his life, he died with a whisper, asleep in his bed in his mistress's residence. The earl had outlived his eldest and favourite child by a mere month.

"I have known for years that Richard would one day be earl, but the notion is still odd. I do not envy the position he will find for himself. His father is certain to have left behind a mess that could take years to be sorted. I thought perhaps he and I could ride to Yorkshire in a week or two and meet with the steward. His mother is bringing the ledgers from the London house, so we can study those for the time being."

Elizabeth rose to her tiptoes and kissed his cheek. "He is fortunate to have your aid with the endeavour." The crooked smile he directed at her made her lips dry. Her tongue peeked out to moisten them, and Fitzwilliam began to lean towards her but straightened in an abrupt fashion.

Hoofbeats carried through the open doors followed by the tell-tale call of a footman. Her husband peered at the grand clock against the wall. "Lady Catherine is as punctual as ever," he said with a laugh. "I do not know how she predicts the moment she will arrive with such accuracy."

His aunt's sharp tones preceded her, her walking stick clicking along the stone floor as she marched into the hall. "I do not believe I have ever travelled on such a sweltering day! I almost boiled in that carriage." She removed her hat, gloves, and spencer, and handed them to the waiting maid. "I should never have made a journey such as this in the heat of the summer."

"We are pleased you could come," said Fitzwilliam, who leaned in to kiss her cheek after bowing.

"Yes, yes, I know." She tapped his shoulder with her fan.

After curtseying, Elizabeth kissed the grand lady's cheek as well. "I am pleased to see you, Lady Catherine. The children are sleeping, but I shall bring them down after dinner so you can visit."

Lady Catherine nodded with an imperious air. "As you should." As much as they knew she was not so difficult, the lady refused to behave without those affectations before the servants. Only with those she trusted the most was she genuinely open and unfettered. "Oh! I have brought my companion with me. If you would place her in the bedchamber across the hall from mine. Forgive me for not warning you before my arrival, but I was not certain she would make the trip until the morning we departed. I trust she will be no bother to you."

"Of course not. Elizabeth motioned with discretion to Mrs. Reynolds, who bustled into the servants' corridor. When she turned back around, Elizabeth gasped at the sight of the young lady standing before her.

"I believe you are acquainted with Mrs. Smith." Lady Catherine peered at Elizabeth with a slight dip to her chin. A hand, which was no doubt Fitzwilliam's, rested upon the small of her back.

Mrs. Smith? Elizabeth pressed a palm to her stomach. "Mrs. Smith?" She glanced at Lady Catherine and lifted her one eyebrow. "Would that be Mrs. Lydia Smith?" They had spent two Easters at Rosings since their marriage, but had never seen Lydia. Where had Lady Catherine hidden her away?

"Hello, Lizzy." Lydia nearly vibrated, she trembled in such a violent fashion.

Elizabeth's eyes trailed from the faded, jagged scar above Lydia's right eyebrow to the long sleeves she wore despite the day being "sweltering." What had happened to scar her so?

Lydia shifted on her feet, her eyes darting to their aunt. "I hope you do not mind, but I—"

Before her youngest sister could finish, Elizabeth jumped forward and enfolded Lydia in a warm embrace. "I am so glad you have come." Her sister's arms wrapped around her and clung as if for her life. Lydia sniffled near Elizabeth's ear, and when they drew back, her eyes were red-rimmed.

Elizabeth took a deep breath. "I am sure you wish to refresh yourselves." She motioned to a maid standing near the wall. "Lottie will show you to your rooms. I thought to have tea in the garden at three, which should give you time to remove the dust from the road and rest if you wish." She faced Lydia. "If you should ever feel overwhelmed, do not hesitate to request a tray. I look forward to becoming reacquainted with you during your stay, but we need not do so until you are comfortable." With a smile, she clasped her hands together. "Do ring the bell if you need help finding your way."

As soon as their guests turned into the family wing, Elizabeth grabbed Fitzwilliam by the sleeve and pulled him into the music room. She rounded on him with narrowed eyes. "How did Lydia come to be your aunt's companion?" He could not claim ignorance. He had to know!

He opened his mouth one, two, then three times before his shoulders dropped. "I cannot lie to you," he said. Then, he told her all. From repeating how he learned of her supposed death to tracking Lydia to the poorest part of Saffron Hill, her removal and virtual adoption by his aunt, and concluding with the hunt for Wickham and the bastard's banishment to the East Indies. "I would have told you, but Lydia begged me not to tell. She made me swear I would never reveal her whereabouts or how I found her to any of her family." When he stopped speaking, he watched her so still and silent, he could have been a statue. Was he even breathing?

"We have spent two Easters at Rosings, and Lydia was not there."

He grimaced and clasped his arms behind his back. "She stayed in the Dower house until we departed. She has needed to heal from her ordeal and was not prepared to face you. Pray, do not be angry with me."

Elizabeth stepped forward and wrapped her arms around his neck. "I am not angry. If I had any doubts of your goodness before Lydia's arrival, I would certainly have none after what you have told me. You saved her and ensured Wickham could never hurt anyone ever again."

"Your uncle helped me with Wickham."

She smiled and held him by the shoulders. "But you found him and contrived the plan. Uncle also had naught to do with saving Lydia. If I were to guess, I would assume he does not know she is well and has been at Rosings these six—no nearly seven years. You kept your promise to her."

"I helped her for you and you alone. I could not let another member of your family be harmed, even if she was who caused the entire debacle in the first place."

Tears welled in her eyes and clung to her bottom lashes. "She would likely be dead if you had not intervened. You could have blamed her for my death, but you did not. You gave her the hope of a better life as you did Jane when you saved us from St. Giles and introduced her to Richard. My dear husband, you are generous and kind—you are simply too good."

He shook his head, but she stopped him by gently taking his face in her hands. "I came to you with nothing. But even now, as your wife, my fortune is not that of jewels or money or even this grand house. My greatest fortune, Fitzwilliam Darcy, is you."

The End

Acknowledgements

Wow! This book has been a crazy ride, and I don't know where to start with this. 2020 was crazy for all of us, and I'm super thankful there's a light at the end of the tunnel. I'm also grateful for the pain management doctor, who made it possible for me to sit again! My back slowly seems to improve, which is another light at the end of a long tunnel. I'm back in the gym and looking forward to being able to teach and really workout again one day.

As always, I wouldn't be publishing anything without the love and support of my family. Yesterday was my birthday, and I spent most of the day editing. I know he would've preferred to be lazy with me and find something to watch on television or take a walk, but he didn't complain once about the fact that I was grumpy and engrossed in my laptop screen. My eldest has started helping to proofread and beta my books a bit. I always appreciate another set of eyes. I'm putting those AP English classes to work for me.

My friends are amazing, but I have a few who are directly involved with my writing. I have been friends with Carol since before I was writing, and she started helping me out as a beta not long after I started writing. We've both grown a lot since then. She began working as an editor, and she does a meticulous job scouring over my books. I don't know what I'd do without her. Having an editor in your corner that you trust and can bounce ideas and issues off of is priceless. Thank you, my dear!

Debbie and I have become friends through JAFF, and she has been helping me out with her mad proofreading skills.

Huge thank you to her for taking the time to help clean up after the editing madness!

Huge hugs to all my friends, old and new, who build me up. This year has mostly been keeping up through Facetime or Zoom, but at least we kept up with each other. I hope we can catch up again soon!

Lastly, to the fans who keep me going. I thank you for every post and message. On those days when I struggle to write, I have you in my head or even on my social media, telling me you're re-reading one of my books or which one is your favorite. Those may not seem like much, but when the words just won't come, your messages make me keep trying until the words are right. To quote Austen: "For you alone, I think and plan." Thank you for reading!

About the Author

L.L. Diamond is more commonly known as Leslie to her friends and Mom to her three kids. A native of Louisiana, she spent the majority of her life living within an hour of New Orleans before following her husband all over as a military wife. Louisiana, Mississippi, California, Texas, New Mexico, Nebraska, England, and now Missouri have all been called home along the way.

Aside from mother and writer, Leslie considers herself a perpetual student. She has degrees in biology and studio art but will devour any subject of interest simply for the knowledge. Her most recent endeavors have included certifications to coach swimming, certifying as a fitness instructor and indoor cycling instructor, personal trainer, and corrective exercise specialist. As an artist, her concentration is in graphic design, but watercolor is her medium of choice with one of her watercolors featured on the cover of her second book, *A Matter of Chance*. She is also a member of the Jane Austen Society of North America. Leslie also plays flute and piano, but much like

Pride and Prejudice's Elizabeth Bennet, she is always in need of practice!

Leslie's books include: *Rain and Retribution, A Matter of Chance, An Unwavering Trust, The Earl's Conquest, Particular Intentions, Particular Attachments, Unwrapping Mr. Darcy, It's Always Been You, It's Always Been Us, It's Always Been You and Me, Undoing, Confined with Mr. Darcy, He's Always Been the One,* and *Agony and Hope.*

Printed in Great Britain
by Amazon

81776962R00154